T0355034

BLOOD MOON

III THE RAVENSCLIFF SERIES

GEOFFREY HUNTINGTON

Diversion Books
A Division of Diversion Publishing Corp.
443 Park Avenue South, Suite 1004
New York, New York 10016
www.DiversionBooks.com

For more information, email info@diversionbooks.com

First Diversion Books edition October 2013

Print ISBN: 978-1-62681-169-0
eBook ISBN: 978-1-62681-075-4

BLOOD MOON

THE
RAVENSCLIFF
SERIES
III

GEOFFREY HUNTINGTON

DIVERSIONBOOKS

PROLOGUE

HALLOWEEN

NEARLY 30 YEARS AGO

The old crones down in the village liked to say that if you made your way out to the farthest crag of Devil's Rock on a stormy, windy night, you could hear the screams of all those who had lost their lives over the centuries to the furious sea below.

On this night, the young man feared, one more death would be added to the legends.

He ran after the woman, desperate to stop her and bring her back to Ravenscliff. Otherwise, he knew the Madman would enact his revenge. *The Madman*—the name Jackson Muir was called down in the village, the word that was whispered in fear in the servants' quarters of the great house. *The Madman*.

That is what he is.

And he will destroy us all.

But Ogden McNutt would not accept that. He wasn't willing to accept the idea of destruction, not yet. There was still time. Perhaps he could avert the fate that had been predicted for them, prevent the cataclysm that loomed over everyone at Ravenscliff. If he could prevent the woman from reaching the cliffs, if he could bring her safely back to the dark mansion atop the hill, perhaps all of what they feared could still be avoided.

"Emily!" Ogden shouted into the wind. "Emily!"

He could see her ahead of him, in her long flowing white gown, heading toward Devil's Rock. Above them a large full moon struggled to break out from the dark clouds that raced against its face as thunder grumbled on the horizon.

"Emily!"

She did not pause, but the young man was gaining on her. He could hear her now: her sobs, her tortured breathing. She had run from the house after finding Jackson, her husband, in the arms of that servant girl—that strange, bewitching creature with the piercing dark eyes and shining black hair. Ogden had witnessed the scene—and in Emily's fair golden face, he had seen something twist, something shatter, as if suddenly, in a glance, she had understood every last nuance of the Madman's evil. She turned and ran.

"Go after her," said Montaigne—the man who had first brought Ogden to this place, who had promised him Knowledge of the ancient arts, who had offered him an apprenticeship with the Guardians. "Bring her back here."

She mustn't be allowed to get near Devil's Rock, Ogden told himself over and over as he ran, remembering the prediction of doom. *I must stop her! I must reach her in time!*

But she was already there, standing at the precipice, her long white dress billowing around her, when Ogden finally reached her. He staggered as he caught his breath, yet still managed to grab the beautiful young woman's arm, just as both were leaning over the edge, staring down into the angry sea crashing below.

"Emily," Ogden said, "you must come back with me!"

She spun on him, eyes wild.

"Back to Ravenscliff? Back to *him*? Are you as mad as he? Why would I go back, knowing what he has planned for all of us?"

"Please, Emily, you must come away from here—"

She pulled out of his grasp, stronger in her fury than Ogden could ever have imagined. How different she was now, how changed from the sweet, innocent, demure girl who had first come to Ravenscliff.

"Are you one of his minions?" Emily's eyes were furious, accusing. "Is that it, Ogden? You and Montaigne—"

"No, Emily, we want to stop him! And we can, if you just come away with me!"

She laughed bitterly. "Stop him? You are a fool. All of you are fools if you think you can stop him now. Ravenscliff will be his—and the Hell Hole beneath it too!"

"No, we can stop him!"

"Look!" She pointed up at the sky just as the first flash of lightning illuminated the night. "See what I have witnessed! Look and see!"

Ogden lifted his eyes to the sky as a loud roar of thunder shook the very rocks on which they stood. And there, as if projected against the clouds by some enormous magic lantern, was the vision that so terrified Emily. From a hole in the sky crawled the creatures of the Hell Hole, eager, slobbering, rancid, malicious demons hell-bent on taking over the world.

"They will become us," Emily cried. "Those filthy, hideous things! They will become us and we will become them!"

Ogden's gaze was riveted to the sky. The demons crawled out of their hole on top of each other like roaches, scrambling across the firmament for as far as the eye could see. Hairy things and scaly ones, too—creatures made of human bone and animal skin—beasts with leathery wings and monsters with eight legs. Most of them were stupid, lumbering brutes, but among them Ogden could discern smiling, crafty devils, too, their malevolent intelligence shining from their eyes.

"That is the world he will bring," Emily said. "That is his plan."

From the distance there suddenly came a voice—the voice of the Madman himself, calling to his wife.

Emily turned toward the sound, her lovely blue eyes staring into the night. The Madman called her name again.

"That is his plan," Emily said, calm now as the vision in the sky faded and Ogden returned his eyes to her. "But not for me."

And before he could stop her, she threw herself from the cliff, her scream fading as she plunged into the night.

"Emily!" Ogden shouted after her.

"Emily!" echoed the voice of Jackson Muir, suddenly emerging from the darkness in a flash of lightning, stepping onto Devil's Rock.

Ogden began to tremble. "I … I tried—"

The Madman rushed to the edge, peering over the side. From below, the sound of the waves against the rocks reached their ears.

"I tried to stop her," Ogden said, shaking terribly now.

The Madman turned to face him. There was rage in his eyes, but shock, too, and grief, terrible grief. For all his powers, he could not bring her back—at least, not to live as she once did. Ogden watched in fear and fascination as a terrible dilemma surged through the Madman's being. Jackson threw his hands out in front of him, gesturing toward the cliff, as if his sorcery might compel his beloved wife to rise from the waves. But then he pulled his hands back, clamping them over his face, and he sobbed.

Making Emily rise might well have been possible, but she would have been broken—in spirit as well as in body. A great Nightwing sorcerer Jackson Muir might be, but he knew he could not bring his beloved wife back to a life of innocence and purity. Worse: he could not make her love him again.

And for that, Ogden knew, someone would have to pay.

"I tried," he stammered, backing away from Jackson. "I tried to stop her."

"And you failed," growled the Madman, his dark eyes flashing.

He spread his arms wide and let out a scream that rivaled the thunder in its power. Indeed, the storm seemed to abate, its fury summoned into the body of the sorcerer on the cliff. Jackson Muir had always been tall and imposing, but now he seemed even more so, as if he stood not six feet but sixteen. His white teeth glowed in the dark, and his eyes blazed red.

"You will pay, Ogden McNutt! You will pay for failing to save my wife!"

"No, let him be," came the voice of another man.

It was Montaigne, having finally reached Devil's Rock himself.

"He is my apprentice, Jackson. I will punish him. Leave him to me."

"You dare instruct a Sorcerer of the Nightwing?" The Madman's eyes burned holes in the night as he threw his gaze at the newcomer. "You, a Guardian, meant only to serve me?"

"And to *teach* you," Montaigne said, defying his anger. "A Nightwing does not use his power for revenge."

Jackson Muir laughed. "But you forget, Montaigne. What was it that my brother called me? A renegade? An *Apostate*?" He laughed again, returning his red eyes to Ogden. "Run, little rabbit! Give me some sport!"

So Ogden ran. It was futile, he knew, but run he did anyway, giving in to the basic human instinct for survival. He ran into the dark night, away from the cliff, into the woods. He blundered into a bramble of thorns, tripped over a log, fell into a puddle of mud. But he kept on, running deeper into the thickness of trees and gathering of shadows. Above him he caught glimpses of the moon, full and gold, appearing now and again in the spaces between branches, a solemn, watchful eye.

He came to rest finally, embracing a tree as a child might its mother's breast. He understood this was the end, that there was no escaping the Madman—but even still, hope found its way to the surface. Might Montaigne have stopped him? Might he have persuaded Jackson to let Ogden go free?

It was quiet. No sound at all except for the distant crash of the surf. Ogden thought of his darling Georgianne.

"A precious little child, isn't she?"

The voice cut him to the quick. Ogden turned, and there, standing not two feet away, was the Madman.

"Do anything you want to me," Ogden said, "but don't harm Georgianne."

Jackson Muir smiled. "Step out into the moonlight, Ogden McNutt."

Ogden hesitated just a moment, but then did as he was commanded. It was useless to disobey, to try to fight him now.

"Look up at the moon," the Madman told him. "Look upon its face. See there your torment, my young fool. See your penalty for failing to save my wife."

Ogden lifted his eyes to the shining orb. It was a moon of

blood, dripping from the sky.

And suddenly Ogden began to itch. A terrible, burning sensation all over his body. He looked down at his hands and saw the reason why.

Hair—sprouting all over. His hands, his arms, under his clothes. He felt his face. There, too. Thick, bristly hair.

Then pain set in. Excruciating, ripping pain. Ogden's body twisted, contorted. His jaw was pulled, stretched out of shape. He saw his mouth thrust forward, transforming into the snout of an animal. In his mouth his teeth grew long and sharp, cutting his tongue.

Ogden McNutt fell to his knees. He could no longer stand. His shoulder blades shifted and expanded. The pain overpowered him. But when he went to scream, it was not a sound that he recognized.

It was the cry of a beast.

And then there was nothing. No pain, no thought.

Just the craving to drink warm blood.

THE PRESENT

INSIDE THE WALLS

Devon March swung the sledgehammer over his head and brought it crashing down into the wall.

"Whoever you are," he called, "we're about to finally meet!"

At last. The answer he'd been after for months. Just who lived behind this wall? Who was it that called his name, who seemed to hold the answer to the mystery of his past?

A woman, Devon thought, from the sound of her cries.

He had first heard her when she'd been kept in the tower of Ravenscliff, when he'd seen a light up there that was routinely denied by everyone else. Then he had seen her moved down here, to this sealed-off room in the basement with no door. And despite his powers—despite all the sorcery that was his birthright as part of the Order of the Sorcerers of the Nightwing—Devon had never been able to penetrate the wall.

That was why he'd had to resort to the sledgehammer.

The plaster crumbled easily under its weight. Devon lifted the hammer over his head and swung again. He broke through this time. He'd smashed a hole into the room.

"Back up," he called to whomever lived inside. "I don't want to hurt you."

But she was silent now. A moment ago she had been sobbing, and she had called him by his name.

Her name, however, remained a mystery despite the fact that Devon's Nightwing intuition—he used to call it the Voice—had told him that he knew her name already.

But what could that name be?

Once more Devon swung the sledgehammer over his head. One more blow and he would have a hole large enough to crawl through, even if he had to break more of the drywall with his hands. He readied himself to hit the plaster with his mightiest blow yet.

But all of a sudden he couldn't move his hands. The sledgehammer remained immobile over his head.

"You mustn't try," came a voice. "Please, please stop!"

Devon knew the voice. It belonged to Bjorn Forkbeard, the caretaker of Ravenscliff, a little gnome who was almost seven hundred years old. Devon twisted himself around and saw that Bjorn, standing on a wooden box, was holding the sledgehammer in place with his stubby but very strong hands.

"Let go, Bjorn!" Devon shouted.

"No, Master Devon! I was brought here to Ravenscliff to guard that room, and guard it I shall!"

Devon relented, loosening up on his grip on the hammer. Bjorn let go as well, jumping down from his box. Devon allowed the sledgehammer to fall to the concrete floor of the basement with a loud clang.

"So, it's just as I suspected," Devon said. "That *was* the reason Mrs. Crandall brought you here. To guard whoever it was she kept in the tower — and then had moved down here!"

"Well," said the little man, shrugging, "that and other reasons. Ravenscliff *did* need a caretaker, you know. And I'm a pretty good chief cook and bottlewasher, as you can attest yourself!"

Bjorn tried to laugh as he looked up at Devon, but the teen sorcerer refused to crack a smile. When he had first came to Ravenscliff, Bjorn had inspired a deep distrust within Devon. He had been unable to determine just whose side Bjorn was on, whether the gnome was good or bad. Too many things had happened in this house for Devon to trust *anybody* on first meeting.

But in the subsequent battle with Isobel—the renegade Nightwing witch from the fifteenth century—Bjorn had shown his true colors, and Devon now considered him an ally. He knew Bjorn was loyal, as all the gnomes were to the sorcerers of the Nightwing. Yet, ally or not, it was clear that the wily Bjorn still had a few secrets he'd been keeping from Devon.

"Who's behind that wall, Bjorn? And why am I not supposed to know?"

Devon lorded over the little man, who stood no taller than three and half feet. His skin was very pink, and his hair was white and unruly. A short beard forked in two under his chin. Hence his name.

"Answer me, Bjorn!" Devon poked his finger at the gnome's chest. "We've been through enough together now that the time for secrets is over!"

Bjorn's struggle with his loyalties betrayed itself on his flat pink face. "Ah, but I have *told* you, Master Devon. I may have been hired as her keeper, but I have never known her name— nor her history."

"Well," Devon said, turning back toward the wall, "we're about to find out."

"Mrs. Crandall will be furious," Bjorn warned him.

Devon smirked. "I've long stopped worrying about Mrs. Crandall's fury."

Whether that was completely true or not, it sounded good, Devon thought. He was tired of living under Mrs. Crandall's thumb. After all, he was the one -hundredth generation of Nightwing since the order's founder, Sargon the Great, and momentous things had been destined for him. It was about time he found out what they were—and he wasn't going to let Amanda Muir Crandall stand in his way any longer.

He reached into the hole in the wall and began breaking apart the plaster with his hands.

Ever since last fall, when he'd come to Ravenscliff to live, Devon had searched for the answers to his past. He'd grown up the son of Ted March, an ordinary auto mechanic—or so Devon had thought. But as his father had lain dying, he'd told Devon that he had been adopted. Not a word about who his real parents were, just the revelation that he was being sent to live with a family Devon had never heard of before: the Muirs. Losing Dad—who was the best father any kid could ever ask for—was hard enough, but to be sent away from his home, his school, and his friends made it ten times more difficult for Devon. A few days after the funeral, Dad's lawyer had placed Devon on a bus and sent him off to a windswept village on the rocky coast of Maine. The place was called Misery Point. Arriving in a raging thunderstorm, Devon had quickly grasped how the town had gotten its name.

Since then, Devon had lived in the mysterious dark house atop the cliff, and bit by bit, he had uncovered clues about who—and *what*—he was. For Devon had never been an ordinary boy. Since he was a toddler, he'd had supernatural powers: being able to levitate his dog, for example, or turn all the desks around in his classroom with just the merest thought. Dad had never explained why he had such powers, only that they were to be used for good. Neither did he explain the presence of the *demons*—those filthy, hideous beasts that lived in Devon's closet and periodically attempted to drag him down into the putrid chasm Dad called their Hell Hole. "You are stronger than they are," Dad had always told him. "Remember that, Devon. You are *stronger*."

Yeah, I'm stronger, all right, Devon thought now. *I've proven that. I've been down a Hell Hole and emerged again to speak of it.* Few people, even Nightwing, could make that claim.

Learning that he was a Sorcerer of the Nightwing had been the biggest revelation in Devon's fifteen years of life. He'd discovered that his father had been no simple auto mechanic, that he was, instead, a centuries-old Guardian who had raised and taught generations of Nightwing. Why, then, had he never told Devon the truth of his heritage?

The teenager had been forced to learn that on his own, with the help of Rolfe Montaigne—the sworn enemy of the Muir family who was, nonetheless, the son of a Guardian himself and who was, even now, trying to uncover as much as he could from his father's books to help Devon understand why Ted March had sent him to Ravenscliff.

Yet the answer to that question, Devon suspected, lay not in any book—but here, behind this wall.

Devon, the woman's voice had called to him many times. *It is you! You have found me!*

And now, Devon thought, *I have found her.*

"Hello?" he shouted through the hole in the wall, his voice echoing. "I'm coming through. Show yourself! Where are you?"

"Be careful, my young Nightwing master," Bjorn cautioned him from behind.

Devon took a deep breath. It was dark behind the wall. And still. As if no one was there, or ever was.

"Don't go quiet on me now," Devon called again. "After all these months of crying and calling my name."

He swung one leg over the broken drywall and pulled himself through the hole.

The dim candlelight from the cellar coming through the hole was not enough to illuminate the dark space behind the wall. Devon cupped his right hand and snapped his fingers. Instantly a glowing ball of white light appeared in his hand. He smiled to himself. When his Nightwing powers worked so effortlessly like this, it pleased him to no end. Sometimes they didn't work. But he was learning to master the powers that had once seemed so unruly and unpredictable.

He glanced around the room. The ball of light in his hand allowed him to see his surroundings very well. There was a bed, recently slept in, and a small table with a tray of dirty dishes sitting on top of it. Devon examined it: a bowl of soup, half eaten. Bread crumbs were scattered across a plate. And beside the plate, a worn, leather-bound book. Picking it up and bringing it close to the light, Devon looked at the cover. It read *Prayers and Meditations*. Opening to the front page, he read a signature in faded blue ink: *Emily Day Muir*.

"Emily Muir?" Devon asked out loud.

He'd seen the ghost of Emily Muir several times since coming to Ravenscliff, a pitiful spirit that had haunted the great house for more than thirty years now. Who would be reading her prayerbook—and why?

Devon turned around, looking back toward the hole. Bjorn was peering through it with anxious blue eyes.

"Someone is being kept prisoner in here," Devon said. "Who is it, Mr. Jailer? And why does she have Emily Muir's prayerbook?"

"I told you, Devon. I have never known her name."

"Then where is she now? How did she get out of here?"

The gnome moved away from the hole, wringing his little hands.

Devon looked around some more. An armoire with one door open. Clothes hung from hangers inside. Robes. And long sheathlike dresses.

"This is inhuman," Devon muttered. "Keeping someone in here like this."

But she was gone. Clearly there was another way in—and out.

"How did you bring her food?" Devon shouted back over his shoulder to Bjorn. But there was no answer forthcoming. The gnome was clearly torn between loyalty to Devon and service to his employer, Mrs. Crandall.

Then the teenager spotted something in the far corner of the room. A shadow. An outline of something.

He approached, holding the ball of light beside his face so he could see.

It was a door. A sliding panel that led from this room into another.

He slid the panel as far as it would move and stuck his face inside to get a good look around. It was completely dark. He moved the ball of light in closer.

And suddenly, revealed by the light, Devon saw a face, just inches from his own.

The face of a wild-eyed, crazy-haired woman, laughing silently at him.

"Whoa!" Devon gasped, taking one step backward.

Now the woman's laughter was heard. She seemed terribly amused that Devon had found her, as if they'd been playing a game of hide-and-seek. She cackled hysterically, then turned and darted off into the darkness behind her.

For a moment Devon was too shocked to follow. But once he'd shaken off his daze, he held the light out in front of him so he could see where she'd gone. He observed that the panel led not into another room but to a staircase, and he caught a glimpse of the woman's feet as she scurried up the steps. Her footsteps faded out as she climbed upward into the house.

"Don't follow her," came Bjorn's voice.

Devon looked over his shoulder. The gnome was leaning through the hole, distraught.

"Do you think I've come this far to just let her go?" Devon's voice was loud and insistent. "Bjorn, that woman knew my name! She clearly knows who I am!"

"She is mad," Bjorn warned him. "Insane. You can see it in her eyes."

That much was true. That face—it had been terrifying. Devon couldn't tell if the woman was twenty or ninety. Long white hair...pale skin...bulging eyes...that maniacal laugh. Crazy she certainly was, and probably dangerous.

But his Nightwing intuition was telling him to pursue her. Danger there might be, but nothing he couldn't handle. He was Nightwing. One-hundredth generation and all that.

"Mrs. Crandall will be furious," Bjorn reminded him.

Devon turned and scowled at the gnome. "If it's your job you're worried about, Bjorn, I can't help you there." He looked back up the secret staircase that led somewhere into the great house. "This is just something I have to do."

"Oh, do be careful, my young friend," Bjorn fretted, his voice trembling.

"Look," Devon said, "in the last few months I've handled two renegade Nightwing and assorted demons of all shapes and sizes. I think I can handle one crazy lady."

But this one crazy lady seemed to know something that none of the others had.

She knew who Devon was, and where he came from.

Yes, he could handle her, Devon thought—but could he handle what she *knew*?

Somehow, his intuition told him, *what I am about to learn will change my life.*

With the ball of light held aloft, Devon started up the stairs.

He was inside the walls of Ravenscliff.

That was what he realized as he continued climbing the stairs. Narrow, twisting passageways, the space so small that he couldn't extend his arms fully in either direction. Looking around, he saw that the woman could have gone any which way. The stairs frequently veered off in different directions, leading all through the great house. By now Devon was certain that he must be on the second floor, as he'd been climbing for at least five minutes. His quarry could have taken a dozen routes different than he had. She might have been anywhere within these passageways. How would he ever find her?

He would use his sorcery, that was how.

He closed his eyes and visualized the house as it stood on the top of the hill, overlooking the sea on one side and the village of Misery Point on the other. It was a creepy old place, to be sure, but pretty majestic, too: floors made of marble, shiny black wood inset with stained glass and crystal. When Devon had first arrived at Ravenscliff, he had been awed by all the ornamentation, what Mrs. Crandall called the family's "trinkets." Suits of armor, crystal balls, carvings of shrunken heads— Devon would later learn that these were the souvenirs from the Muir family's many years of sorcery.

But most wondrous of all were the ravens—those black-eyed familiars of the Nightwing, which had long roosted all over the house, but which had disappeared when the Muirs had renounced their sorcery. That renunciation had come after a terrible event—a tragedy the Muirs called the "Cataclysm"— in which Mrs. Crandall's father had died in the Hell Hole that existed under the great house. The decision was made at that point to end the family's long association with the Nightwing.

Accordingly, the ravens had flown off into the darkening skies that very night, with the belief that they would never return.

Yet they had. The ravens had come back. They had settled all over the house, taking up their former places of honor, when Devon March, his Nightwing powers intact, had come to Ravenscliff to live.

And Mrs. Crandall had been none too happy about it. More than once Devon had seen the lady of the house angrily shooing the birds away from the terrace. But she knew that so long as a Sorcerer of the Nightwing lived at Ravenscliff, the ravens would remain.

Good thing, too: the ravens had saved Devon from a demon attack not long ago. He'd come to feel a great fondness for the black birds with their shining dark eyes. They were his; they were part of who he was and where he came from.

If only they could talk.

For despite all that he had learned during these past several months at Ravenscliff, Devon still did not know the answer to the central mystery. If Ted March hadn't been his real father, then who was? And his mother—who was she? Had they both been Nightwing? What had happened to them? Why had they sent Devon away to be raised by Ted March? And why had Dad, on his deathbed, sent him here to Ravenscliff? What was the connection between this house and Devon's past?

She knows, his Nightwing intuition told him. *The woman I'm pursuing now ... she knows. She knows who I am.*

Devon paused to listen. He thought he heard a sound, a footstep. He couldn't be sure. He listened intently, as Sargon the Great might have—using not just his ears but all his other senses as well. A Nightwing could track someone through the slightest scent. Could he find her that way? If not by sight, then by scent?

But all he kept getting was Cecily's perfume.

Cecily—the girl he was in love with. Devon tried to block out Cecily's scent but found he could not. It was getting in the way of tracking down his quarry. And he knew why. As stupid as it sometimes made him feel, Cecily intoxicated him. She

21

fascinated him. Sometimes he couldn't think of anything but her. Cecily was not only pretty but strong, too—and smart, and crafty. She was also Mrs. Crandall's daughter.

The mistress of the house wasn't pleased by Cecily's budding romance with Devon. Maybe that was because she didn't want her daughter trying to reclaim the Nightwing heritage she had renounced for her before she was born. In fact, if Mrs. Crandall had her way, Devon would be forced to give up his powers, too—so terrified was she that, by using them, he'd bring back the Madman.

The Madman who had killed her father in the Hell Hole.

Devon admitted her fear was not without reason. The Madman had already come back once; who was to say he couldn't come back again? But Devon had defeated him—he, Devon, just a novice sorcerer, had kicked Jackson Muir's butt straight back to his Hell Hole. And he could do it again, too, he thought cockily to himself—but he'd really rather not *have* to, just the same.

He would never forget what it was like descending into the darkness of the Hell Hole. The feeling of utter misery and despair—not to mention the stink of death. The demons had attacked him, eaten parts of his flesh, infiltrated his mind. But he'd *had* to go down there; the Madman had taken little Alexander, and Devon was the only one—the only Sorcerer of the Nightwing left—who could save the boy.

Since then, Alexander, who'd just turned nine years old, had become Devon's pal. Despite all the horrors he'd had to face at Ravenscliff, Devon had still found a home here. There was Cecily, Alexander, and his friends from school: D.J., Marcus, Natalie. And of course, there was Rolfe Montaigne, who was the key to helping Devon unlock the secrets of his past.

But finding Crazy Lady might prove to be even more effective than Rolfe's research.

Blocking Cecily's perfume as best he could from his nostrils, Devon tried to concentrate. Where was she? Where was Crazy Lady? He stood on the dark, stuffy, cobwebby staircase and trained all of his sorcerer's senses on finding the woman.

He heard something. Definitely a footstep this time.

He turned, and behind him he made out a figure ascending the stairs. He held up his ball of light to get a better look.

And what he saw made him gasp.

It was not a woman climbing the steps at all. But a man.

A transparent man—with Devon's light shining right through him.

"Who are you?" Devon asked.

The ghost didn't answer. Devon knew the figure was a ghost because he had seen enough of them in this house to recognize them. But just whose ghost this was he couldn't be sure. It was some Muir ancestor, perhaps, but the face was unfamiliar from the portraits that hung on the walls of the parlor. This man was quite young, only a few years older than Devon, perhaps: eighteen or nineteen, possibly, certainly no older than twenty. He was dressed in jeans and a shirt.

"Who are you?" Devon asked again.

Ghosts didn't frighten him. He'd seen things way more frightening than ghosts in this house. Still, this one made Devon uneasy. The way the apparition just stood there on the steps, looking up at him. He reminded the teenaged sorcerer of someone, but he couldn't quite figure out who.

"Why don't you speak?" Devon was growing impatient. "Are you just wandering through walls or did you appear to me for a reason?"

"The moon is full," the ghost finally intoned. He sounded English.

"Um, yeah, I think it was." Devon stopped to think. It had been storming earlier, but he remembered looking out his window before the storm began. "Yeah," he said. "It was definitely a full moon. Is that supposed to mean something to me?"

The ghost suddenly raised his right hand and moved it up, then down, then up and down again in front of Devon's face. It was like he was making a sign of some kind.

"What are you doing?" Devon asked. "Do it again. It's dark, I can't see …"

But the ghost had faded away.

What was the sign he had made in the air? What did the moon have to do with anything?

That was when Devon felt the hand on his shoulder.

He turned—and screamed into the decomposing face of a long-dead corpse.

It took Devon too long to recover from his shock—too many seconds wasted to get his heart under control, to stop its racing. He knew how disappointed Sargon the Great would be in his reaction. Sargon had tested Devon once before, and he had expected better from his one-hundredth generation descendant. No matter that Devon had just seen a ghost and hadn't flinched. A Nightwing sorcerer could never permit his opponent the element of surprise. But still, he was a fifteen-year-old kid, and rotting corpses were his weakness. He'd take a ghost or a demon over a zombie any day.

But after about thirty seconds (twenty-nine longer than he should have allowed himself) he managed to concentrate on what he had just seen, and he realized it was no corpse at all. It was the woman, the one he sought. She had played some kind of trick on him. She was standing a few feet away from him now, laughing hysterically over the fright she'd caused him.

"Devon!" Her laughter was crazy, the sound of a disturbed mind. "I scared Devon!"

"Yeah," he grumbled, "and you won't get that chance again!"

"Scare *me* now!" the woman cried, her eyes wild, her hands waving in the air.

"How did you do that? How did you make yourself look like a corpse?"

She just giggled insanely.

"What is your name?" Devon asked. "You know mine, so tell me yours."

"Only if you can catch me!" Crazy Lady said, still laughing, bolting off once more down the corridor into the darkness.

Devon ran in pursuit of her. He thought about using a burst of sorcery to catch her. Maybe he could reach out his hand and cause his arm to stretch long enough to grasp the back of her neck. Or maybe he could turn his hand into a kind of magnet that would just draw her back to him. Could he do it? Should he try?

He was still mastering this stuff, after all. He'd learned how to do some things just by willing them to happen: making himself invisible, for example, or disappearing and then reappearing somewhere else. This would be a new trick. He concentrated on the magnet idea—but as soon as he did he felt the heat. The heat—which was the sign that either demons or another sorcerer was near.

He paused in his pursuit. If the demons were loose again—

But his intuition reassured him that was not the case. The heat that pressed against his cheeks must have indicated instead that some sorcery other than his own was present. It must have been that the woman whose laughter echoed through the dark was a sorceress herself!

"Show yourself!" Devon suddenly demanded.

And all at once, ahead of him in the darkness, the figure of the woman emerged. In her hands she held the same kind of glowing ball of light that Devon held.

"So many years," Crazy Lady said, looking at Devon and not sounding so crazy any more. "So many years ... I had forgotten the allure of sorcery ..."

"Who are you?"

She smiled at Devon. "You really do not know, do you?"

"No, but you know me. You know about my past."

Her eyes danced in the reflected glow. "Your past ... is that what you have come to Ravenscliff to find, Devon?"

He took a few steps toward her but she backed up, skittish, like a cat. He didn't want her to flee again, so he stayed in place, keeping a distance between them.

"Yes," he said. "I want to know the secret of my past. Who my father was. My mother."

She smiled again, almost kindly. "Is that so important

to you?"

"Of course it is. I deserve to know!"

The woman seemed almost sane as she approached him. Long white hair framed her face, but of her age Devon still couldn't be sure. Twenty? Forty? Eighty? Her eyes were dark but her skin was pale, pale white—smooth as a baby's while as brittle as ancient parchment.

"And you have learned nothing, nothing at all, while you have been at Ravenscliff?" Crazy Lady asked, only a few inches now from Devon's face. He did not move, not wishing to startle her.

"I have learned some stuff, but not all," he said, holding her gaze. "I have not learned the names of my parents, or what connection they had to Ravenscliff."

"Your parents?" She seemed to consider the idea. "Do you seek the names of your parents?"

"Yes." He was growing impatient. "How many times do I have to tell you? I want to know my father, my mother."

Crazy Lady began to laugh again, low and tittering. "Your mother ... why, she has always been right here, Devon, all along!"

He stared at her. "What do you mean?"

"All along," she echoed.

"You can't mean—" Demon stammered as an idea took shape in his mind. "Not her—"

The mysterious sorceress just laughed.

"You can't mean—*Mrs. Crandall?*" Devon asked, his voice a bitter croak.

Crazy Lady clapped her hands together, letting out a long hideous cackle, thrilled to have finally revealed the deepest, darkest secret of Ravenscliff.

THE BEAST

Devon couldn't respond. His voice—all thought—was gone.

He said nothing, did nothing as Crazy Lady turned and ran off back down the corridor into darkness.

"No," he finally said.

It can't be.

Not Mrs. Crandall—

He reacted suddenly to a noise. A scraping sound. The wall beside him began to move. A panel opening. Devon readied himself, as a sorcerer should, for an attack.

But it was Cecily.

"Devon," she said, scrunching up her face as she peered into the darkness at him. "What are you doing inside my *wall?*"

Behind her a soft light glowed from the side of her bed. Devon just stared at her, unable to speak.

"I heard voices from inside here," she said. "They woke me up." She examined the sliding panel. "I haven't used this old secret door since I used to play on this staircase as a little girl." She looked back at Devon and frowned. "You still haven't answered me about what you're doing in there."

He couldn't seem to form any words.

"What is the matter with you?" Cecily took his arm and coaxed him forward into her room. He followed numbly. She shut the panel and then turned to face him, crossing her arms over her chest. She looked especially pretty in the soft light from her lamp, her red hair down around her shoulders. She was wearing a pink flannel nightgown.

"Oh, I get it," she said, smiling. "You were sneaking up to see me. Didn't want my mother to know. Oh, Devon—"

She reached out to take him in her arms but he recoiled.

"No!" he shouted, pushing her away.

She made a face. "What's up with you?"

"Nothing. I mean, everything. I mean—"

He covered his face with his hands and staggered away from her.

"What *is* it, Devon? Tell me."

He dropped his hands and stared into her eyes. "We can't— we can't be—I mean, we can't—we can't see each other any more, Cecily!"

"What?"

"I got behind the wall in the basement," he said. "I met the woman we've heard behind there. I was right. She *did* know who I am!"

"You met the sobbing woman?" Cecily's eyes sparkled with interest. "The one I've heard all my life? Who *is* she?"

"I don't know. But it doesn't matter right now."

"Doesn't matter? Of *course* it matters, Devon. Mother's always denied her existence. Claimed it was a ghost. If she's *real*—"

"Didn't you *hear* me, Cecily? She knew who I was! *That's* what matters here!"

"Oh," Cecily said in a small voice. She looked at Devon with sudden fear in her eyes. "What did she tell you?"

"That—that my mother is—" He couldn't bring himself to say it. He finally forced the words out. "My mother is your mother!"

Cecily covered her mouth with her hand.

"I can't see you any more, Cecily. You're—you're my sister." The words burned his lips. He felt sick.

"No way," Cecily said, her eyes holding his in horror.

"That's what she just told me," Devon said.

Cecily suddenly gripped Devon by his shoulders. "Are you sure? Is that what she said? Are you absolutely sure?"

"Yes! She said my mother had been here all along and when I asked if she meant Mrs. Crandall—"

"What did she say, Devon? What did she say then?"

"She laughed," Devon told her.

"So she didn't confirm that's what she meant. She didn't actually *say* Mother was your mother."

"But that *was* what she meant."

"You don't know that," Cecily said, grasping.

"Come on, Cess—I've suspected your mother was my mother before!"

"Yes," the girl said, "and each time you have you've decided it was ridiculous. I mean, *look* at us, Devon. We look nothing alike!"

It was true: Cecily with her fair skin, green eyes and red hair, Devon with his olive complexion, brown eyes and hair so dark it was almost black.

"Different fathers," Devon said in response. "We probably had different fathers."

"But we're the same age. You were born in March and I was born in August. Sorry, but that's not quite enough time for Mother to have had you and then had me. Check Biology 101 if you're still not sure."

Devon had an answer for that, too. "Who's to say that I'm not already sixteen? I might be a year older than you are, Cecily. There's never been any birth certificate for me, remember. Your mother could've had me a year before you were born, and given me to Ted March to raise, and for whatever reason they decided to tell me that I was a year younger than I really was."

"And why would they do that?"

"I don't know. To throw us off the track."

Cecily sniffed. "Now you're just talking stupid. I won't hear any more of it. And who is she anyway, that crazy sobbing lady? Why should we take her word for anything? Until I know who she is, I'm not believing anything she said."

"Cecily, I believe her ..."

"Why? Did the Voice confirm it?"

She meant Devon's Nightwing intuition. "Well, it's not telling me she's wrong."

Still Cecily refused to accept it. "Well, I have my own intuition, and it's telling me she is. I don't know if it's some Nightwing remnant of my own family sorcery, but it's just as real as yours, Devon. And mine says we are *not* brother and sister."

"I don't know," Devon said, and his heart broke. "I can't take that chance any more."

She looked at him. "What do you mean?"

"What I said before, Cecily. We can't go on together. Not like we were. Not until I know for sure …"

Cecily looked aghast. "Are you breaking up with me, Devon March?"

He felt worse than he'd ever felt before. Even worse, if that was possible, than the day Dad died.

"Yes," he managed to say. "I guess I am."

Cecily grabbed her pillow from her bed and threw it at him. "Then get out of my room! You have no business being here! Get out!"

He did as he was told.

When one goes seeking answers, a voice told him—Sargon's? Dad's? His own?—*one has to be prepared for what those answers might be.*

Of course, back in his own room, he couldn't sleep. He lay there staring up at the ceiling.

Mrs. Crandall is my mother. A woman who has shown such little regard for me that when the demons have struck, she's barely lifted an eyebrow. A woman who has tried to bully me into forgetting my past and renouncing my powers. A woman who has kept secrets from me, lied to me, discouraged me in everything.

This was the mother that Devon had looked for all his life? This—*ogress*?

He couldn't even begin to process the horrible sensations roiling through him. Worst of all—he had lost Cecily.

I've kissed her. My own sister.

Devon felt as if he might be sick. He tried to push the memory far out of his mind.

He had to stop thinking about Cecily and Mrs. Crandall and instead concentrate on the mystery of the woman who was now running around inside the walls. With his sharply attuned Nightwing hearing, he could hear her scuttling from room to room and floor to floor. Who was she? Why did Mrs. Crandall—

his mother!—keep her locked away?

Suddenly he heard a sound from outside. It pulled him away from his thoughts and focused him on the present. Lying in the dark, he listened for the sound again, and finally it came: a long, low howl. The sound of some animal. A cry of agony, Devon thought.

He threw his blanket off and stood up. He wasn't going to be able to sleep anyway. He hurried over to his window. The howl came again. It rose up from the village at the bottom of the hill. The sound of a dog—or a wolf—or a bear—

"Devon," came a voice behind him.

He turned. It was Alexander. The chubby little boy stood there in his blue flannel pajamas, his big button eyes wide with fear.

"Do you hear that sound?" he asked. "What is it, Devon?"

"I don't know, buddy," Devon said, unfastening his window and opening the panes. Cold air rushed in at them as they heard the howl again, far off and ferocious.

"Is it a demon?" Alexander asked, coming up beside Devon.

"I don't think so. I don't feel any heat, and I always feel heat when demons are present." He tousled the boy's hair. "Maybe it's just a dog."

"I never heard any dog sound like that," Alexander told him.

It occurred to Devon that if Mrs. Crandall was his mother, Alexander was his cousin, the boy being the son of Mrs. Crandall's brother, Edward. Devon had met Edward Muir. He was an irresponsible playboy always off traveling the world, leaving his son here at Ravenscliff under his sister's care. Although Alexander worshipped his absent father, Devon felt sorry that the boy had to grow up with such a distant, uncaring parent.

At least I grew up with a great dad, even if he wasn't my blood father, Devon thought, remembering Ted March. *Dad was always there for me. He was the best parent anybody could ever have.*

But if Mrs. Crandall was his real mother, Devon asked himself as he stared out the window, then who was his real *father?*

The howl came once more, louder and longer and more anguished this time.

"Do you think it's hurt?" Alexander asked.

The sun began to rise over the horizon, casting a pink glow over the rooftops of the village.

"Could be," Devon said. "It sounds pretty distressed."

"But you're *sure* it's not a demon?"

Devon nodded. Alexander had seen a few of the nasty creatures; he knew enough about them to be afraid. And even though he had no memory of being taken down into the Hell Hole by Jackson Muir, the boy's subconscious seemed wary of another attack by the Madman.

"I'm sure it's just a dog," Devon said, trying to reassure him. "Maybe a bear caught in a trap."

"Poor thing," Alexander said.

"The sun's coming up," Devon said, moving away from the window. "I might as well start getting ready for school."

"Yeah, me too," Alexander said. "Hey, it's stopped now. The howling."

"Maybe somebody rescued it," Devon said.

The boy nodded, heading back to his room. "See you at breakfast, Devon."

"'Kay, buddy."

Of course, Devon knew he wouldn't just see Alexander at the breakfast table. He'd see Cecily, and he was not looking forward to that.

But the free-spirited, redheaded teenager was nowhere to be found when Devon made his way downstairs. The first one he spotted was Bjorn, who was setting out the scrambled eggs and French toast on platters. Devon helped himself to some as the gnome peeked up at him with a reproving eye.

"You see what you went and did," Bjorn whispered. "Now she's loose. Running through the insides of the house. How am I going to explain that to Mrs. Crandall?"

"Tell her I did it," Devon said defiantly.

"If I tell her that, she'll have your head!"

"Tell her not only did I do it," Devon said, sitting down at the table with his breakfast, "but now I know everything. The truth!"

Bjorn squinted his little eyes as he looked at Devon. "What do you mean, the truth?"

"Mrs. Crandall will know what I mean. Tell her."

"Oh, she's going to be furious with me." Bjorn clenched his fists together. Devon could see the gnome's long fingernails, used for carving tunnels through earth and stone, pressing into the skin of his palms. "I might even lose my job over it."

"I won't let her fire you," Devon assured his friend. "I'll take all the blame." He forked some eggs his mouth. "So why didn't Crazy Lady have access to the secret panels inside the walls before? Why wasn't she *always* running so freely through the house?"

"Somehow, whatever spell was put on that room was broken when you smashed your way through," Bjorn said. "There was a hex on wherever they kept her imprisoned, but you've destroyed it."

"It's inhuman the way she kept her prisoner," Devon said. "I have a mind to report Mrs. Crandall to the police. If she tries to fire you, that's what I'll do."

Bjorn sat down beside Devon. "Oh, she was really very kind to her. She and the late Mrs. Muir both. They'd spend long sessions down there with her, or up in the tower when she was kept there. They'd read to her, or play games with her ... she loved playing cards. Crazy Eights was her favorite."

Devon smirked. "Why am I not surprised?"

"And they'd go for long walks in the courtyard or in the woods when you kids were at school."

"But to keep somebody imprisoned like that, Bjorn ..."

"It was for her own good," the gnome insisted, "her own protection."

"Protection from what?"

"I don't know." Bjorn sighed. "They never told me."

"Mrs. Crandall only does what's good for *her*," Devon said

bitterly. "She thinks of her own welfare first. Whatever reason she kept poor Crazy Lady locked up was purely selfish, I'm sure of that."

The gnome was staring into Devon's eyes. "What has turned you so hard against her?"

"Look, Bjorn, ever since I came here to Ravenscliff, she's fought me. You know that. She's tried to keep the truth of my Nightwing heritage from me."

"That's because she fears the return of the Madman," Bjorn reminded him.

Devon couldn't eat any more. He'd lost his appetite. He pushed his plate away. He didn't have the heart to keep up this conversation. "I'll be in the parlor," he told Bjorn, standing. "Call me when it's time to leave for school."

Devon headed out of the dining room and through the foyer. He passed the tall paneled windows that looked out onto the front driveway and spied D.J.'s vintage red Camaro. Devon was glad; he could use a friend. He hurried to the front door and threw it open.

"Hey, Deej!" he shouted. "Man, I've got to talk with you! You here to give us a ride to school?"

His friend, sitting behind the wheel of his car, rolled down his window. "Hey, dude," D.J. said, the early morning sunlight glinting off the metal piercing in his upper lip. He was wearing a Red Sox baseball cap low on his eyes, and his voice was a little less exuberant than usual. Most mornings D.J. would greet Devon with a hail and hearty clap on the back. Today he seemed quiet and reserved.

Devon immediately saw why. In the passenger seat next to D.J. sat Cecily. She abruptly turned her face away, long hair flinging, when Devon approached the car.

"Listen, dude," D.J. said, looking up at him plaintively from the car window, "Cess—well, she called me—and well, you know, she asked me to come by and give her a ride to school."

"I see," Devon said. "So she didn't have to ride with me."

"Well, uh, I just, well, you know, man, I just figured I, well, that—"

Devon let out a long sigh. "It's okay, D.J. It's probably just as well."

"See you at school, man," D.J. said. "Still friends, right, dude?"

"Yeah," Devon said sadly. "Still friends."

Before Devon had arrived on the scene, D.J. and Cecily had been an item. Cecily had always been toying with him, and Devon was sure she'd start doing so again. It made him angry, the idea that Cecily would use D.J. to get back at him.

So he made his way over to Bjorn's old Cadillac and climbed in the backseat. Alexander sat up front, chattering all the way to school about the howling he heard during the night. Bjorn had heard it too, but he echoed Devon's belief that whatever it was, it wasn't a demon.

They dropped Alexander off first, at the new elementary school he'd just started, and then continued on to the high school. "Look," Devon said, "I'm sorry about Crazy Lady. I don't want to get you in any trouble."

"Let's hope I can round her up," Bjorn said as he pulled up in front of the school.

"If you can't, I'll try to catch her when I get home. Maybe we can get her back into the room before Mrs. Crandall even finds out." He got out of the car. "But in the meantime, maybe we ought to just let her run free for a while. It must feel good after being cooped up for so long."

The gnome just shuddered and drove away.

Devon looked up at his school. The kids were all milling around, talking in their little cliques. It was still cold enough that their breath steamed between them, but there was a hint of spring in the air, too. Devon could smell it. Maybe it was his heightened Nightwing senses that perceived it, but it was there: the smell of a thawing earth. He couldn't wait for spring, for summer. He wanted this winter over and done with, forgotten.

"So what's up between you and Cecily?"

He turned. It was Natalie, walking up to him, holding her books against her chest. The sunlight caught specks of blue in her jet-black hair and made her deep brown eyes sparkle.

Devon smiled.

"We broke up," he said simply.

"She said you claim she's your sister."

Devon sighed. "That seems possible, yeah. Maybe even likely."

Devon expected Natalie to make a wisecrack. She and Cecily were friends but also sometimes catty rivals. Devon figured she'd come back with some insensitive quip and he'd just grunt and move on. But Natalie surprised him.

"I'm really sorry, Devon," she said. "I told that to Cecily, too. That must be really hard. I know you guys had thought maybe—"

Devon laughed bitterly. "Yeah. We thought maybe."

"I can't imagine what you must be going through. I'm really sorry."

He looked over at her. Maybe he'd never given Natalie enough credit. She was being genuine and compassionate. After all, they'd all been through a lot together: coming close to being slaughtered by a pack of demons had a way of bringing people together. He was grateful to Natalie for her kind words. He definitely felt the need for her friendship right now.

He put his arm around her shoulders and they walked into school together at the first bell.

And there, leaning with his forehead against his locker, was the fifth member of their little band of warriors: Marcus.

"Hey, man, what's up?" Devon asked, coming around behind his friend.

Marcus turned his face slowly to look at him. Devon made a little sound as their eyes met. There it was again. The pentagram. The five-pointed star that Devon had seen hovering over Marcus's face from time to time.

And as Devon saw it again, he realized something else: *that* was the sign the ghost had made last night! The ghost he'd seen in the secret passageway. He had made *a five-pointed star* with his hand!

"Are you okay, man?" Devon asked, leaning in close to Marcus.

His friend had deep black circles under his eyes and red,

raw scratches on his cheeks and the bridge of his nose.

"I had a wicked bad night," Marcus said. "Really bad dreams."

"How'd you get so scratched up?" Natalie asked, peering in now herself.

"I must've done it myself. When I woke up, I had dried blood under my fingernails."

"What kind of dreams?" Devon asked.

Marcus shook his head. "I can't remember. Running … Fighting. I just know I tossed and turned all night."

Devon knew something was up. Too many things were happening all at once: the ghost had made the sign of the pentagram, and now Devon saw it on Marcus's face. Marcus had bad dreams and scratched himself in the night. Could there be a connection between all of this and the fact that Devon had broken whatever spell had kept Crazy Lady imprisoned? Had Devon disturbed some kind of force by doing so?

The second bell rang. "Look," Devon said to his friends. "We need an emergency meeting after school. I don't care what plans you have. We need to meet."

"Demons?" Marcus asked.

"Possibly. Or something." Devon turned to Natalie. "Tell Cecily and D.J., too. Whatever attitude Cecily is throwing my way will have to be put aside for now. It's Marcus's safety we're talking about."

His friend grabbed his shoulder. "Then you saw it again on my face. The pentagram."

"Yeah," Devon told him. "I did."

"What pentagram?" Natalie asked. "What are you talking about?"

"I'll tell you everything after school. We'll meet at Gio's for pizza. Tell D.J. and Cecily, too."

They hurried off to their various classes. Devon's first was geometry—neither his favorite nor his best—and he struggled to pay attention as Mrs. Bouchier droned on about acute versus obtuse angles and intersecting perpendicular lines. Devon prayed she wouldn't call on him because when he looked up at the chalkboard all he saw was one big floating pentagram—a geometric shape itself, but not one being discussed at the moment. At least not by Mrs. Bouchier.

What did it mean? For months he'd seen the pentagram occasionally on Marcus's face. Yet despite his and Rolfe Montaigne's best efforts, they had discovered nothing about what it meant, or what it might portend. The best they'd learned was that the pentagram was usually seen as a sign of protection, that wearing the pentagram or staying within its boundaries kept one safe from supernatural harm. Maybe Devon needed to find a pentagram for Marcus to wear.

But what was it that threatened him? Were the dreams Marcus had significant? Why had that ghost appeared to Devon—and who was he? And was there some connection between all of this and the woman who was now running madly between the walls of Ravenscliff?

He had to talk to Crazy Lady again. He had to ask her about—

"Mr. March?"

Devon blinked. The teacher. Damn. She'd called on him.

"Um, I'm sorry," he said, "would you repeat the question?"

Mrs. Bouchier folded her arms across her chest. "I've already asked you twice. I think instead you ought to come see me after the last bell."

"Oh, but I can't then. See, I have to—"

"See me after the last bell, Mr. March," she insisted, returning to the lesson.

Great. Just great. Now he was going to have to be late to Gio's. He had to get a message to his friends. If he wasn't at D.J.'s car at the end of the day, he could just see Cecily stalking off, still filled with spite. She could be very impulsive like that.

He knew he couldn't pull out his phone without Mrs. Bouchier noticing. She detested cell phone usage in her class. But he needed to send a text.

Well, he thought, a small smile slipping across his face. I don't need my thumbs for that.

He visualized his phone in his jacket pocket. He concentrated on Natalie's name in his contact list. And he texted her with his mind.

wait for me. i've got to deal with bouchier but i'll be there asap.

Then he hit send with a simple thought.

In his mind he could see the text coming through on Natalie's phone. She was in her English literature class down the hall. He could see her surreptitiously turning over her phone and reading Devon's text. He smiled to himself. Yes, he was definitely getting better and better at this sorcery stuff.

After school, he endured a lecture from Bourchier, agreeing to do an extra-credit homework assignment to show he wasn't entirely clueless about all that geometry stuff. Then he tore out of the room and ran down the hallway toward the parking lot—he couldn't pull his disappearing-reappearing act in front of so many kids. He skidded the last few feet to D.J.'s car, where his friends were waiting for him.

"Whoa, Speedy Gonzales," D.J. cracked.

"You were like going *really* fast, Devon," Natalie told him. "People were noticing. You could've given your powers away."

"I was afraid you guys would take off," he said.

Cecily glared at him coldly. "Take off? We wouldn't do that, not if it's true that Marcus might be in danger." She smirked. "See, *we're* loyal. We don't give up on friends so easily."

Devon ignored her sarcasm. "Let's go to Gio's."

Over pepperoni pizza, Devon filled them all in. About the ghost, about Crazy Lady, about her revelation about Mrs. Crandall being Devon's mother. Cecily just snorted, hoping the others will join her in dismissing the theory, but nobody did.

D.J. wasn't happy about something else, however. "Dude, it was not cool that you kept us in the dark so long about Marcus's pentagram."

Natalie defended Devon's decision to keep it quiet. "We've

had enough to deal with," she argued, "what with the Madman and then the demon witch Isobel."

Devon gave her a look of gratitude. It was nice to be defended. Cecily never did that.

"And besides," Marcus added, "Devon told me, and that's what counts. We planned to tell you all when we found out more." He tried to suppress a shudder. "And if I turn out to be some kind of danger to you all, I won't blame you if you want— "

"If we want what?" D.J. asked. "Dude, we're in this together. That's the way it's always been and always will be."

In this together, Devon thought as they piled into D.J.'s car after finishing their pizza. Cecily continued to give him the cold shoulder. So much for togetherness.

Devon asked D.J. to drop him off at Rolfe Montaigne's. "Do me one favor," he said to Cecily. "Cover for me with your mother. She'd be furious if she knew I was with Rolfe, but I'm hoping he can help us figure out what's going on."

Cecily huffed. "I'll do it for Marcus, not for you."

Devon watched them drive off. He couldn't believe how much this breakup hurt. He'd really been starting to like Cecily—a lot. Now, in a way, he was glad she was acting so childishly. It would make it easier to get over her, he hoped—to stop thinking of her as a girlfriend and more as a sister. A bratty, spoiled sister, but a sister nonetheless.

He turned and looked behind him at Rolfe's house. It was made of stone, set into the side of a cliff, facing the sea. It was a house filled with books on magic and strange glowing crystals that contained the knowledge Devon needed to gain if he was to become a master sorcerer. He trudged toward the house, the crashing sea in his ears. The sun was already quite low in the sky, the shadows of the bare, twisted trees lengthening around him. Once again Devon longed for spring. He was so tired of cold, dark, short days.

He was looking forward to seeing Rolfe—the mysterious man who'd been the first person he'd met in Misery Point, and who'd turned out to be the key to Devon's past. For Rolfe was a Guardian—like Ted March, one of those ancient, noble teacher-protectors of the Nightwing. But Rolfe, like Devon, had been deprived of much of his heritage by the untimely loss of his father, with centuries of knowledge failing to be passed on to the next generation. Despite helping Devon enormously over the last few months, Rolfe was still trying to learn as much as he could about the arcane lore of Nightwing magic so he might be an effective Guardian and guide Devon in his development as a sorcerer.

But this afternoon it was a much more mundane, much more human question that Devon needed to ask Rolfe—a question that had been gnawing at him all day. He just wondered if he'd have the guts to bring it up.

"Devon!" Rolfe called out in greeting when he saw the teen approaching the house. "You've come just in time. Look what I've discovered!"

Rolfe was in his study, the one made almost entirely of glass and jutting out over the sea. Whenever Devon visited, the sea was roiling and restless, crashing hard against the rocks. A flash of silent lightning zigzagged across the sky, then disappeared, leaving the moon to rise on its own.

"What is it, Rolfe?" Devon asked.

"Come down the stairs and let me show you!"

Devon descended the spiral staircase that led from the main part of the house into Rolfe's study. He could see the older man below. Rolfe was tall and handsome, with dark eyes and hair and a cleft chin. In his hands he was holding a crystal, pinkish and blue and pulsing with light.

"Watch what I can do," Rolfe said, as excited as a little boy.

Instantly, images flashed against a sheet that Rolfe had pinned up against his bookcase. It was sort of like an old-fashioned magic lantern. Images of birds—ravens—were flying furiously. Devon squinted his eyes to make out the blurry picture. The ravens were landing on a house …

"Ravenscliff?" he asked.

"Yes indeed!" Rolfe looked from him back to the makeshift screen with obvious thrill. "I think my father must have used this crystal to teach Randolph Muir the history of his family."

Devon now stood at Rolfe's side, watching raptly. Randolph Muir was Mrs. Crandall's father. A great sorcerer, Randolph's tragic death had been the reason his family had eventually renounced their powers—why Cecily had had no clue of her Nightwing heritage until Devon had revealed it to her, much to her mother's chagrin.

"Keep watching," Rolfe said.

Devon didn't have to be told. His eyes were transfixed. Suddenly the images of the ravens were replaced with that of a man, somber-faced and serious, in top hat and gray muttonchop sideburns. Devon recognized him instantly as Horatio Muir, the founder of Ravenscliff and one of the greatest Nightwing of all time.

"This is awesome!" Devon exclaimed. "Finally I can learn more about the Muir family!"

My family, he thought wryly to himself. It was an odd idea to get used to.

But he was distracted by a sound. As fascinated as he was by the images of Horatio Muir, his sharply attuned ears picked up a disturbing commotion from outside. Howling. The same as last night. That strange animal howling—

"Rolfe, do you hear that?"

But his Guardian was focused on the images being projected by the crystal. "Look! There's Horatio with his children. Randolph, and his second son, Gideon—and there, look! It's Jackson—the Madman—as a young, innocent boy!"

Devon admitted it was uncanny to see Jackson Muir as a teenager not much older than he was now. But he didn't look so innocent to Devon. There was a glint in his eye, a hard, calculating ambition, even then—

Once more, Devon was distracted by the howling. It was closer this time. Almost as if it was right outside the house.

"Rolfe, do you hear—?"

"Devon, pay attention to these images! They may reveal so much about the Muirs and hopefully your own sorcery ... I'm hoping we'll see my father and yours ..."

Devon returned his eyes to the sheet, in anticipation of

seeing Dad.

But the howling came again then, louder than ever.

"Rolfe," Devon said, "I really think that sound is—"

But before he could finish, the large window to their right was smashed, the glass shattering everywhere—

And a beast—stinking, wet, hairy, and snarling—had leapt upon Rolfe, grabbing him by the throat with an enormous furry hand.

A BIRTHDAY SURPRISE

"Back!" Devon commanded. "Back to your Hell Hole!"

But even as he shouted, he knew the beast was not going anywhere. This was no demon, no minion subject to a Nightwing's power. This was something else, something Devon didn't recognize—something that might kill Rolfe right here, right in front of his eyes.

The crystal had fallen from Rolfe's hand and the images had disappeared from the screen. Rolfe tried to fight back as best he could, grabbing the beast's hands—more like paws, giant bear paws—and struggling to wrest them from his throat.

With his powers having no effect on the thing, Devon felt helpless. In desperation, he grabbed a candlestick from Rolfe's table and whacked it hard against the thing's hairy head. The beast howled, dropping Rolfe to the ground and turning to face Devon.

Its eyes, Devon thought. *Why do I recognize its eyes?*

The thing dropped down onto all fours. It was preparing to pounce.

It did resemble a bear, but also a wolf. *But also a man*, Devon thought. The face was hairy, but human, too—like one of those Neanderthals Devon had studied in school.

The beast snarled, ready to lunge. Devon remained locked in its gaze, holding the candlestick over his head.

The thing pulled back, growling low. It had seemed to reconsider its attack on Devon.

Rolfe, meanwhile, had gotten to his feet. With one eye, Devon watched him move slowly across the room, while keeping his other eye firmly trained on the beast. Rolfe reached his desk and carefully pulled open a drawer. Devon knew he was going for his gun.

"What are you?" Devon asked the beast, wanting to keep its attention. "Where are you from?"

The beast only growled down deep in its throat.

"What kind of creature are you?"

Once again the thing stood on its hind legs, hissing.

"Come on, ugly. Communicate with me. What brought you here?"

All at once it let out a howl and lunged. Yet it didn't leap directly at Devon; it made a grab instead for the candlestick, as if to dislodge it from the teenager's hands. Devon instantly disappeared and reappeared behind the creature, causing it to spin around in frustrated confusion.

"That's what you get for tangling with a sorcerer!" Devon taunted, waving the candlestick at him. "Come on! Try and get it! I might not be able to overpower you, but I can still tire you out!"

The thing recoiled, as if the candlestick somehow had the power to hurt him.

"Move out of the way, Devon," Rolfe shouted. From the corner of his eye, Devon could see the older man leveling his gun at the beast. "I've got a good shot from here."

"No!"

It was a woman's voice from upstairs. Devon saw Roxanne, Rolfe's lady friend, who had some mysterious powers of her own, standing at the top of the spiral staircase. She was watching the scene with alarm.

"Don't shoot it, Rolfe! You'll regret it!"

"Regret it? The thing just tried to kill me!"

"I suspect unless those bullets are silver," Roxanne said, "they'll do nothing more than enrage the poor creature." She started down the staircase, holding a large silver amulet in front of her. It was one of the necklaces Devon had seen her wear many times. "Devon, just keep approaching with the candlestick. If we both close in on him …"

Devon obeyed. The two of them walked slowly toward the snarling, slobbering beast. It looked between the two of them, then raised its hideous face to the ceiling and howled. They weren't two feet away from it now, Devon with just his candlestick and Roxanne with just her amulet. But it was enough to make the thing tremble and cry out. Devon actually felt sorry for it, so pathetic did it sound. Up close he got another look into its eyes. Black and glassy, but still somehow familiar …

And then the beast jumped—smashing through another window and landing on the sand below. They watched as it lumbered down the beach and disappeared into the night.

"What," Rolfe managed to say, catching his breath, "was *that*?"

Roxanne had rushed up to Rolfe and was examining his neck where the beast had grabbed him. Devon looked over at her. "You seem to know what it was," he said.

"Not in any specifics." She touched Rolfe's throat and he winced a little. "The wound is not serious, my love. Thankfully you'll only have a bruise."

"So what *do* you know?" Devon persisted, coming up behind her.

She left her hands on Rolfe's neck for several seconds, almost as if she were healing him. She looked over her shoulder at Devon. "On the way back from the village," she explained, "the moon spoke to me. I knew as soon as I saw the beast that it was a creature of the moon."

Devon scratched his head. "Uh, Roxanne. You know I think you're cool and whatever powers you've got going on there, they're totally awesome. But—" He made a face. "The moon *spoke to you*?"

She laughed in that hearty, musical, Jamaican way she had. She moved away from Rolfe and stood in the moonglow, seeming almost ethereal, as if she weren't so much flesh and bone but smoke and light. Devon watched her intently.

"Yes, Devon March, the moon spoke to me. The whole world, the entire universe, will speak to you if you only listen." Roxanne smiled. "Isn't that right, Rolfe?"

"Yeah, yeah," he grumbled, rolling out some sheets of plastic from the closet. "Right now the world is telling me that thing made a mess of my study. Help me cover these broken windows before my books get wet. It's started to rain."

"Hey, Rolfe," Devon said, smirking. "Don't put yourself out. I can fix 'em."

With a wave of his hand, he sent out a silent command that the windows repair themselves. It was a snap. A simple enough Nightwing trick.

But the windows stayed broken; the glass remained shattered across the floor. A gust of wind swept in rain and sleet.

Rolfe rolled his eyes. "Showing off, Devon. You know your powers won't work if you're trying to show off."

"Okay, okay, let me try again."

Still nothing.

"Forget it, buddy, too late. Being cocky won't win you any Nightwing medals. Now help me do it the old-fashioned way."

Chagrined, Devon helped Rolfe tack the plastic against the wind. He saw Roxanne suppress a small laugh.

"So, go on," Devon said. "Finish telling us what that thing was. How is it the moon's creature?"

"Look outside," Roxanne said. "Even in its second night of its full phase, the moon is still round and vivid and bold in the sky. Even the most supernatural-denying scientists acknowledge the power of a full moon."

"So you mean," Devon asked, an idea coming to him, "it was kind of like ... a werewolf?"

Rolfe snorted. "More like a were-*bear*. Or were-*beast*."

"Yes, exactly like that," Roxanne said. "The old legends say only silver can ward off a creature of the moon. Hence the reason you could repel him with a simple candlestick but not with your great mystical powers."

"You keep calling it a *him*," Devon observed.

She nodded. "You know the stories. You've seen the movies."

"You mean ...?" Devon turned, leaving Rolfe to finish tacking up the plastic himself. Part of it unfurled and smacked Rolfe on the head, leaving him grumbling. "That thing—it was really some guy who turns into a beast when the moon is full?"

Roxanne smiled. "What is the old rhyme? 'Even a man who is pure at heart, and said his prayers by night, may become a wolf when the wolfbane blooms, and the moon is full and bright.'"

Rolfe sighed, stepping back to look at the plastic. "Well, that should do it until I can get it repaired."

"Sorry I couldn't be of more help," Devon said.

Rolfe grinned. "Don't worry about it, kid. That's what I have homeowner's insurance for." He laughed. "Though what I'll put on the claim, I'm not sure. Am I covered for attacks by were-beasts?"

"I wonder who the poor guy is," Devon said, glancing off into the night, "and how he got that way."

"A curse, usually," Roxanne told him.

"We should call the police." Rolfe looked out onto the beach to see if the beast was still lurking nearby. "Last night John Harker reported a sighting of some kind of large animal at his farm, and he found a dozen of his chickens slaughtered and his cow attacked. That thing needs to be caught."

"But why would it attack you, Rolfe?" Devon wondered. "Why jump in here like it knew what it was doing? Or—what *he* was doing." He looked over at Roxanne. "I'm sure you're right. It *was* a man. Because I sensed I'd met him before."

Rolfe was considering this. "Then … there must be a Nightwing connection. I'll try using the crystals again, see what they might tell us …"

Devon sighed. "Stuff is happening again, Rolfe. That's why I came over here."

"You two should talk," Roxanne said. "I'll call and report a sighting of the creature. I'd worry that the police might kill the creature, but without silver bullets the best they can do is capture it—and come morning, we'll see who the poor soul really is."

"Yeah, and I should be getting back to Ravenscliff," Devon said. "I've got a showdown looming with Mrs. Crandall."

Rolfe eyed him, curious now. "I'll drive you home and we can talk on the way," he said.

They headed down the winding narrow road along the cliffs, the windshield wipers of Rolfe's Porsche struggling to keep the rain and sleet from obscuring their vision. Devon figured he might have just pulled one of his disappearance-reappearance acts, landing himself nice and dry back in Ravenscliff's parlor. But after his last flop, he wasn't keen to try another showy routine. Besides, he needed time to talk with Rolfe.

There was still the matter of that very important question he needed to ask. *If* he had the guts.

So he told Rolfe everything that had happened: breaking into the secret room, the ghost and the sign of the pentagram, the encounter with Crazy Lady and her revelation that Mrs. Crandall was his mother.

"That one's hard to swallow, Devon," Rolfe said.

"Wait, just let me finish."

He told him about seeing the pentagram on Marcus's face again this morning at school, and that Marcus had reported a night of bad dreams.

"But you have no idea if the pentagram is connected to any of this," Rolfe said. "You've seen it before on Marcus's face and nothing has happened."

"Yeah, but now, with the ghost making the sign and talking about the moon and then this beast showing up—"

Rolfe was silent as he drove. He seemed lost in thought.

"Well?" Devon asked. "What do you make of it all?"

"I just—" He shook his head. "The part about the crazy woman …. Are you *sure* she said Amanda was your mother?"

Devon sighed. "She said my mother had been at Ravenscliff all along, and when I asked if she meant Mrs. Crandall, she clapped her hands and smiled."

Rolfe looked over at him. "So she didn't say yes. She didn't actually confirm that Amanda was your mother."

"But that's what she meant, Rolfe! It was obvious!"

"She's insane, Devon. You said so yourself."

"But she's a sorceress, Rolfe. I felt the heat. I saw her do tricks …"

Rolfe raised an eyebrow as he glanced over at Devon.

"Nightwing?"

"I don't know for sure if she's Nightwing, but she's got some kind of powers. And she *knew*. She knew about me! She's been calling my name for months. And my inner Voice, my Nightwing intuition, confirms that she knows the truth."

Rolfe went silent again.

"It makes sense that Mrs. Crandall is my mother," Devon argued. "That's where I get my powers. Through *her*. And Dad sent me here to live because he knew the truth."

"If Amanda is your mother, Devon," Rolfe said, his voice calm and steady, "you shouldn't *have* any powers. She renounced her own before you were born. That's why Cecily has no powers."

That was a good point, Devon realized—and one he hadn't considered before. "Still," he said, shaken only a little in his conviction, "I know what the woman was telling me and I know it's true."

"Why are you so determined to believe Amanda is your mother?"

Devon couldn't answer. He looked out the car window into the cold, driving rain. They were quiet again for several minutes, unspoken words hovering in the air.

"Rolfe," Devon finally said.

"Yes?"

"If Mrs. Crandall is my mother …"

"Yes?"

"Well, you know, I have to wonder …"

"About?"

"Well, I know that, well, that you and she … a long time ago …"

Rolfe turned to look at him, and his face was kind. "You're thinking that, if she's your mother, I might be your father."

"Well," Devon said, and his voice was thick, "it kind of crossed my mind."

Rolfe reached over to squeeze the teenager's shoulder. "I'd like nothing more than to be your father, Devon. Nothing more. But you see, well … Amanda and I were in love, yes. I hoped someday to marry her. But we never …" His voice trailed off.

"Oh," Devon said in a small voice. "I get it."

"We never did anything more than kiss," Rolfe said, returning his hand to the wheel. The roads were becoming extra slippery through this pass. Devon realized it was the very spot where, soon after the young Amanda Muir had broken up with him, a distraught and drunken Rolfe had run his car off the road. He had survived the plunge into the waters below, but two passengers in his car, a boy and a girl, servants at Ravenscliff, did not. It would be Amanda's testimony—that she had seen Rolfe at the wheel—that had sent him to jail for manslaughter for ten years.

It was an act of betrayal for which Rolfe had never forgiven her, and for which he had sworn revenge—on her and on the whole Muir family. He insisted he was *not* driving that night. He'd been too drunk to remember who was, but he knew it wasn't him. He hadn't been too drunk to remember the horror of their deaths, however. Rolfe had been fooling around with the girl, Clarissa Jones. That was the reason that Amanda had ended their relationship. Jealousy, spite, hatred—these had been the motives behind her testimony against him, Rolfe had always believed.

"If Amanda *is* your mother, Devon," he said now, breaking the silence, "who your father could be is a complete mystery. I was in prison, of course, so I don't know who she was seeing. But she would have had to give birth to you very soon afterward, for within a year or so after I had left she had married Peter Crandall and had Cecily."

Devon nodded. "That's why I'm starting to believe I'm a year older than I've always thought. Instead of being almost sixteen, I'm almost *seventeen*."

Above them the lights of Ravenscliff had begun to glow through the rain. "I don't know, Devon," Rolfe sighed. "I just don't know about any of this ..."

"Well, I *do*," Devon said, looking up at the house.

"For now," Rolfe said, "the more immediate mystery is who that woman is, and what her powers are, and why Amanda has kept her locked up so long." He smiled deviously. "Wouldn't the authorities be interested in learning about this …"

"Don't, Rolfe. Don't say anything yet. Not until I can get some answers from her." Devon continued staring up at the glowing windows of the great house. "After that—mother or not—you can do whatever you want with her. Send her to prison. It would serve her right."

Yet despite his anger at her, Devon immediately felt guilty for saying such a thing. She *had* taken him in after all, and certainly Cecily would be devastated by her mother going to jail …

Rolfe was looking over at him. "You think she's actually going to give you answers to your questions? She's never answered you straight before."

He had stopped the Porsche halfway up the driveway. It was best that Devon got out here; Mrs. Crandall was already going to be angry enough as it was. No use further perturbing her by letting her see him get out of Rolfe Montaigne's car.

"I'm going to try," Devon said, opening the door. "Now that I've met Crazy Lady, she's going to have to admit *something*."

"Good luck, buddy," Rolfe said.

"You, too. See what the crystals have to say about all of this."

"I'll finish watching the little home movies and let you know."

Devon gave a little salute and pushed out into the rain. He watched as the Porsche turned and headed back down the hill, its headlights sweeping past him, then disappearing beyond the crest of the hill.

He began to trudge toward the house.

And in the distance, he heard it.

The howl of the beast.

And something else, too.

The sounds of moaning close by. A strange wailing, as if another animal was in pain. It came from behind him, then in front of him, then off to his left. Something out there in the woods along the driveway. Devon began to walk faster, anxious to be inside the house and out of the cold rain. Away from these sounds …

But then he saw it. In front of him, standing directly in his way.

The ghost. The same from last night. The man in the jeans and tee shirt. He writhed and twisted and contorted, the moonlight seeming to single him out like a spotlight. He moaned and cried out—and before Devon's eyes, he transformed into the beast.

The thing fell to all fours and growled up at Devon, yellow saliva dripping from its lips, ready to spring.

I haven't any silver, Devon thought in a panic just as the thing leapt.

Devon screamed.

But it never made contact. It simply disappeared into the night.

Devon ran the rest of the way into the house.

"*Well*," Mrs. Crandall intoned imperiously, her arms folded across her chest, "you finally came back to face what you've done!"

"Can I just take off my wet coat before you start yelling at me?" Devon asked, yanking himself free of his drenched denim jacket and hanging it on the coat rack.

She was standing in the doorway to the parlor. As ever, she was dressed as if she were going to a ball instead of just hanging around the house on a stormy night. She wore a green satin brocade gown that came to the floor, emerald earrings, and a long pearl necklace, her strawberry blond hair swept up in an elaborate 'do. She was beautiful, all right, green eyes set deep into her pale face. Devon could see why Rolfe had found her hot. But she was also his *mother*, and he was angry at her, and he just couldn't look at her with any objectivity.

"You have no *idea* what you have done, Devon," she said, glaring at him.

Just then there came a mad thumping, followed by hysterical laughter. It was Crazy Lady, running behind the wall of the parlor. She banged her fists against the wall a couple of times to let them know she was there, emitting a high-pitched cackle. Then Devon heard her footsteps running up some secret stairs and then—bang, bang, bang!—across the ceiling above them.

"She is running wild within the walls of this house thanks to you," Mrs. Crandall snapped, turning and striding into the parlor. "Come in here! We need to talk!"

"Yes, we certainly do," Devon agreed.

He followed her into the parlor. It was a wondrous room, presided over by the stern portrait of Horatio Muir hanging above the mantel. Musty old books were stacked from floor to ceiling on shelves that were imbedded with skulls and crystal balls, shrunken heads and stuffed birds—souvenirs of generations of sorcery. An ancient suit of armor stood beside stained glass double doors, beyond which lay a terrace overlooking the cliffs and choppy sea below. In the air hung the heavy aromas of incense and oils, while in the stone fireplace a furious fire snapped and popped.

"You had no right—*no right!*—to break that wall," Mrs. Crandall shouted now, facing Devon. "That's willful destruction of property!"

The teenager stood his ground. "So have me arrested. Wouldn't the sheriff like to know you kept somebody imprisoned in this house?"

"Don't play games with me, Devon. This time you have gone too far. You know the dangers of this house, the horrors we have faced here from the Madman. Do you want to bring that all back?"

"So is there a connection between Crazy Lady and Jackson Muir?"

Amanda Muir Crandall let out a long sigh as across the ceiling above her came the sound of running footsteps.

"Look," Devon said, "she's been calling my name for months. How could I *not* investigate? If she's a danger, *tell* me. I've got powers. I can take care of her. I've handled crises here *before*, you know."

"Oh, Sir Galahad," Mrs. Crandall said sarcastically. "But

maybe this time you've gotten a bit over your head."

Devon made a cocky sound of disbelief. "Crazy Lady is more dangerous than Jackson Muir? Than Isobel the Apostate? I don't think so."

"Oh, Devon," Mrs. Crandall said, suddenly appearing utterly exhausted. She sank down into her wingback chair. "Do you really believe we would have kept her safely secured and hidden away in the tower, and then in the basement, if our very lives hadn't depended on doing so?"

Devon made a sound of frustration. "Why don't you just tell me who she is? Every secret you've tried to keep from me has eventually come out …"

Mrs. Crandall stood again, pacing across the room. The footsteps behind the wall, the laughter, the bang-bang-banging, was grating on her nerves. "Oh, *why* hasn't Bjorn caught her yet? Every time he manages to contain her, she slips away. She is crafty. She's remembered how to disappear …"

Devon nodded. "I assume whatever spell kept her confined for so long also kept her from the use of her powers."

"Not any more," Mrs. Crandall conceded.

"Is she Nightwing?"

"Her powers … they're different from yours, Devon. She was never properly trained in them. And she has forgotten even the rudiments of how to use them correctly, which only makes her more dangerous. If you met her, Devon, you would understand how unbalanced she is—"

"Oh, I did meet her," Devon said. "Didn't Bjorn tell you?"

Mrs. Crandall's head suddenly spun around to look at Devon. "No. He only told me that you had seen her run into the secret panel …"

Devon gave a little laugh. "I imagine he was trying to keep both of us out of more trouble than we were already in. But yes, I met Crazy Lady." He held his gaze with Mrs. Crandall. "We had *quite* the conversation."

Her face went completely pale as she looked at Devon.

"In fact, she told me who I was," Devon said calmly.

Mrs. Crandall steadied herself against the back of her chair.

"Devon," she said, her voice trembling now, "she is insane. You must remember that …"

"She told me who my mother is."

The mistress of Ravenscliff seemed almost as if she might faint. Still holding onto the chair, she managed to sit back down, her eyes never leaving Devon's face.

"She … told … you …"

"Yes," Devon said. "She told me that *you* were my mother."

Mrs. Crandall was silent, just staring up at him.

"Don't you have anything to say to that?" Devon asked.

She finally broke her gaze, looking off across the room. "She told you that I was your mother? She really said that?"

"Yes, she did."

Mrs. Crandall stood. Her face had shifted from anger to kindness in a matter of seconds. She approached Devon, cupping his cheeks between her palms and looking down into his eyes.

"Oh, Devon," she said. "How difficult it must be for you, not knowing who your real parents are. I do feel for you. Please don't ever think that I don't. But I'm not your mother. She is insane. She is insane and dangerous, and we must find her and keep her safe, so we, too, will be safe."

And with that, she moved off, her long gown rustling as she walked out of the parlor and across the foyer to the staircase. Devon watched her ascend to the second floor like an empress, regal and poised.

What is the truth? Devon couldn't be sure. If Mrs. Crandall was his mother, why didn't she just admit it?

Well, for lots of reasons, he supposed, *prime among them probably Cecily.*

Mrs. Crandall didn't want her daughter to know that she'd had a child before she was married. And by admitting it, she'd then have to deal with the question of Devon's father, and maybe she just didn't want to be reminded of whoever he was.

Or maybe—all sorts of ideas flooded Devon's mind over the course of the next few days—maybe Devon's father was some powerful sorcerer, and by reconnecting him to Devon all the sorcery would come back to Ravenscliff.

Which, come to think of it, was Devon's birthright as much as it was Cecily's and Alexander's. If Mrs. Crandall was his mother, Ravenscliff was as much his as it was anybody else's.

That's why Dad sent me here.

But in the days that followed, Devon's heart continued to hurt as Cecily cold-shouldered him. How much he wished Mrs. Crandall was not his mother and Cecily not his sister. He tried to convince himself that was Rolfe was right, or at least to entertain the possibility that Mrs. Crandall was not his mother. After all, why would Devon have powers if his mother had renounced hers before his birth? And Crazy Lady hadn't exactly confirmed the theory, as everyone kept pointing out—even if Devon was certain that was what she meant.

Okay, ninety-nine percent certain.

What's the matter with my inner Voice? It's supposed to intuitively tell me things that I can trust. Why is there a nagging little doubt now?

Even with his doubts, however, he could not bring himself to reconcile with Cecily. There were still too many questions, too many fears. So he spent his time with Natalie. It was actually not so unpleasant. Natalie was extremely pretty, but even more important, she was sweet and considerate. Cecily had often had temper tantrums and punished Devon with the silent treatment. It was actually pretty nice to hang out with someone less mercurial. They could talk about a million things, and Natalie never got all cranky and annoyed at anything. At lunch, he sat with Natalie in the cafeteria; Cecily sat at another table with D.J. Their little band of demon hunters was in danger of breaking up.

Especially with Marcus's absence. The day after Devon's confrontation with Mrs. Crandall, they'd all been alarmed to see that Marcus wasn't in school. He wasn't answering any of their texts and hadn't tweeted or posted anything online in more than twenty-four hours. Devon was worried. After class, he'd headed over to Marcus's house.

His father had answered the door. "Marcus is in bed. He's … uh, not feeling well."

"Can I see him?" Devon asked.

"Um, well," Marcus's dad had said, looking back over his shoulder. "It's Devon, Gigi. Can he go up and see him?"

"Have him come inside," Marcus's mother had called.

It was a plain, ordinary house, no skulls or crystal balls, just a simple, flowered sofa, a La-Z-Boy recliner, and a television set. Marcus's school photos hung on the wall. It had reminded Devon of the house where he'd grown up, that small little two-bedroom place in Coles Junction, New York, where he'd lived with Dad. There'd been no secret panels and portraits of somber, mysterious ancestors. Devon had felt a pang of homesickness walking into Marcus's house, and not for the first time did he wish he could go back in time. Things were so much simpler then.

Marcus's mother had stood in front of him in a housecoat, wringing her hands. She had looked terrible, as if she'd been up all night. "Marcus is sleeping," she had told him. "He's … he's had a rough time."

"What's wrong with him?" Devon had asked.

"The doctor isn't sure. He's been … sleepwalking. Has he seemed any different to you?"

"Well, he told me he'd had some bad dreams the other night," Devon had replied, wondering if he should reveal anything about the pentagram to Marcus's parents. He'd decided against it; they never would have believed it.

"Bad dreams, bad dreams," Marcus's mother had said, putting a hand to her head and sitting down on the couch. She'd started to cry.

"It's okay, Gigi," her husband had said, placing a hand on her shoulder.

"Can't I go see him?" Devon had asked.

"No," Marcus's mom had said between tears. "I don't want you seeing him. It'll be a while before he gets back to school. He needs to recover …"

Devon had left there feeling helpless. He'd tried to will himself into Marcus's room but found he couldn't. There was something shielding his room. Devon worried that he was failing his friend.

Now, days later, it struck him what Marcus needed.

A pentagram.

To protect him.

How could I have been so stupid not to realize it before?

That's why I had seen it on his face.

A pentagram was for safekeeping. And Marcus needed to be kept safe—from what, Devon wasn't sure, but he was in some kind of danger.

If only I had a pentagram to give him …

But I'm a Sorcerer of the Nightwing. Of course *I have one to give him.*

Devon stopped back at Marcus's house again after school. The kid's poor mom seemed even more haggard when she opened the door.

"No, he's still not feeling well," she said.

Devon dropped his hand into the pocket of his denim jacket. Sure enough, there was something in there that wasn't before. He withdrew a silver necklace with a small five-pointed star hanging from it.

"Would you give this to him?" Devon asked, handing the necklace to Marcus's mother. "Tell him it's from me. He'll recognize it. He should wear it."

"Wear it?" she asked, accepting the gift.

"Yeah, it's kind of like a good luck charm."

The mother agreed to give it to Marcus. Devon turned to leave, imagining the worst about his sick friend and cursing the limits of his powers to find out what was really going on.

In the days that followed, the earth continued to thaw, and spring made its stealthy return to Misery Point. There were still some cold, windy days, and a couple of dustings of snow, but in the village shutters were being removed from the windows of shops that had been closed for the winter. Flower boxes were suddenly sprouting blue and yellow pansies, and getting a table for lunch at Stormy Harbor restaurant sometimes now meant waiting in line.

The moon was no longer full, so there were no more sightings or encounters with the beast. Rolfe, after much effort, had given up on the crystals: although they offered some intriguing portraits of the Muir family, they'd told him nothing about sorcery—or about the creature or its origin. The night it had attacked him, the beast had also apparently killed a couple of dogs and frightened a girl who was walking home from Stormy Harbor. If the girl hadn't managed to get into her car as quickly as she did, the thing would certainly have attacked her, too. The police followed up on several leads, including Roxanne's call, but they were unable to find the beast.

Devon knew they wouldn't have to worry about it for another month, when the moon was once again full.

Except for the fact that Marcus remained out of school, things seemed, in fact, to fade back to normal. That was, if the occasional rampage through the walls by Crazy Lady didn't count. Any discussion of her identity was strictly forbidden; whenever Devon tried to raise it, he was silenced by Mrs. Crandall, who snarled he'd "done enough damage." Nor did she permit Devon to try to see her—even when he argued that with his powers, he might be able to contain her. On his own, Devon found himself just as frustrated in his attempts: trying to encounter Crazy Lady again in the secret passageways, hoping to press her for more answers, he met with failure every time.

She's avoiding me, Devon thought. *She knows how to give me the slip. I have to remember she's got powers, too.*

For a while, Bjorn managed to get her confined to one room, playing games with her and bringing her some of her favorite treats, like hot fudge sundaes. But inevitably Crazy Lady disappeared on him again and took to running through the walls of the house, making Mrs. Crandall absolutely wild. Alexander thought it was a hoot, banging on the walls back at her, making a game out of it. Cecily complained that the noise was giving her a migraine, and so she was out of the house as often as she could be, ordering D.J. to drive her to the mall or take her to the movies.

Devon tried not to process any lingering feelings he might have had for Cecily. It was best to just forget them. Instead, he concentrated on Natalie, with whom he texted until two a.m. every night.

After about a week, they were all thrilled when Marcus returned to school. But he was reluctant to talk about his illness. He was kind of bruised and he'd lost some weight, but otherwise he seemed okay. Devon noticed he was wearing the pentagram and made his friend promise not to take it off. Marcus agreed, but also insisted that it was over—that whatever had ailed him was done, finished, and they should all stop worrying about him.

With the arrival of spring came Devon's birthday. As he fell asleep the night before the big day, he wondered again if he would be sixteen or seventeen when he woke up in the morning. He dreamed of his dad—Ted March—the only father he ever knew. "Dad," Devon asked him, "will I ever know the truth?"

"Maybe you already do, my son," his father told him.

It became one of those long and meandering dreams, where images flowed together, where one thing led to another without any rhyme or reason. Dad's image was followed by Cecily, then Natalie, and then the beast, howling at the moon. Its howling became drawn-out, almost musical, until, absurdly, it was as if the beast were singing "Happy Birthday."

"Happy birthday, dear Devon …"

He opened his eyes. Someone was stroking his face.

A dream, or …?

It was dawn. Pink light streamed into his room, flickering against his wall.

Devon looked up.

Yes, someone really was sitting on the edge of his bed, stroking his face and singing to him.

It was Crazy Lady!

"Happy birthday ... to yooooooou!"

And then she threw back her head and laughed. That shrill, maniacal sound.

Devon sat up in bed.

That wasn't the light of dawn flickering on his wall.

His room was on fire!

DEAD MAN'S HAND

Devon leapt out of bed. His dresser, his desk, the curtains at his window were all aflame. The fire crackled, hopping impishly from the curtains to the wall.

And Crazy Lady, her hair teased out wildly, just stood there and laughed.

"You're trying to burn the house down!" Devon screamed. "You're trying to destroy Ravenscliff!"

She laughed even more hysterically now.

Devon spread his arms wide and concentrated. *You better not think this is showy,* he told whatever Nightwing forces were out there. *I'm doing this to prevent this whole place from going up in smoke!*

Instantly, the fire snuffed itself out, leaving only blackened, smoldering debris.

Crazy Lady covered her mouth and giggled, then turned and slipped through an open panel in Devon's wall. He started after her, poking his head into the panel that he'd never even known was there, when he heard a scream.

Cecily.

He hurried quickly into the hallway. Smoke billowed down the corridor.

"Fire!" he could hear Cecily shouting. "My room is on fire!"

Alexander, too, was running into the corridor in his pajamas, his round pudgy face contorted in terror. "There's fire in my room! The house is burning down!"

"Oh, no, it's not," Devon said, once again stretching out his arms and concentrating—this time on extinguishing every flame in the house.

He succeeded—only too well. Even the pilot lights in the stove and the hot water tank were snuffed out. Mrs. Crandall was none too pleased at such an ostentatious display of his powers.

"But if Devon didn't do what he did, the whole house would've burned to the ground," Alexander said later that morning as the household gathered in the parlor. "He has such cool powers."

Mrs. Crandall just sighed and sent the boy upstairs to get ready for school.

"Well," Cecily said after he was gone, "Alexander is right. I have to give credit where credit is due." Her green eyes made contact with Devon's as she wrapped her pink terrycloth robe tightly around her. "Thank you, Devon."

He looked away, not wanting to be reminded of how he once felt about her. "Do you want me to fix the fire damage?" Devon asked Mrs. Crandall. "I can probably repair most of it …"

"If you are going to use hammer and nails and paint, fine," said the mistress of Ravenscliff. "But not any sorcery."

Devon made a face. "Then I guess you'll need to call a carpenter."

"If I may be permitted to say so, ma'am," Bjorn said to Mrs. Crandall, "she's getting to be a real danger. One never knows when she'll strike. I thought she was happy and content last night. I brought her a hot fudge sundae. She seemed so good-tempered. But she must have been plotting, even then. Next time we might not be so fortunate. Master Devon might be at school …"

"Well, what do you propose we *do*, Bjorn?" Mrs. Crandall snapped. "Every time you capture her, she slips away again, since the spell of confinement has been broken." She shot a withering look Devon's way.

"Well, if I may be so bold to suggest, ma'am," Bjorn offered, "maybe a new spell ought to be cast."

Devon knew Bjorn meant him. He was the only one at Ravenscliff—other than Crazy Lady—who had any powers left.

"No more spells," Mrs. Crandall said weakly, sinking down into her chair. "It stirs things up. It lures things this way …"

"But if she tried to burn the house down once," Cecily argued, "she'll do it again."

"Can I even *do* it?" Devon asked. "I mean, if she's got powers, too, who's to say I can contain her?"

"She's never known how to use her sorcery properly," Mrs. Crandall said. "She was never adequately trained." She eyed Devon coldly. "Not that you *were*, Devon, but you have, over my objections, been making progress."

Making progress? Devon could really get into it with her on that point, arguing that rescuing Alexander from a Hell Hole and defeating an undead demon witch was considerably more than just "making progress." But he held his tongue.

"I would be willing to try," Devon said, "on the condition that you tell me who she is, and what she knew about me. It seems only fair, if I'm to be the one who contains her."

Mrs. Crandall seemed appalled. "You would bargain over the safety of this family?"

"Yeah, Devon," Cecily said, coming around to stand beside her mother. "That seems really selfish." She crossed her arms over chest and thrust her chin up. In that moment, Devon thought, mother and daughter had never looked more alike.

"Look," Devon argued, "you're asking me to imprison someone against her will."

"A *sorceress*, Devon, who is becoming more dangerous by the day." Mrs. Crandall slapped the arm of her chair. "What if she gets it into her mind to open the door to the Hell Hole? What then?"

It was a thought that took Devon aback. Yes, what then? In his mind's eye he could see the portal in the West Wing— that bolted metal door behind which the demons slithered and scratched, begging to be set free. Only a Sorcerer of the Nightwing had the power to open that door, or seal it shut.

"All right, all right, I'll do it," Devon said. "But I still want answers. And if you won't give them to me, I'll find them elsewhere."

"Just locate her and keep her in one room," Mrs. Crandall said. "I hate the very thought of allowing you to use sorcery in this house, but I've no other choice. Just bind the basement room with mystical energy to keep her from breaking free, energy that would also surround her even on walks we might take in the courtyard."

"No," Devon said. "I'm not putting her back in the basement. Or in the tower, either. Now that we know she exists, she ought to live in a normal room. She can't be treated like a prisoner, even if she is. She needs help. There must be some kind of help we can get for her."

Mrs. Crandall laughed derisively. "What? Like some Nightwing psychiatrist?"

"Well, yeah." Devon turned to Bjorn. "There are doctors for sorcerers, aren't there? There must be."

"Well, yes," Bjorn said, nodding his little head, "there are shamans and other practitioners of the mind and body who work with Nightwing. In fact, ma'am, I recommended one for the lady when I first came here …"

"She needs no quack doctors, Nightwing or otherwise," Mrs. Crandall insisted, cutting him off. "Devon, you may put her in my mother's old room. I'll allow that. It's well appointed, with a lovely view, but far enough removed from the rest of the house so as to keep us out of harm's way."

Devon figured for now that was as much as he'd get out of her. "Okay," he said. "So what do I do? Just concentrate …?"

"There was a time," Mrs. Crandall said, a certain wistfulness creeping into her voice, "when all I would have had to do was blink one eye and all this would be accomplished. It's an easy task, easily performed, when one has had the best teachers."

"Which you *did*, right, Mother?" Cecily asked, eager for stories of her mother's Nightwing past, stories she was usually so reluctant to reveal.

"Oh, yes," said Amanda Muir Crandall, a faraway look in her eye. It was the first time Devon had ever seen her nostalgic for her days as a sorceress. "Thaddeus brought in some wonderful teachers …"

"Thaddeus," Devon said softly. He knew Thaddeus Underwood was the name his father, Ted March, had used while he was a Guardian here at Ravenscliff. If only he had taught Devon in the way he had taught the Muirs, educating him in all the mysteries and majesty of the Nightwing, rather than keeping his heritage a secret for so long ...

"Oh, Mother, I so wish you hadn't renounced your powers," Cecily said. "Then I could be a sorceress, too ..."

"No!" Mrs. Crandall snapped out of her reverie. "It was too dangerous a life! We are better off as we are, living as ordinary people." She stood and pulled her daughter to her. "I couldn't bear losing any more of my family."

She looked over at Devon deliberately.

"And that means you, too, Devon," she said, her voice tender. "So please be careful. Do what you must, and then let us be done with it."

Devon didn't have time to ponder Mrs. Crandall's words long, whether by calling him a part of her family she was admitting he was her son. She was out of the room before he could say another word, hustling Cecily upstairs and leaving Devon in the parlor to concentrate on corralling Crazy Lady.

Everybody seemed to have forgotten it was his birthday.

He sighed. It was a lot to ask a guy to do: summon energy to contain a fellow sorcerer, all before getting ready for school. *School*—it hit him that his books and geometry homework were on his desk. They were just smoldering ashes now. Great, just great.

"Concentrate," he told himself, trying to block out any other thoughts. He stood in the middle of the room, surrounded by the relics of the Muir family's Nightwing past. Horatio Muir's eyes stared down at him from the wall. Devon took a deep breath. "Concentrate on finding Crazy Lady."

But he couldn't see her. He wasn't concentrating hard enough, he supposed. He pressed his palms against his temples and closed his eyes. "Come on, Crazy Lady, wherever you are," he murmured. "Fun and games are over. You went too far this time, trying to burn the house down. Waking me up and singing—"

He opened his eyes.

"How did she know it was my birthday?" he asked out loud.

She's a sorcerer, he told himself. *She has an inner Voice of intuition, too.*

But maybe she was *there,* when Mrs. Crandall gave birth …

"Concentrate," he commanded himself again, but now there was a sound to distract him. The soft sound of crying. His eyes darted around the room. They came to rest on the portrait of Emily Muir.

Jackson's wife—whose ghost haunted this house and Devil's Rock. Whose prayerbook had been in Crazy Lady's room …

Devon approached the portrait. How pretty Emily had been, so blond, so innocent. And yes, the eyes of the portrait were dripping tears.

"Are you trying to tell me something, Emily?" Devon asked. "Something about what's happening here with Crazy Lady? What was your connection to her?"

The tears just rolled down the oil paint, one after another.

Devon knew the legends. He'd heard them the first day he came to Ravenscliff. How, one stormy Halloween night, Emily had found her husband with another woman and, in despair, had thrown herself from Devil's Rock. Devon knew, having confronted Jackson Muir in the Hell Hole, that the tragedy profoundly determined the course of the Madman's subsequent evil, so great was his grief and guilt.

Devon returned to concentrating on finding Crazy Lady, but again had no luck. She'd kept herself hidden from him before; she clearly did not want to be found. She was pitting her sorcery against his.

He sought out Bjorn and told him that if he couldn't find her with his mind, they'd have to do it the old-fashioned way—with their eyes and ears. He also determined that he'd need to miss school—who knew how long finding an insane sorceress would take? It was just as well, since his homework was charred beyond recognition.

Bjorn took the basement and first floor; Devon headed into

the West Wing. It always creeped him out going in there. This was where the portal to the Hell Hole existed, in the secret room with no windows. There was a portrait in there, too, that Devon found fascinating: of a boy who looked exactly like him, in the clothes of an earlier time, further evidence of a connection between himself and Ravenscliff.

He didn't need to check the secret room, however; if Crazy Lady were at the Hell Hole, he'd feel it. Every cell of his body would be vibrating. Instead, he explored the passageways within the walls of the West Wing. He slunk down the narrow, cobwebby corridors, sometimes not more than a foot wide, holding his magic globe of light in his hand. What better place for her to hide out in, in a part of the house that had been closed off, unused since the time of Emily Muir.

Of course, Devon reasoned, Crazy Lady might have discovered the sorcerer's trick of invisibility. He could have been walking right past her and never have known it. A sorcerer could make himself or herself invisible to all senses, including the sense of intuition. Rolfe called it the "Cloak of Obscurity"— he'd read about it in one of the books. Devon had used the trick to avoid detection by Isobel the Apostate.

So Crazy Lady knew her sorcery. *She's good*, Devon thought. Mrs. Crandall might claim she'd never been trained adequately, but it was clear that she'd learned enough to remain undetected.

There must be another way to find her, Devon told himself. If she was physically invisible *and* shielded from his Nightwing gaze, she was going to win their game of hide-and-seek every time. *There's got to be another way ...*

How he wished he'd had a Guardian in the way most Nightwing kids had. Not that Rolfe hadn't been trying to do his best, but he was often as much at a loss as Devon. If only Devon had been able to go to the great Nightwing school run by Wiglaf in the fifteenth century. Devon had met Wiglaf during his trip into the past and had seen firsthand how awesome it would have been to have a Guardian who'd really known his stuff, who could have taught him all the finer points of sorcery. Wiglaf would have known what to do, how to nab Crazy Lady ...

And maybe I do, too, Devon thought, an idea suddenly coming to him.

Once, in a test with none other than Sargon the Great, the founder of the Order of the Nightwing, Devon had failed miserably because he had failed to see the obvious, because he had let fear and doubt get in the way.

I am a Sorcerer of the Nightwing, Devon told himself. *Not only that, I am the one-hundredth generation from Sargon, destined for greatness.*

If I can't find Crazy Lady, Devon reasoned, *I'll find everything* else.

He emerged from the secret panel into what had been Emily Muir's upstairs sitting room. A dust-covered chandelier hung forlornly from the ceiling. Shutters kept out most of the light, with only slivers of the sun's morning rays slipping through. Devon stood in the middle of the room, trying to empty his mind of all other thoughts than the task at hand.

"Everything in this house," he said, "wood, glass, marble, furniture, electrical wires, carpet, plumbing, books, appliances, food, portraits, clothing, people—everything *other* than Crazy Lady—fade from my consciousness!"

At first nothing happened. Then, bit by bit, the room around him began to shiver. First a corner off to his right, then a section of the floor beneath him. Then the chandelier trembled and disappeared, and then the ceiling was gone, replaced only by a stark white nothingness. Devon looked down at his feet. The floor was gone. He stood on white air. The rest of the room gave one last shudder, then was gone, too.

The whole house had vanished. Devon was enveloped in a stark white void. No sound, no smell, nothing to see.

"Now," Devon said, "what can I discern?"

With the distraction of everything else gone, he could concentrate on locating Crazy Lady. She might have been invisible, she might have wrapped herself in a cloak of mystical privacy, but now she did so in a chasm of nothingness.

And Devon immediately detected a clue. A scent, recognizable only to his Nightwing nose.

Hot fudge.

Bjorn had said he'd given her a hot fudge sundae last night. There must have been a slight remnant on her lips or fingers.

Devon honed in on the smell. He couldn't tell exactly where he was going, as he had no relation to the house around him— which way was the floor and which way was the ceiling. Still, he moved through the whiteness with ease. At first he had the sense that he was descending, but then it changed to a sensation of rising. Up, up, up. The tower? It would make sense. It had been home to Crazy Lady for a long time …

He stopped. The smell was strong here. He reached out his hands and touched flesh. A face. He heard Crazy Lady's startled shout.

"How did you find me?" she shrieked, and the whiteness suddenly disappeared. They stood facing each other in the tower room. Crazy Lady cradled a headless plastic doll in her arms.

"I'm a sorcerer," Devon told her. "It was easy."

She backed away from him, clutching the doll to her breast.

"I'm not going to hurt you," Devon said. "You don't have to be afraid of me."

"You're here to make me a prisoner again, aren't you?"

She didn't seem insane now. She seemed merely frightened, and so much younger than ever before, as if she might not be all that much older than Devon. Her gray hair was pulled back into a ponytail; her eyes were cast down at that deformed little doll. Devon's heart ached for her.

"You tried to burn down the house," he said. "Why did you do that?"

"I don't want to be kept prisoner any more," Crazy Lady told him, still gazing down lovingly at the doll, rocking it back and forth in her arms. "My baby and I want to be free. We want to go back out into the world."

"I don't think you're quite ready to do that yet. But maybe we can get you some help …"

Her eyes reacted, darting up to meet his. The madness was there again, shining through. "I won't be put in that room again!"

"No, not that one," Devon said, "a nice one …"

"No!"

"Calm down, please," Devon said kindly, reaching out for her. "I want to be your friend."

She eyed him cagily. "My friend?"

"Yes. You know my name, so why don't you tell me yours?"

Crazy Lady glared at him for several seconds, then suddenly leapt backward, onto the windowsill behind her. She crouched there like a bird.

"I've learned how to fly," she told him, turning the latch on the window. "Do you know how to fly, Devon?"

"Please, don't try it," he begged her. "We're at the top of the tower. It's a long way to the ground."

"But I told you," she said calmly. "I've learned how to fly."

She turned, thrusting her head and shoulder out the window.

Devon made a lunge for her, but she was prepared for him. He was suddenly repelled backward, falling onto his butt.

"Oh, and Devon," she said, looking back one last time, "my name is Clarissa."

With that, she flew off into the morning sky.

"Are you sure?" Rolfe asked him after Devon had told him the story. "Are you absolutely sure that's what she said?"

"She told me her name was Clarissa," Devon said once again.

Rolfe sat down in a state of stunned silence.

"That was the name of the girl in your car," Devon said. "The one you thought drowned, who has a gravestone in the cemetery on Eagle Hill."

"It can't be," Rolfe muttered.

Devon took the seat next to him. They were in the office of Rolfe's restaurant, one of several he owned in the area. Devon had come to see him right away, as soon as Crazy Lady had disappeared into the air. He'd just closed his eyes in the tower and reappeared at Rolfe's. He loved it when his powers worked.

"It can't be Clarissa," Rolfe said again.

"You told me her body was never recovered."

The older man's eyes grew dark. "I went to prison for her death. Amanda testified—all the while she was keeping the girl hidden away at Ravenscliff! *That's* why she kept her imprisoned! So she could convince the police that Clarissa was dead and make sure I was locked up in jail!"

Devon held a lot of things against Mrs. Crandall, but this seemed too much even for her. Utterly destroy a girl's life merely for revenge? Have a gravestone made for her just so it would keep up the illusion of her death and keep Rolfe in jail? Was she really capable of such hatred and viciousness?

"Look," Devon argued, "Crazy Lady—whatever her real name is—has powers, powers that need to be controlled. Did Clarissa have powers when you knew her?"

"No, of course not. She was just a girl. A servant girl ..."

"Who you were fooling around with ..."

Rolfe nodded. "It was a stupid thing." He sighed. "When Amanda discovered what was going on, she was furious. And rightly so. I apologized and promised never to see Clarissa again. I did everything I could to make it up to her. But she was so stubborn, so strong-willed, so determined to hold a grudge ..."

"It runs in the family," Devon said, thinking of Cecily.

"But to do *this*," Rolfe said, standing up now, slamming his fist into his palm. "It staggers the imagination! She sent me to jail for a death she knew didn't occur!"

Devon decided against bringing up the fact that there was another person in the car that night—a boy—who, for all they knew, really *did* drown. But everything now seemed open to question, including Clarissa's identity.

"If this is the same person," Devon reasoned, "why didn't she have powers then? Why does she have them now? And when did she go insane?"

"Clarissa Jones was no sorceress. She was not Nightwing. She was just a village girl." Rolfe looked at Devon intently. "Only Amanda will have the answers to those questions." He was rubbing his hands together, obviously itching for a showdown. "And I can't wait to ask her."

"Not yet, Rolfe," Devon said. "Let me try to—"

"*Ten years of my life, Devon!*" Rolfe snarled. "That's what she took away from me! Ten years I sat in that stinking place! I'm going up to that house to demand some answers!"

Rolfe moved as if he meant to leave right away, then stopped. He turned to look at Devon. He seemed to calm down, but Devon could still see the rage in his eyes.

"It's your birthday today, isn't it, Devon?" he asked, more softly now.

The teen nodded. "Not so that anybody remembered."

"I remembered, Devon, and tonight I will bring you a birthday gift."

Devon smirked. "And that's when the explosion will take place?"

"After I give you your gift," Rolfe said, a devious grin stretching across his face, "I'll take Amanda aside and we'll have a nice little chat."

Devon decided to walk back to Ravenscliff. No car, no disappearing-reappearing trick. He needed to clear his head and think about a few things.

The village continued its headlong rush to spring. Green daffodil bulbs sprouted alongside sidewalks. Freshly painted shops boasted signs reading, Opening in 2 weeks! Seasonal workers were arriving, standing in line to apply for jobs at the Clam Shack and Frosty Fingers Creamery. Devon couldn't imagine sleepy Misery Point as a bustling summer tourist spot, but that was what they all told him it would be, and soon.

Climbing the steep, crumbling staircase that was built into the side of the cliff, Devon got a good view of the village, its sea-washed white clapboard houses and scrubby, gnarled black pines. Dad had sent him to this place without telling him why, but Devon understood now that it was his home—his real home, more than Coles Junction had ever been. *When I lived in Coles Junction, I was just biding my time*, he thought to himself as he climbed. *I was just waiting for my destiny to kick in. Waiting to come here.*

At the top of the staircase was Eagle Hill cemetery, the Muirs' private burial ground. They were all here: Horatio Muir, the founder of Ravenscliff, and Mrs. Crandall's parents, Randolph and Greta Muir, and others of the family. Overlooking the sea was a memorial to Emily Muir, and—making Devon's skin crawl every time he saw it—the grave of Jackson Muir himself. Master of Ravenscliff was etched upon its surface, though the title had never been his in life.

I was down there, Devon thought, shuddering, as he stood looking at the grave. *I was down there with Jackson's skeleton, trapped in his coffin.*

The Madman had put him there. Sometimes Devon still woke up at night in a panic and a cold sweat, imagining himself back in that terrible place.

But I got out, Devon reminded himself. *I got out because I was stronger than he was.*

Stepping past the hideous marker, he cleared away some dried leaves with his foot. He peered down at the simple, flat marker bearing just one word: Clarissa.

"Why?" he asked out loud. "Why did Mrs. Crandall pretend Clarissa was killed in the car accident? Why did she go to the trouble of having this stone placed here? Was it really just to have revenge on Rolfe?"

He turned. His eyes were drawn, as ever, to the obelisk in the center of the cemetery. On its base was carved the single most enticing clue to his past. His name, Devon, in bold, raised letters.

No record of who's buried there, Devon thought, staring down at the name. At least, none that Mrs. Crandall was willing to share.

Is it my father? Is that who it is? My real, blood, Nightwing father?

"And who might you think that would be?"

Devon spun around.

"Who said that?" he called out. "Who's here?"

A low, mocking laughter drifted over the gravestones.

"Do you want to look upon his face? The face of

your father?"

The voice terrified him. Who was it? Devon couldn't even tell if it was male or female.

"Yes," Devon said. "Yes, I want to see him!"

"Very well," came the voice, deep and gravelly, as if it came from the earth itself.

Devon braced himself. No one appeared. But then he heard a sound, a stirring at his feet. He jumped back in horror.

A hand was pushing up from the ground.

The hand of his dead father!

BLOOD ON THE MOON

This has happened before, Devon thought. *An army of zombies attacked me here once ...*

But this time it was just one dead man sitting up in the soil. A horrible, stinking dead man, with holes where his eyes once were.

Decomposing corpses—they freaked Devon out more than just about anything else. More than demons, more than renegade sorcerers, more than were-beasts. Devon recoiled as the dead man staggered to his feet.

"Back off," he commanded, his heart thudding in his chest. "Back off!"

But the zombie lumbered blindly forward, its decaying hands flailing about in an attempt to grab the teen. Devon managed to evade its grasp but got a whiff of its rotting flesh. That was the worst thing about zombies: they *reeked*.

"Back to your grave!" Devon shouted, but still the thing staggered on, grossing him out more with every step it took. Devon considered just disappearing to get away from it, but figured leaving a zombie to roam the grounds of Ravenscliff wasn't such a good idea. Besides, it would be cowardly—

That's when it hit Devon—why he couldn't overpower the dead man. *I'm scared*, he said. *I'm freaked out by it. I'm freaked out that this stinking, rotting corpse might be my father—and that's why my powers aren't working.*

Fear, he had been taught many, many times, was the only thing that could incapacitate him, render his Nightwing powers useless.

He heard Dad's voice: "You are stronger than anything out there. Always remember that, Devon."

"Yeah," he shouted now, standing in place against the encroaching zombie, no longer backing up out of fear. "I'm stronger than you, mush-face!"

The dead man's hands made contact with the teenager's flesh. Devon choked back his revulsion and stared defiantly into the empty black eye sockets, trying to disregard the maggots that crawled through the dead flesh.

"Back to your grave!" Devon commanded again, and this time the thing disappeared. The earth at his feet looked as if it had not been disturbed. Devon let out a long sigh of relief.

I was being tested, the teenager realized. *And I passed the test.*

But who was doing the testing?

Trudging through the woods back to Ravenscliff, he realized he was going to have to explain to Mrs. Crandall that Crazy Lady had gotten away from him. He wasn't sure if he'd reveal that other bit of information—that she had told him her name was Clarissa. He might wait for Rolfe to do that tonight, because after that, his whole world was going to fall apart.

Mrs. Crandall might well kick him out of Ravenscliff for defying her order about not seeing Rolfe Montaigne. Where Devon would be sent then, he wasn't sure. He had to be prepared for anything.

It was mid-afternoon. He'd missed lunch, but he didn't have much of an appetite after seeing—and *smelling*—that dead thing. He just felt like taking a nap.

As he crossed the driveway toward the front doors of the mansion, a car's horn honked at him. "Yo, Devon!"

It was D.J. He screeched the Camaro up the driveway and stopped right in front of the house. He hopped out of the car while Natalie, Marcus and Cecily stepped out the other side.

"Happy b-day, dude!" D.J. said, slapping him on the back. "We had a cake and everything waiting for you at school, but you never showed up!"

Marcus, looking a little more like his old self, presented him with what was left of it. A slice of Sara Lee chocolate cake on a paper plate, one candle lopsidedly stuck on top.

Devon smiled. "Thanks, guys."

Natalie came up beside him. "You didn't answer my texts."

Devon removed his phone from his jacket pocket and saw he had a mess of texts from her, and from D.J. and Marcus. "I had it on silent," he said, kind of chagrined that he'd been feeling sorry for himself that no one remembered. "I was doing some investigating and figured I shouldn't be distracted."

"Well, I hope you didn't think we'd forgotten," Natalie said.

Devon looked over into her dark eyes. How pretty they were. "Naw," he said. "I knew you would remember."

They held each other's smiles for several seconds.

"Well, if you want to eat your cake, then come inside," Cecily said coldly, and marched in through the front door of the old mansion. The rest of them followed.

At the enormous mahogany dining room table, Marcus lit the candle. "Go ahead," he told Devon, "make a wish and blow it out."

"Before he does that," came another voice, "maybe he ought to save his breath for this."

It was Bjorn. The little man waddled into the room carrying a gigantic chocolate cake on a silver platter, so wide and high it was practically bigger than the gnome himself. He eased it onto the table. It was loaded with flickering candles.

"Sixteen candles," said Alexander, rushing in behind Bjorn. "I lit 'em all myself."

"Sixteen, huh?" Devon asked. He looked over at Cecily, who leaned uncomfortably against the far wall. She alone had failed to say "Happy Birthday" to him.

Devon reached over and plucked the lone candle out of the Sara Lee cake. He stuck it onto the cake that Bjorn had brought out.

"Maybe we ought to make it seventeen," he said, and proceeded to blow them all out.

Cecily turned her face away.

"Did you make a wish?" Natalie asked, keeping close to Devon's side.

"Yeah, I did."

"Bet it's to find out who your real parents are," D.J. said.

Devon smiled. "If I tell you what it was, it won't come true."

He caught a quick glimpse of Cecily looking at him, but once again, she turned away.

"Old superstitions," Bjorn intoned. "There's something to them. I take them very seriously."

"Well, let's chow down," D.J. said. "Cut me a big slice, Devon, my man."

For a while that afternoon, it was just a teenager's birthday party. Chocolate cake and Coca-Cola—Diet Coke for the girls—and silly, sugar-buzz laughter. There was no talk of sorcery or demons or beasts or zombies. Instead D.J. promised to take them all to Florida this summer. His parents were buying a condo, he said, to get away from the misery of Misery Point winters, but it would be empty and available for their use in the summer. "The demons will never find you in West Palm Beach," D.J. laughed.

Devon laughed, too. His appetite returned, and he devoured three slices of cake. Sitting against the wall on the floor next to Natalie, he felt high and happy, and when he noticed she had frosting on her upper lip he reached over and kissed it off.

"Devon!" Natalie giggled and kissed him back.

"Okay, you two," Marcus said, pointing his fork at them. "No PDAs."

Devon grinned, looking up. He saw Cecily walk out of the room, D.J. following after her. For a moment, he felt guilty. But then he figured it was for the best; they had to forget about each other. Besides, he couldn't deny how nice it was to be with Natalie, who was so much calmer, so much sweeter than the volatile Cecily Crandall ...

But thoughts of love and romance were quickly displaced by alarm when he noticed, once again, the pentagram floating in front of Marcus's face.

"Hey," Devon said to his friend. "You still wearing that star chain I gave you?"

Marcus smiled, patting his chest through his sweatshirt. "I never take it off."

"Good," Devon said.

"But whatever that was, it's over," Marcus insisted. "It was just the flu or something. You don't need to worry about me."

"Whatever," Devon said. "Just keep wearing that pendant."

Marcus held his gaze. "I promise, Devon."

The reality of his life came flooding back to him then, and he stood up, breaking contact with Natalie. "Listen, you guys, this was all really cool and everything," he said. "But maybe you all ought get going. Rolfe is going to be here soon, and stuff is going to happen. Things might get nasty."

"All the more reason to stick around and watch," Marcus said, grinning.

"No, it wouldn't be cool," Devon said. He turned and faced Natalie. "Thanks for my birthday cake. Why do I figure it was you who brought it to school?"

She smiled. "I was hoping maybe you could come over to my house tonight and I'd bake you a real one."

"More cake?" Devon laughed. "After all this?"

"Well, then we can just hang out," Natalie said. "Watch TV …"

Devon sighed. "I'd like to. I really, really would. But this stuff between Rolfe and Mrs. Crandall … it could get pretty intense. I need to be here."

She smiled. How understanding she was. She reached up and gave Devon a quick kiss on cheek. "Okay. Then maybe tomorrow?"

"Yeah," Devon promised. "Let's plan on tomorrow."

D.J. and Cecily were already in the car. "Tell Mother that D.J. is taking me to the movies," the red-haired girl shouted from the car window as Devon, Natalie and Marcus walked outside. "I'll be home later."

"Yeah, okay," Devon said, figuring the less people in the house the better.

"Oh, and happy birthday, Devon," Cecily said.

"Thanks, Cess."

Their eyes held. Devon felt terribly confused. What were his feelings toward her? Toward Natalie? He was a Sorcerer of the Nightwing. But he had no powers over teenage hormones.

"Oh, and did you deal with Crazy Lady?" Cecily asked. "I

really don't feel like getting burned in my bed tonight."

Devon sighed. "We're safe for now, I guess."

"Good." She nodded crisply, then rolled up the window.

He waved goodbye to his friends before turning and walking forlornly back inside.

Maybe he'd get to move in with Rolfe if Mrs. Crandall threw him out. That would be cool, and it would make sense, Devon figured, if Rolfe was seriously going to be his Guardian. But would Mrs. Crandall ever sign over legal rights to Rolfe Montaigne? Devon doubted it. Dad had left him in Mrs. Crandall's care. It would be up to her to determine where he would go if she decided to kick him out of Ravenscliff. And Rolfe was the last person she'd send him to.

Truth was, Devon didn't want to leave. As freaky as this place could get, it was home now. This was where Devon's past lay, and his future, too. He was sure of it.

Of course, if Mrs. Crandall went to jail—and she just might, if Rolfe could prove she perjured herself and then kept Clarissa a prisoner all those years—then there would be no telling what would become of Devon. Or Cecily. Or Alexander.

Or Ravenscliff.

But the fact was, Clarissa was gone. Devon could feel it, and his Nightwing intuition confirmed it. She was free. Finally and truly free. Flying on her own. What he just told Cecily was true. They were safe, until Clarissa decided to come back.

And without Clarissa around, Rolfe would have a hard time proving that her body wasn't washed out to sea. No charges against Mrs. Crandall would stick.

That wouldn't stop Rolfe, however, from making them.

"How *dare* you walk into this house?"

Mrs. Crandall was on the landing on the top of the stairs, looking down with wide, outraged eyes at Rolfe Montaigne, who was standing with Devon in the foyer.

Devon had answered the door when he heard Rolfe knock, hoping to ease into the clash he knew was inevitable. But Mrs. Crandall had apparently seen his Porsche from her window upstairs, and she was not pleased by his arrival, to say the least.

"As ever, Amanda," Rolfe said, looking up at her, "you're especially beautiful when you're angry."

His flattery only ratcheted up her rage. She moved down the stairs, her voice icy but her eyes filled with fire. "The last time you were here," she seethed, "I told you never to come back."

"But I had to bring Devon a birthday present," Rolfe said innocently.

She stood in front of him. "I suppose it will be some magical trinket that will only encourage him in practicing what I have forbidden."

"Now, now, Amanda," Rolfe said. "Can we all just be civil for the boy's sake? I mean, it is his birthday."

Mrs. Crandall's lips tightened as she looked from Rolfe to Devon. "Give him the gift and then go."

"May we go into the parlor, at least? Standing here in the foyer seems so formal."

She just sighed. They all proceeded into the parlor, Devon's heart pounding in his chest. He wished Rolfe would cut the act and just get to it.

He didn't have to wait long.

"By the way, Amanda," Rolfe said as the mistress of the house sat down in her wingback chair, "have you heard from Clarissa?"

Devon watched the expression on Mrs. Crandall's face. She was emotionless, just staring at Rolfe coldly. She betrayed nothing.

"Clarissa is dead," she finally said, "and you of all people should know that."

"So it's been her ghost banging on the walls these past few weeks?" Rolfe asked.

Mrs. Crandall's eyes shifted over to Devon.

"I'm sorry," the teenager said. "I had to tell him. I saw her again today, Mrs. Crandall. And she told me her name."

"She is insane," she said calmly. "You know that, Devon."

Rolfe was standing over her, glaring down. "So you're denying that your mystery lady is in fact Clarissa Jones?"

"Our mystery lady has the powers of a sorceress," Mrs. Crandall said, still apparently unperturbed, though Devon's Nightwing ears could detect a racing heartbeat. "Did you ever know Clarissa to have powers?"

"None," Rolfe admitted. "Except the ability to bewitch a boy who was otherwise in love with you."

At that Mrs. Crandall could keep her composure no longer. She stood, pushing past Rolfe and striding across the room. "This is all nonsense!" she said, her voice shrill, her hands quavering. "Give Devon his birthday present and then go."

"Not until you tell me the truth, Amanda." Rolfe's voice was cold and final. "I went to jail for ten years for Clarissa's death. If she's out there, she will come to me. Tell me the truth now, Amanda, before I learn it on my own!"

"*All right!*" Mrs. Crandall spun around to face him. "Yes, that was Clarissa! Yes, I kept her here secretly all these years! What do you propose to do about it, Rolfe?"

He smiled evilly. "Maybe give you a taste of what I went through for those ten years. Perjury is a crime, Amanda."

"I testified that I saw you driving, which I did," she said, defiant. "No perjury involved."

"That's a lie and you know it. It must have been Clarissa who was driving!"

She laughed at him. "You were so drunk that you couldn't even walk!"

"But hiding Clarissa here when I was on trial for her death—"

Mrs. Crandall pushed away from him again, moving across the room with the forcefulness of a cheetah. Devon jumped out of her way.

"Clarissa didn't return until after my testimony, after your trial was all over. I had no idea until that point that she was alive." She turned to glare at Rolfe, then over at Devon. "Imagine my surprise when she showed up at the front door."

"Where had she been?" Devon ventured to ask.

"She could never tell us," Mrs. Crandall said. "She was insane. The shock of the accident, I suppose."

"And her powers?" Devon asked. "How did she get them?"

"Again, we never knew," Mrs. Crandall said. "All I know is that when she came back to Ravenscliff she was a different person—and she went straight to the portal in the West Wing and tried to open the Hell Hole! She was obsessed with the idea of it. It was all she wanted to do—let the demons free, and the Madman, too!"

Neither Devon nor Rolfe could speak after hearing that.

Mrs. Crandall gave them a small, tight smile. "Now perhaps you can understand why my mother and I needed to do what we did. Why we kept Clarissa here, safe and protected. Why we never let her learn the extent of her powers. If she were allowed to be free, she would open the Hell Hole. It would have meant the death of us all!"

Rolfe was scratching his head. "Why do I have the feeling we're only getting part of the truth here?"

"I'm telling you all I know."

Rolfe sneered. "I just find it awfully convenient that in protecting Ravenscliff from the Madman you also managed to get revenge on *me*."

She held his gaze. "That's your own narcissism, Rolfe. Thinking everything is about you."

"You could have found a way to keep Clarissa from the Hell Hole and still let the authorities know she was alive."

"Why? To get you out of jail?" Mrs. Crandall moved in, her face only inches from Rolfe's. "Why would I care to do that? You seem to forget there was someone *else* in that car, too. That servant boy. *He* never turned up alive. Oh, no. That poor boy really *did* drown because of your negligence, your disregard for human life. So whether Clarissa lived or not, you *deserved* to be in jail."

Rolfe looked away, saying nothing.

An awkward, unhappy silence settled over the parlor. Devon realized that neither of them enjoyed this battle of wills. Neither truly wanted to be cruel to the other. Devon could plainly feel that.

"Well," the teenager said, breaking the silence, "at least we don't have to worry about her any more. There's no need to try to contain her. She flew out of here. Literally. Flapped her arms like a bird and flew. I tried, but I was unable to stop her. And my inner Voice assured me she's really gone."

"We can only hope that is true," Mrs. Crandall said.

Rolfe had recovered himself. "You'd better *hope* that's true, because imprisoning someone is against the law, too."

"She was a *guest* here, never a prisoner. She was treated very well."

Devon wasn't sure how true that was, remembering all the times he heard Clarissa's sobs echoing throughout the house. But then again, she *was* insane. Who was to say what her tears meant?

Mrs. Crandall leveled her eyes once more at Rolfe. "I want you out of this house in ten minutes. Give Devon your gift and then please leave."

She walked quickly out of the parlor, her long green gown rustling behind her on the floor. Once she was gone, Rolfe sat down, exhausted, in her chair.

"She's still in love with you," Devon said, sitting on the couch opposite the older man. "It's so obvious."

"She hates me," Rolfe said, none too convincingly, "just as I hate her."

"Yeah, right." Devon sighed, rolling his eyes at the absurdity of his elders. "So do you think maybe the mystery of Crazy Lady is over? Maybe there's nothing more to worry about. Maybe Clarissa has taken her powers, whatever they are, and gone off to live as a sorceress somewhere else."

Rolfe laughed. "Like you haven't had enough experience at Ravenscliff to really believe that. Come on, Devon. Clarissa is tied up in the mystery of this house as much as any of us. She'll be back." He shook his head. "What I don't understand is how she got the powers of a sorceress. She was just an ordinary girl."

Devon leaned forward on the couch, a little grin playing with his lips. "So, um, not to change the subject or anything, but … do you really have a birthday present for me?"

Rolfe laughed. "Sure do."

He reached into his pocket and produced a small box. Devon accepted it gladly, removing the lid and peering inside.

"It's my Dad's ring!"

"I think I've gotten it working," Rolfe said. "I consulted several books and learned that if the crystals in a Guardian's ring become erratic, they should be placed in close proximity with other crystals and they will, in effect, 'recharge' themselves."

Devon looked down at the gold ring in his hand, a sparkling blue crystal in its center. It was Ted March's ring, and Devon had been thrilled to receive it. But the ring had proven weak and unreliable in its visions. If Rolfe had indeed fixed it, it could prove to be a font of information for Devon.

"Thank you, Rolfe," Devon said, slipping it onto his finger. "I'll try it tonight."

"Happy birthday, my friend." Rolfe glanced out into the foyer and up the stairs. "Now I'd better get out of here. My ten minutes are almost up, and I think we've antagonized Amanda enough tonight."

"Listen, Rolfe," Devon said as they walked toward the door, "there's going to be a full moon again in a week or so. We need to be prepared that the beast might come back."

Rolfe nodded. "I've been trying to find out more about such things in my library but haven't come up with much. I'll keep looking."

Devon looked down at the ring on his finger. Maybe this would offer some answers. He said goodnight to Rolfe and hurried upstairs to give it a try.

His room smelled like fresh wood. Mrs. Crandall had wasted no time getting carpenters in to repair his room. They had begun repairing the charred floorboards and window frames. Tomorrow they'd be back to finish the job. Devon hated the new curtains Mrs. Crandall had picked out, however. Yellow with pink roses—what was she *thinking*? He pushed them back as far as they would go and opened his windows outward. He cast his eyes up to the sky.

It was lightly raining, but he could still make out the partial moon. Devon held his hand out into the air, extending his ring finger as he concentrated.

At first, there was nothing. Devon feared that Rolfe really didn't get it working again. But then he felt a tingling sensation in his hand, which traveled up his arm and into his head. Everything around him became sharply delineated. Devon kept his eyes on the moon.

And suddenly the bright white orb turned red.

Blood! The moon was covered with blood!

Long and syrupy, it dripped from the face of the moon, staining the night sky. The misty rain turned into blood, too, and Devon's arm got covered with the sticky stuff. He pulled back, shutting his windows tightly.

Once closed off from the night, the blood disappeared, but it had left a sickening feeling in Devon's gut. What did the vision mean? What was it supposed to tell him about the beast?

He sat on his bed and closed his eyes. "Show me more," he commanded. "Tell me what I need to know."

He was suddenly no longer in his room. He was walking down some cobwebby corridor, probably in the closed-off West Wing. He could hear his breathing, loud and in his ears, as if this were a movie and the soundtrack had been amplified. He felt fear, not knowing what it was he was walking toward, but he tried to keep a lid on that fear, realizing it could render him powerless.

Finally, at the far end of the corridor, Devon made out the figure of a man. Approaching, he recognized it as the ghost he'd first met in the secret panel. The young man in the jeans and tee shirt. He was standing there, just staring at Devon. He looked terribly sad and weary.

"Who are you?" Devon asked.

The man made the sign of a five-pointed star in the air again.

"Yes, I know, I know, the pentagram," Devon said impatiently. "But who are you? What do you have to do with the beast? And are you connected to Clarissa in any way?"

The man didn't answer. He just lifted his eyes upward. Devon followed his gaze. Suddenly they were no longer standing in a dusty old corridor but in the woods. The smell of dead leaves and wet earth assaulted his nostrils. Devon's eyes looked up at the moon in the dark night sky. It was no longer a partial moon as it was earlier. It was now full.

And once more dripping with blood.

Devon returned his eyes to the man opposite him. But the man was gone, replaced by the snarling beast. It roared at him, baring its long, sharp teeth. Then it lunged.

Devon opened his eyes.

He was still on his bed, in his room. Outside the rain tapped against his windows. He let out a breath, expelling the fear the vision had inspired. He was suddenly tired, inexplicably so.

"I'll leave the ring on," he said to himself as he undressed for bed. "Maybe it will give me some answers in a dream."

He fell asleep as soon as his head hit the pillow.

"Devon."

He heard the voice from somewhere, far off, but couldn't make out who it was.

"Devon."

"Dad?"

Through the fog he recognized his father's face. Ted March, with his round, red, chubby cheeks, his bright blue eyes. His arms were outstretched toward him.

"Dad, is it really you?"

"Yes, Devon, it's me."

Devon was aware that he was dreaming, but that didn't make the sensation of seeing his father again any less thrilling. Devon had come to realize that his dreams were often as real as anything he experienced while awake. He might have been asleep, but Dad was still very much there with him.

But as in so many dreams, time and distance held no logic; the more Devon approached his father, the farther away he became.

"Dad, so much is happening," Devon called to him through the mist. "So much I need to figure out."

"You can do it, Devon. You can put all the pieces together. I know you can."

His voice was far off. Devon ran faster, trying to reach him, to get closer. But his father kept fading farther and farther away.

"Dad! I need your help! I need you to tell me who Clarissa is! What does the blood on the moon mean? Please tell me, Dad!"

He could barely make out his father's words now, as his form rapidly disappeared into the thick, moist fog. "My ring," Ted March said, but what he said after that, Devon couldn't hear.

"Dad! I'm losing you! Dad!"

The face of Ted March shimmered, fading in, fading out, merging with something else. His voice was nothing but a whisper now, overpowered by a new sound. A low, crackling sound that got louder and louder.

Laughter.

The laughter of a madman.

"Dad!" Devon shouted.

"Dad!" mocked the laughter. "Dad! Dad! I'll give you Dad!"

And suddenly it was no longer Ted March's face in the fog but the face of Jackson Muir, in all his decomposing horror. His skeletal teeth chattered as the Madman laughed at Devon.

"So much is happening," Jackson Muir said, still mocking him. "So much you need to figure out."

"You're dead and gone," Devon insisted. "You're never getting out of the Hell Hole again!"

"I'll get out, Devon," the Madman's voice purred, as thick and heavy as molasses. "Because *you* will let me out."

"Never!"

"Oh, but my boy, never is an awfully long time."

Maniacal laughter filled the space of Devon's dream. He was trying to force himself to wake up, but he couldn't. He felt trapped, and the Madman sensed it.

"Well, then, if you will never let me out, perhaps I will have to keep you *here*, in your dreams," Jackson Muir said, his voice giddy with the idea. "Poor little Nightwing boy, they'll say as they watch you writhe and twist and thrash about in your bed. Trapped in an eternal nightmare!"

"You can't do that," Devon shouted.

"Oh, no?"

Now it was the human Jackson Muir, the tall dark man in his black cape and shiny leather sorcerer's boots, who stood before Devon, not a foot away. His eyes blazed red as they gazed down on the teenager.

"You forget all the practice I've had, Devon. How I've had many more years than you to perfect my sorcery. I can do things you can't even imagine." He smiled demonically. "And you forget how real the dreams of a Nightwing are."

Suddenly the Madman's hands were closed around Devon's throat. They began to tighten.

"Now, Devon March, prepare to die in your dreams—a death you will live over and over for eternity, here in the Hell Hole of your own mind!"

A Kidnapping

Devon gasped for breath, his hands useless in their attempts to pry the Madman's cold fingers from his throat.

"You can try all you want, little boy, little sorcerer, but you will fail," Jackson Muir told him, his thumbs pressing in against Devon's adam's apple.

This is it, Devon thought, overcome with fear. *He's found a way to kill me.*

It's your fear, Devon, came the voice of his father. *It is always your fear that leaves you weak.*

I know, I know, Devon screamed in his mind, ready to lose consciousness. *But I'm getting killed here, Dad. How can I help being afraid?*

"Let him go, Apostate."

It was another voice, one Devon didn't recognize. Jackson's grip around his neck loosened slightly, allowing Devon to suck in one meager, twisted breath.

"Who dares—?" the Madman snarled, looking back over his shoulder. "I rule here! Who dares enter?"

"I dare," said the voice, plain and simple.

"You!" Jackson Muir was startled into dropping Devon to the ground. But there was no ground, of course, only mist. Still, Devon recovered himself and managed to stand.

And to look upon the face of his savior.

It was the ghost from the secret passageway. The young man in the blue jeans and tee shirt who, standing there now, once again made the sign of the pentagram with his hand in the air.

"You dare to interfere, McNutt?" the Madman bellowed. "You should know by now that you are ineffectual in saving anyone, least of all yourself."

"You have no power here," the ghost told him calmly, rationally, without any fear. "This is the province of Devon's dream. Only he has the power to command us."

Jackson Muir laughed. "*Devon?* Look at him! A shaking, trembling child! Unworthy to call himself Nightwing!"

"Unworthy?" Devon sputtered. Hearing his voice restored his confidence, and he found the Madman's grip loosening. "I imprisoned you in the Hell Hole, Muir! I think that qualifies as worthy enough for a Nightwing."

Already Jackson Muir was fading from view, his power ended.

"I'll get you, my fine young boy, and your little friends, too!" The Madman laughed, and then he was gone.

All that was left was his stink.

"So much for him," Devon said. He turned to face the ghost, who the Madman had called McNutt. "Thanks for dropping by."

"I'm sure you would have recovered your courage even if I hadn't."

"I appreciate the confidence," Devon said. "But now tell me about you. Tell me what I need to know."

"Devon."

Now whose voice was intruding?

"Devon, wake up!"

No, I need to talk to this McNutt guy ...

"Devon!"

Devon opened his eyes. It was Bjorn.

"You're going to be late for school," the gnome told him.

"School?" Devon sat up in his bed. The morning sunlight filled his room. "You woke me up for *school?*"

"When you sleep through your alarm and miss breakfast, yeah, I do," Bjorn said. "Don't you have a geography quiz today?"

"Bjorn, I was doing something much more important than a geography quiz."

"How is snoring like a buzz saw more important than a geography quiz?"

Devon stumbled out of bed, muttering. "Why does

everyone forget that I am a Sorcerer of the Nightwing? That my sleep might be *important*?"

Bjorn smirked. "Get dressed. We're all waiting for you in the car."

Devon was quiet and moody all the way to school. Once again Cecily had ridden with D.J. Devon just slunk down in the backseat, grumbling to himself. He was grumpy all through first period. He had been *this close* to finding out what he needed to know. Now he'd have to wait until tonight for more answers. He couldn't exactly go into a trance sitting at his desk. And certainly not during his geography quiz, which he feared he flunked, given that he'd never studied for it.

"Too bad that I can't just summon my Nightwing power to pass all my tests," Devon said later, in the cafeteria, squirting ketchup in a spiral onto his hamburger. "It would make this school stuff a lot easier."

"Uh, careful there, Devon," Marcus told him.

"What? I like a lot of ketchup."

Marcus rolled his eyes. "I don't mean about the ketchup. About what you wish for."

They settled their trays down at the table. "What are you talking about?"

"Wanting to use your powers for your own personal gain." Marcus sat opposite him, fixing his eyes onto Devon. "You could probably do it, if you really wanted to. But you know what that would make you."

"Yeah," Devon said, smirking. "It'd make me the Honor Roll."

"It would make you an Apostate," his friend said. "Like Isobel. Like Jackson Muir. Like all those Nightwing who went bad and who never won in the end."

"I wonder," Devon said.

Marcus took a bite into his turkey rollup. "Wonder about what?"

"That's what they teach us: that the Apostates all were defeated. That none of them made good on their bad deeds. You know, the old 'crime doesn't pay' moral. But is it true?

Maybe there's some Nightwing-gone-bad somewhere who's living it up, who's got it made."

"I don't like how you're talking."

"Don't worry, Marcus. I'm not going bad. I'm just wondering."

He looked across the table. There it was: the pentagram on Marcus's face. This was happening way too often now.

"Look, Devon, you're my hero," Marcus said. "Not just because you routinely kick demon butt back to their Hell Holes. You're my hero because you aren't afraid to do the right thing. To stand up and be counted." He smiled with meaning. "To sit at a table in the cafeteria with the fag."

"Hey," Devon said, startled back into the moment. "Don't use that word."

"Others do. I hear them. But you, Devon, you never think twice about hanging out with me—the gay kid—no matter how it might look to somebody else."

Devon grimaced. "If those idiots knew what's out there—what they should *really* be afraid of—if they saw how you kicked demon butt right along with me—well, then, they wouldn't be calling you any names."

The pentagram still hovered in front of Marcus's face. Devon couldn't ignore it any more.

"You still wearing the pendant?" he asked.

Marcus nodded, patting his chest. "Always, Devon. Ever since you gave it to me."

"Good. Don't take it off."

"Never," Marcus promised.

Natalie arrived with her tray. She took the seat next to Devon.

"Are you boys talking normal stuff or demon stuff?"

"Both," Marcus said.

She drizzled a little vinegar across her salad. "Well, I had a dream last night and I just want to make sure everything is okay."

"What kind of dream?" Devon asked.

"It was stupid," Natalie said.

"Tell me," Devon insisted.

"Well, it was like a little kid's dream. The big bad monster. It was coming after me. That's all. I'm sure it was nothing."

"What kind of monster?"

Natalie sighed. "I shouldn't have even brought it up. Devon, it's sweet of you to be concerned, but we can't be getting alarmed every time one of us has a nightmare. It was just a dream."

"There's no such thing," Devon told her. "Not in this group. Tell me what the monster looked like."

Natalie smiled wryly. "Well, then, let's see. I can't really remember. Hairy, I think. Big and hairy. That's all I remember."

Devon looked over at her round, pretty face with her dark, sparkling eyes.

The pentagram now hung in front of Natalie as well.

What did it mean? What did the sign of the five-pointed star mean for his friends?

It was a question that haunted Devon all through the next week. Things were quiet, terribly so. No more dreams, no more visions, no more intrusions by Clarissa or anything else. If it weren't for the pentagram popping up periodically over the faces of Marcus and Natalie, it would seem as if they were all leading very ordinary lives.

Ordinary lives. Devon couldn't imagine what that would be like.

His father's ring had proven helpful. At least, Devon thought it had. While it hadn't given him any concrete answers to the origin of the guy called McNutt and hadn't answered anything specific about the pentagram, it had filled in a lot of other blanks.

One night, for example, it showed him a vision of Horatio Muir, the founder of Ravenscliff, while he was still a young boy in the little village of Romney Marsh in Kent, England. There, in the background, had sat Horatio's father, a stern-faced Victorian gentleman named Quentin Muir. He had been sitting in a high-backed chair, almost like a throne, and perched on his shoulders had been several large ravens, occasionally fluttering their wings.

As Devon watched, a series of men in long purple robes—Guardians, he presumed—entered the room and looked down at the young Horatio, sitting on the floor.

"To America," they each said in turn. "To the New World."

"Such is my son's destiny," intoned Quentin Muir.

"To found a branch of Nightwing in the Western Hemisphere," said the most wizened Guardian, probably a thousand years old, "and to cap the egregious Hell Hole that has emerged along the coast of New England."

"But I must correct you, O Wise Ceolwulf," another Guardian interrupted. "We believe there have long been Nightwing in the New World, but we have lost touch—"

"The Nightwing of the original Americans have gone their own way," acknowledged Ceolwulf, "and it is our hope that Quentin Muir's heirs will find a way towards reunification with our long-lost brothers."

Later, Devon shared the vision with Rolfe. "So there are Nightwing among the American Indians," he said. "Wouldn't it be awesome to find them?"

Rolfe agreed. But for the moment, he was more interested in the mystery of the beast. All he'd been able to find, however, were old werewolf legends. Roxanne, watching them as quiet and still as a stone sentinel, could only add that they would get more answers—the next time the moon was full.

On another night, the ring showed Devon a scene from soon after Ravenscliff had been built. Horatio Muir stood on the front steps as hundreds of ravens landed, cawing and flapping their wings. The birds took up their posts all over the house, from the roof to the gargoyles to the windowsills. Horatio, now a man in his twenties, held open his arms and welcomed his wife to their new house. She was holding their baby son in her arms.

The baby Jackson Muir.

Yet as Devon stared into the vision, it wasn't the incongruity of seeing the Madman as a cooing, innocent baby that held his attention most. Rather, it was the face of the infant's mother. A strong, broad-shouldered woman, vivacious, full of life.

He found Cecily in the parlor after that. Outside an early spring storm shot hard rain and hail against the windowpanes. The pretty redhead was lying on the couch with her iPad. "Hi, Cess," Devon said. "What're you doing?"

"Posting some pics." She looked up at him with one eye. "Don't you follow me?"

"I haven't been online much lately. Been spending most of my time with my father's ring."

"Well, here's what you're missing." She turned her tablet around to display a photo of herself and D.J. hunkered down in a booth at Stormy Harbor. They looked very cozy together. "I took it myself. I think I'm getting pretty good."

"Cecily," Devon said, "do you really have feelings for D.J.?"

"What's it matter to you?"

"Well, he's my friend and I don't want him to get hurt."

"Who's going to hurt him?"

Devon sat down next to her. "Cecily, I'd like you and me to be friends again."

She laughed. "Of course we're friends, Devon. Siblings should always be friends."

He looked at her. He couldn't deny the feelings he still had for her. She was tempestuous and cocky, not nearly so thoughtful as Natalie, but she was sweet and kind underneath, and Devon hadn't forgotten how he'd once felt about her. But so long as there was a chance that she was his sister, he had to push those feelings out of his mind.

"We've been through a lot, Cess, and we may be through even more," he told her. "Let's not be hostile to each other."

She looked over at him. Her green eyes looked full of pain. She'd had feelings for him, too. "All right, Devon," she said. "Let's be friends."

They gave each other small smiles.

"Why do you say we may go through more?" she asked. "Is something happening? Is your father's ring telling you something I should know about?"

"I'm learning a lot," he told her. "I'm not sure about a lot of things, but I'll let you know what I find. But tell me something. What was Horatio Muir's wife's name?"

"Well, let's see, she was my great-grandmother. Chloe, I think."

Devon nodded, then waved his hand toward the bookshelves across the room. A large dusty tome slid out from the others and levitated across the room, attracted toward him as if his hand were magnet.

"Show-off," Cecily said.

Devon set the heavy book down on a table with a thud. Dust rose up into the air as he flipped through the pages. "Yeah," he said finally. "Here she is."

"Why are you interested in her? She wasn't Nightwing. She was just an ordinary woman who died young." She looked over at Devon and made a face, as if suddenly figuring something out. "Oh, I get it. You're thinking *my* great-grandmother was also *your* great-grandmother."

"I don't know what I think any more," Devon said.

"It's not true, Devon," Cecily said. "We're not siblings. You've got to believe that!"

"Cecily, we don't know—"

She scowled. "I hate seeing you with Natalie. I hate it!"

"Well, I hate seeing you smoking." He saw the surprise on Cecily's face. "I've seen you and D.J. puffing away. I can smell it on your coat when you come in. You used to hate cigarettes and get on D.J.'s case all the time about his smoking, and now you're doing it, too. Real smart."

"I can do what I want and see who I want, Devon."

"Be my guest. Get lung cancer. Turn yourself into a smelly, stinky, slacker mess."

"I thought you said you wanted to be friends!"

"I do. I'm sorry. I shouldn't have said anything."

"Neither should I," Cecily grumbled.

Why was talking to her so hard? Why did they seem to fight all the time now?

He'd talked about it with Rolfe, about these crazy, mixed-up feelings he had for Cecily and Natalie. His Guardian had assured him that it took a long, long time to get over a girl. It had taken years, Rolfe said, for him to really fall out of love with Mrs. Crandall and to fall in love with Roxanne. *Years.*

Except, Devon was convinced, Rolfe never really did stop loving Amanda Muir Crandall. He was still smitten, no matter how much he denied it.

Is that what it's going to be like for me? Devon shuddered at the thought as he sat down at the table, trying to return his attention to the book. *Am I going to keep having these feelings for Cecily the rest of my life, no matter how much I care about Natalie?*

Horatio Muir had two women in his life, too.

That much was obvious as Devon concentrated on the old photographs of Horatio and his family that were printed in this book. There they were: Master of Ravenscliff, with his demure wife, Chloe, beside him, holding their third son, Randolph, in her arms. In this photo, Jackson was a boy of eight or so, already reaching his father's shoulder, a cocky grin on his dark face. Next to him stood the gaunt middle son, Gideon, about whom no one seemed to know much about. But as the teen sorcerer stared down into the face of the frail Chloe—who would die only weeks after this picture was taken—Devon was equally certain of something else:

That was not the woman he had seen in his vision.

So Jackson Muir had had a different mother from his two brothers, a woman not recorded in the family history books. A woman who was not frail and delicate like Chloe, but instead vibrant and powerful. A woman, Devon was certain, who was every bit as Nightwing as her husband.

The next day, the ring gave Devon a final peek into Ravenscliff's history—of yet another Muir wife, everyone's favorite ghost, Emily Muir.

Except for the day her portrait had cried real tears, Devon hadn't seen Emily in a while. But ever since he'd found her prayerbook in Clarissa's room, he'd known she was connected somehow to the mystery of the imprisoned sorceress. In the vision shown to him by his father's ring, Devon watched as Emily sat alone in her room in the West Wing, waiting for her husband, the Madman. She stood and started to pace, glancing up at the clock. It was past midnight, getting close to one in the morning, but still she waited, growing more frantic all the time.

And then Jackson returned, his black cape swirling around him, his voice soft and reassuring. He took his wife in his arms and kissed her. Jackson loved Emily. Devon had learned that much—but that didn't stop him from treating her badly. In his arms, Emily melted. She forgave him his indiscretions, took him back time and time again. Until that fateful day, Devon knew, when, having finally had enough, poor Emily flung herself from Devil's Rock.

Maybe I really am part of this family, Devon thought, a little amused, as he drifted off to sleep. *Because none of its male members seem to have had an easy time with women, either.*

"Devon, it's going to be a full moon tonight."

On the morning that Alexander awakened him with that report, Devon felt the temperature in his room rising. His sheets were damp with sweat. He bolted upright, looking around.

Something was about to happen.

"Did you hear me, Devon?" Alexander asked. "A full moon. Tonight."

"Yeah," the teen said. "I heard you. I already know that tonight's a full moon."

He stared over at the boy, dressed for school, face freshly scrubbed and glowing. Alexander didn't know Devon had been waiting for the next full moon, counting the nights until the beast returned.

"So what's it to you?" Devon asked, swinging his legs off the bed and placing his feet against the floor. "What's with waking me up with the weather report?"

"I just thought you'd like to know." The boy smiled. "About the moon, I mean."

Devon looked into Alexander's round button eyes and

his breath caught in his throat. The look on the boy's face—
Devon had seen it before. A cold, knowing stare. The last time
Alexander had looked like that, the Madman had been playing
games with the kid's mind.

"You okay, Alexander? Something going on?"

The boy smiled again. "I just thought you'd want to know
about the full moon."

He turned and walked out of the room. The heat ratcheted
up another couple of degrees.

"Great," Devon said. "Just great."

Not only did he have the beast to contend with that night,
now he might have another potential possession going on with
Alexander, too.

We all ought to just move away, Devon thought as he made his
way into the bathroom. *Get outta this house. Buy a condo in Florida
with D.J.'s parents.*

He couldn't help but smirk. Somehow he couldn't picture
Amanda Muir Crandall in her jewels and gowns living in a condo
in Florida.

But his levity didn't last long. The heat troubled him, and not
just because it turned him all gross and sweaty once again after
he stepped out of the shower. It meant one of two things: there
were demons present, or another sorcerer was nearby. He knew
from last time that the beast wasn't a demon, so he wondered
if it signaled a return of Clarissa. Or worse: the Madman. His
dream the other night made him question how securely Jackson
was imprisoned in the Hell Hole. Could Alexander's weird
behavior mean the Madman was loose again?

But he couldn't spend too much time pondering all these
questions; he had to get ready for school. He would just have to
stay on his guard all day.

Sitting in the backseat of Bjorn's old Cadillac, Devon kept
glancing over at Alexander, sitting next to him. The boy was
stiff and quiet, his hands folded in his lap. Normally he was
squirming, digging into his lunchbox and munching on candy
bars. Today he sat glassy-eyed staring straight ahead.

"So you want to talk about anything, buddy?" Devon

whispered, not wanting to draw attention from Bjorn up front.

Alexander's head turned almost robot-like to look at Devon. "How about if we talk about the moon?"

Creepy. The kid had turned all creepy on him again, like he was when Devon had first come to Ravenscliff. He shook off a shudder and asked, "So what's got you so fascinated by the full moon all of a sudden?"

"It has such power," the boy said, in a voice not his own. It was deeper, lower, too modulated for a boy of nine. "Such power, don't you think, Devon?"

Devon leaned in toward him and spoke in a low voice so Bjorn couldn't hear. "Okay, buddy. No more fooling around. Something's got a hold of you again. I'm not sure if you can hear me, Alexander, but I'm not going to let whatever it is remain for very long. As soon as I figure out what's going on—"

The boy began to laugh. A low, shuddering sound that bubbled up from his chest and spilled from his lips.

"What's so funny?" Bjorn asked, an eyebrow lifted at them in the rearview mirror.

"Nothing," Devon said, and he meant it.

They dropped Alexander off at his school. For a moment Devon considered telling Bjorn what he suspected, but his intuition, which he always trusted, warned him against it. Alexander would be fine for now, he told himself. He'd get through the school day without any incident.

It's tonight—when the full moon has risen—that I've got to watch out.

Coming up behind Marcus at his locker, Devon placed his hand on his friend's shoulder. "You wearing the pendant?"

"Never without it," Marcus assured him, and he tugged it out from under his shirt to prove it.

But Devon had also seen the pentagram in front of Natalie. He found her just as she was about to go into her advanced literature class. "Here," Devon said, pulling from his pocket another necklace with a five-pointed star, one that hadn't been there a moment before. "I want you to wear this."

"For *me*?" Natalie's beautiful brown eyes, lacy with dark eyelashes, flickered up at him.

"Yeah, for you."

"Oh, Devon, thank you."

She placed it over her head and dropped it over her blouse. Then she reached up to encircle Devon's neck with her arms. She kissed him full on the lips.

"I'll wear it always," she purred.

Devon's eyes moved past her and suddenly locked onto Cecily's. She was in the corridor, walking beside D.J., and she'd witnessed the whole thing.

The last bell rang. "I've got to get to class," Natalie said, pulling away from him. "But I want you to know, Devon, that I really, really like you. I have ever since you first came to Misery Point. This necklace means so much to me. Thank you so much."

He managed to smile. He couldn't exactly throw cold water on her romantic moment by explaining that the necklace was for protection, not anything else. Except maybe it was. He *did* like Natalie. Giving her something special—even if it was the same exact pendant that Marcus was wearing—wasn't such a bad idea after all.

So why did the fact that Cecily saw them bother him so much?

After school, D.J. gave them all a ride home. They stopped at Gio's for pizza. Their little gang hadn't hung out much in the last several weeks. They used to be like glue: while the other kids had headed to after-school sports or activities, the five of them had met at Gio's to strategize their demon hunting. Now the crisis they faced wasn't nearly so specific—Devon wasn't even sure what they were up against—but he figured it was time to bring his band of comrades up to date.

He told them all about Alexander's strange behavior, about the heat he'd felt at Ravenscliff, about the fear that the beast would return tonight, about his strange dream of the Madman.

"He's getting restless in the Hell Hole," Cecily said, shuddering. "It's what Mother's always feared. That he won't stay in there, that he'll come back."

"He can't come back, not unless someone opens the Hell Hole," Devon assured her.

"And only a Sorcerer of the Nightwing can do that," D.J. added.

"And this is the only Nightwing we know," Natalie said, gripping Devon's arm. "And he's not about to do any such thing."

"Excuse me, Ms. Santos," Cecily said, "but I'll point out, yet again, that *I* am also Nightwing. You seem to keep forgetting that fact."

"Yeah, but, Cess," D.J. told her, "you haven't got the powers so—"

"I *know* I don't have my rightful powers!" Cecily snapped. "Thanks for rubbing it in, D.J. Sheesh!" She pulled away from him in the booth.

"Look, we've got to stop bickering with each other," Devon said. "Let's all meet at Rolfe's tonight. If the beast makes a return appearance—"

"Did you know there was a beast like this once before in Misery Point?"

It was Marcus, who hadn't said much since they arrived at the pizza joint and Devon began telling his stories. He had just sat there, peeling the cheese off his slices and then rolling it up and eating it with his fingers.

Devon turned to look at him. Sure enough, there was the pentagram. It was there almost constantly now.

"What do you mean? When?"

"My mother told me. She remembered when she was a real little girl almost getting attacked by a beast just like the one the newspapers were describing last month."

Devon was fascinated. "What else did she tell you, Marcus?"

"Nothing. It was like she was almost sorry she even brought it up. Guess it left her pretty traumatized."

Natalie was looking at Devon with her big brown eyes. They were filled with fear, and he wanted to protect her. "Do you think there's a connection, Devon?" she asked.

"I don't know. There's so much we don't know. But I have a feeling that tonight, when the moon rises, we're going to start learning a whole lot of things."

The plan was to meet at Rolfe's shortly before sunset. So D.J. pulled up in his Camaro, which he called Flo after his grandmother. Devon and Cecily told Mrs. Crandall they were going to a movie; she would never have allowed them to head over to Rolfe's with her blessing. Devon found it definitely weird to sit in Flo's backseat while Cecily, up front, kept making a point to reach over and stroke D.J.'s hair or rest her head on his shoulder. Devon sulked as he stared out the window. Why should he care? Besides, he had a lot more important stuff to worry about than Miss Cecily Crandall.

"Where are the other two?" Rolfe asked as they converged in his glass study overlooking the sea. The windows had all been repaired, and the setting sun had turned the waves into a wash of golds and oranges.

"Natalie and Marcus were planning to walk over together," Devon said. "I didn't want to say anything to freak them out yet, but they're the ones I'm most worried about."

"As if *that* wasn't obvious," sniffed Cecily.

Devon ignored her. "You know I've seen the pentagram in front of Marcus's face. Well, it's been there almost constantly the last few days. And now I've seen it on Natalie as well."

"Oh," Cecily said, and a flash of fear crossed her face. For all her surliness toward Natalie of late, Cecily was clearly concerned for her friend.

They waited. And then they waited some more.

"She's not responding to my texts," Cecily announced.

"Marcus either," D.J. echoed.

The sun sank over the hills.

"Where *are* they?" Devon asked, pressing his face against the window. "I don't like them walking out there alone in the dark."

Cecily whipped out her cell phone and called Natalie. She got her voicemail. So she rang Natalie's house. She was told by Natalie's little sister that Natalie had left an hour ago to meet Marcus.

"That's way more than enough time to get here," D.J. observed.

Devon tried Marcus's house. There was no answer.

"We're going out looking for them," Devon announced, standing up.

"What exactly are you concerned about, Devon?" Rolfe asked.

Just then, from the distance, came the long, low howl of the beast.

"That," Devon replied.

"I don't want you going out there alone," Rolfe said. "We'll go in my car."

Roxanne promised to stay at the house and keep a lookout in case Natalie and Marcus showed up. Rolfe rolled out a Range Rover from his garage instead of his usual Porsche sports car. They all piled in.

Devon noticed Rolfe had a gun strapped to his waist. "You're thinking you'll need that?"

"Silver bullets," Rolfe said. "Specially made. Just in case."

"Don't shoot it," Devon insisted.

"We might have to."

Rolfe was right, of course. But Devon felt certain that to kill the beast would be a tragedy none of them would ever get over.

From somewhere in the woods outside the village they heard it again: an agonizing, horrible, fingernails-on-blackboard kind of cry.

"Drive in the direction of the sound," Devon said, shuddering. "I'm going to try to find them in my mind."

They started off down the road into the village. Devon concentrated. He couldn't see Natalie or Marcus, but he could see the beast. It was lumbering in the shadows. But just where it was, he couldn't determine quite yet. "Keep driving," he told Rolfe. "Maybe I'll pick up something as we get closer, like radar or something."

But they didn't get far. A police barricade prevented them from reaching town. Flashing red lights from six cruisers parked in a V sent shivers through the night.

"What's going on?" Rolfe asked from his car window.

A sheriff's deputy shone his flashlight into the car. "Oh, hello, Montaigne." The beam of his light caught Cecily, sitting up front next to Rolfe. "Oh, hey there, Cess."

It was that annoying Joey Potts, a pimply twentysomething who was always giving Cecily the eye. Devon sneered. They ought to have thrown the creep in jail.

"What's going on?" Cecily repeated Rolfe's question. It was more likely that Potts would answer her than anyone else.

"Some wild animal, the same one that was around here last month." The deputy made a face. "Don't know if it's a bear or what, but it apparently got some girl."

"No," Devon said, feeling the fear inside him rise up like bile.

"Where do they think it is?" Rolfe asked.

Potts shrugged. "In the woods somewhere. We can hear it howling from time to time. But I'm afraid the road is closed."

"Well, I need to get back to Ravenscliff," Cecily said, clearly trying to flirt her way through the barricade.

"Sorry, Cess, but you'll have to go the long way around."

"That could take an hour! Please, Joey!"

He stood his ground. "They won't move those cruisers for no one."

"Then I'll just have to go around them," Devon said under his breath.

"Dude," D.J. whispered, leaning into him, "are you about to pull one of your disappearing acts?"

Rolfe overheard. After the deputy backed away from the window, Rolfe turned around in the seat to glare at the teen sorcerer. "You don't have power over this thing, remember," he told Devon. "Don't be charging in without thinking."

"I have to," Devon said, suddenly absolutely certain about what he was about to say. "The girl the beast has with it— it's Natalie."

"What?"

"I'm sure of it. It just came to me. I have to go, Rolfe."

"Devon." It was Cecily. Their eyes met over the seat.

"Please be careful."

"Wait, Devon," Rolfe urged. He unstrapped the gun at his belt. "At least take this."

Devon accepted the weapon, looking at it with revulsion. But he would have been a fool to refuse it. "I'll meet you back at the house," he said, and then he disappeared.

He heard the thing before he saw it: a low, angry growl. Deep in the woods the moonlight was blocked by the tall black pine trees. Covered with a thick carpet of needles, the earth smelled rich and new, spring unthawing the frozen crust. Devon stood completely still, breathing in and out, concentrating all his senses on the beast. He heard it again. A raspy breath. The gnashing of teeth.

"Show yourself," he demanded.

He knew the beast didn't have to obey him. Whatever it was, it was no demon, bound to the will of the Nightwing. But he was pretty certain it wouldn't remain in hiding. It wanted to confront Devon. *We're connected*, Devon knew. *Just how is uncertain. But we are.*

"I'm here!" He turned his head to look through the dark shadows but kept his feet firmly placed on the ground. He held the gun tightly in his right hand. "Come on, I'm *here*! Don't keep me waiting!"

In front of him there were eyes.

Red eyes, blinking once, then twice, in the dark.

"Hello, ugly," Devon said, keeping his voice calm and steady.

Then came the roar, a deafening sound, causing Devon to pull back, gripping the gun even more tightly in his hand.

The beast was suddenly looming over him, its twisted, hairy body a cross between an ape and a bear and a wolf. And, Devon recognized once more, a man. Saliva dripped down onto Devon's face from the creature's yellow teeth. Lifting its snout, the beast howled into the trees.

And in that moment Devon was suddenly encased in a solid silver armor.

"Hey, nice work," he muttered to himself. He hadn't even planned it. It had just happened instinctively. *That's the way good sorcery works*, his intuition told him.

The beast wasn't nearly so pleased with his handiwork, however. It hissed at Devon, recoiling from the brightness of the silver. It lumbered backward into the bushes.

Devon followed.

"No, no, get away from me!"

A girl's voice from somewhere in the darkness.

Natalie's voice!

Devon could see her clearly now, her clothes torn, terror burning in her eyes, as she tried to crawl away through the pine needles.

"Natalie!"

The beast bared its fangs, ready to bite down upon her.

And suddenly Natalie was gone. The beast, outraged and confused, reared up to its full height and roared.

"Yeah," Devon said as the thing turned to look at him. "I did that. That was me. Natalie is now back with my friends, safe at Rolfe's house. In the future, you ought to pick on somebody your own size."

The beast leaned back, faced the moon, and let out a long, horrible howl.

"Who are you?" Devon demanded. "What connection is there between you and me and everything that's been going on?"

The beast lowered its face and leveled its eyes with Devon's. *Yes, something familiar there*, Devon thought. Definitely something familiar …

"The cops want to kill you," he told the creature. "Do you understand what I'm saying? I have a gun right here that could do the job, too. If I can't make communication with you I may have to turn these silver bullets over to the police and let them do what they want. Because I can't let you keep threatening my friends."

He studied the thing.

"Speaking if which, where is Marcus? If you've hurt him, I swear I'll pump you full of silver myself."

There was no recognition, no flicker of understanding, in the thing's brutish black eyes. It was a beast, nothing more. If it had been a man at some point, as Roxanne supposed, then all human intelligence had departed. It was nothing more than a dumb animal, with an instinct to kill—a realization confirmed when it suddenly leapt at Devon, his silver armor be damned.

With one elbow Devon sent the thing sprawling into a tree, but it was back on its feet again within moments. It went down onto its haunches, ready to lunge again, like a coiled spring.

This time Devon was ready for it. He jumped into the air in a preemptive strike, bringing the soles of his silver feet crashing down onto the thing's hairy chest, knocking it to the ground before it had the chance to pounce.

"Face it," Devon said, standing over the beast, one foot planted on its rib cage, "we are not evenly matched."

The creature was enraged. It grabbed Devon's ankle, no matter that the silver was scalding its flesh. It took hold and wouldn't let go, upsetting Devon's balance and sending the teen sorcerer sprawling down onto his silver butt.

Now it leapt at him in blind fury. *It will tear me apart, even if the silver kills it in the process*, Devon thought.

Devon raised the gun. He had a clear shot, straight through the heart. He could kill it, right here. Of course, he could also just disappear, but that would leave the beast still roaming the village. Better to take it down right now ...

But he couldn't pull the trigger.

He couldn't kill it.

Instead he deflected the beast with his feet once again, slapping them against its torso at it lunged, and sent the creature back into the trees. The thing was on its feet quickly, but this time it simply retreated, howling back into the woods until Devon could hear it no more.

"I was waiting for Marcus," Natalie said, her whole body shuddering, "and this thing just came out of nowhere and grabbed me."

Bjorn had come down from Ravenscliff, and he'd treated her cuts and bruises with the salves and potions from his medicine bag. They worked much more quickly than traditional Western treatments. A cut along Natalie's shoulder healed visibly in front of their eyes.

"Where *is* Marcus?" Devon asked.

Natalie's eyes flashed with fear. "He never showed up. You think he's in danger, too?"

"I do," Devon admitted. "I've tried to hone in and find him, but I can't. It's like he's nowhere."

"Oh, God," Cecily cried. "Does that mean he's dead?"

No one answered her, because that was what they all feared.

"Somehow that thing knows who my friends are," Devon said, overwhelmed once again by the danger his sorcery brought to the people he cared about. "It wanted to confront me, and it knew that going after my friends would bring me out."

"I just tried calling Marcus's house again," Cecily said, "and still no answer."

"Then the whole family must be out," Rolfe said. "Let's not jump to any conclusions yet."

"He was supposed to meet us," Devon said. "He wouldn't just not show up."

He tried again to see Marcus in his mind's eye. But all he came up with was blackness.

Is that what the pentagram meant all along? That Marcus was marked for death? Had the beast killed him before it grabbed Natalie? Were his parents out looking for him now—or were they down at the morgue, identifying his body?

Devon needed to focus and not let his fears overtake him. "Natalie," he said. "Where's your pendant?"

She looked up guiltily at Devon. "I wanted to wear it! I planned on it! You gave it to me, Devon, and I treasured it!" She sobbed. "But when I went to put it on tonight, it was gone! I had placed it on my bureau, but it was gone! Just gone!"

The same thing must have happened to Marcus, Devon thought. Who would take it? And why?

Devon gave her a new star pendant; in fact, he gave one to everybody, including Rolfe and Roxanne, just in case. He ordered them to sleep with them around their necks. Whether the pendants would do any good or not, Devon didn't know. But they sure couldn't hurt. And clearly they had some power, if someone had taken the time to snatch them from Natalie and Marcus.

Back at Ravenscliff, Devon called Marcus's house again. This time his mother answered.

"Hi, it's Devon. I'm sorry to call so late but I'm looking for Marcus …"

"Why?" Her voice sounded strained, edgy.

"Well, he was supposed to meet us tonight and he didn't reply to any of our texts …"

"He's asleep!" Marcus's mother was practically shouting into the phone. "He's sound asleep in his room!"

Devon heard Marcus's father in the background. "Who is it, Gigi?"

"It's Devon," she said. "I told him Marcus is sound asleep!"

"Get off the phone," her husband told her.

"Is Marcus okay?" Devon asked.

"He's asleep in his room!" Her voice cracked. "Why *wouldn't* he be okay?"

"All right," Devon said. "I'm sorry to have bothered you."

Marcus was *not* okay.

But if he was in his room he was at least safe. Devon tried once more to see him, to see into Marcus's house, but he couldn't. Something was blocking his Nightwing vision. And when he tried teleporting himself into Marcus's bedroom, he found he could not. Something was definitely interfering with his powers. Who was strong enough to do that? Clarissa? Or— something else?

The Madman?

It couldn't be! Jackson Muir might have tried to reach Devon through his dreams, but he couldn't affect them while awake. He was trapped in the Hell Hole. He was powerless.

Wasn't he?

Devon let out a long sigh. He'd have to take Marcus's mother's word that her son was okay, and check in with his friend about what really happened tomorrow at school.

There was one thing more, however, that Devon needed to do before trying to fall asleep. He needed to look in on Alexander.

The boy slept soundly. To look at him one wouldn't have imagined some entity had taken control of him again. He slept like a little baby, buzzing with soft, steady breaths.

Devon was about to close Alexander's door when something caught his eye. A glint of light on the boy's dresser. He knew he needed to look closer.

He gasped when he saw what was there.

Two star pendants. The ones he had given to Marcus and Natalie.

"Hahahahahahaha."

Devon turned. Alexander was sitting up in bed now, laughing in a low, deep, horrible voice not his own.

A Terrible
Transformation

Devon got nothing out of the boy but maniacal laughter. Alexander just kept laughing at him, his eyes wild. Devon backed out of the room, horrified.

He *was* possessed. Alexander was once again possessed by some malevolent spirit.

The Madman?

No, it couldn't be!

Please don't let it be! Not again!

As Devon suspected, he barely had any sleep after stumbling in fear and confusion back to his room. Why would Alexander steal the pendants? How had he gotten into Devon's friends' rooms? What force made him do it? Devon's eyes remained wide open and staring at his ceiling even as the sun broke over the horizon.

Everything's coming to a head, Devon thought, getting dressed. *Alexander, Marcus, the beast ... tonight everything came together.*

When he got to school, he discovered Marcus wasn't there. Just like what had happened last month when the moon had been full.

"I'm out of here," Devon whispered to D.J., deciding geometry class was of secondary importance to everything else.

"Truancy can lower your final grade, you know," his friend told him wryly. D.J. swung open his locker door to give Devon cover. "Go on. Disappear. Find out what the hell is going on."

"Meet me at Rolfe's after school," Devon said.

D.J. gave him a little salute. "Aye-aye, capitan."

Devon knew he couldn't will himself to appear at Marcus's

house; that route was somehow blocked. So instead he just trusted that he'd materialize wherever he was supposed to, wherever there might be some answers. He nodded to his friend, then faded out behind D.J.'s locker door.

It took him a couple of seconds to realize where he had reappeared.

"The Misery Point public library?" he asked out loud.

"Shh," scolded a librarian with short gray hair and blue cat's-eye glasses sitting at the reference desk.

Why here? Devon asked himself. *What possibly can I find out about the beast and Marcus's condition in the Misery Point public library?*

Libraries have answers to everything, he heard his intuition tell him.

And maybe I can learn something about when the beast appeared here in Misery Point before, the way Marcus's mother remembered ...

"May I help you, young man?" the librarian was asking, looking at him oddly. "I didn't even see you come in. Shouldn't you be in school?"

"I'm—I'm here on a school project," Devon said.

"A school project? What is it on?"

"Um, it's on—well, it's—kind of hard to describe—"

She narrowed her eyes at him suspiciously. "I hope you don't think you're going to use the public library as a hideout for playing hooky."

"No, no, it's not like that at all. I'm doing a research project. Really I am."

I am, Devon realized. *That's no lie.*

"I'm researching unexplained phenomena," he blurted out. "You know, strange occurrences that have no explanation. And they have to have occurred right here in Misery Point."

The librarian's eyebrows pushed up into her forehead above her blue glasses. "Unexplained phenomena? You mean, like UFOs?"

"Maybe. Or anything. Sightings ... like Bigfoot maybe."

"Bigfoot? In Misery Point?"

"Or whatever."

A small smile crept across the librarian's face. "All right, young man. Let's see what we can find."

She stood, walking over to a row of metal filing cabinets. The third drawer down was marked local ephemera.

"If we have anything, it'll be in here," she said, pulling open the drawer.

Devon watched intently as she riffled through the manila folders, reading each tab. "I clip the local newspaper every day. I've been doing it for twenty years, and my predecessor did it for twenty years before me."

"Cool," Devon offered.

"Beach erosion," the librarian read. "Crime statistics. Murders. Restaurants. Tourism. Watercraft." She shrugged. "Nothing for unexplained phenomena. But I know there *have* been stories …"

"Stories like what?"

The librarian removed her glasses and looked at Devon closely. "Well, strange things. Like those ravens that for no reason at all clung to Ravenscliff up on the hill. And then disappeared."

"And then returned," Devon reminded her.

"And then returned," she echoed, still looking through the folders. "There have been so many legends about the Muir family, so many ghost stories. The villagers love to gossip about strange rich folk. I know I've clipped stories …"

She suddenly extracted a folder and handed it over to Devon.

"They must be in here," she said. He took the folder. It was marked miscellaneous and bulged with faded newspaper clippings. "Go through that and see what you find."

He settled down at a table. Sure enough there were several stories about the ravens, and one, dated 1964, included a photograph of the great house covered with the birds, far more than even roosted there currently. tourists flock to see house of ravens read the headline.

But Devon could only glance at it. He didn't have the time to read it thoroughly, or any of the other stories told by villagers of seeing strange sights, ghosts, and visions in the woods around Ravenscliff. He'd want to come back and read them all at a later point, of course, but for now he was hunting for something in particular. Just *what* he was hunting for he wasn't sure. But he was certain that when he found it, he'd know.

He turned a clipping over and gazed down at the one below.

He sat back in his chair in surprise. The newspaper clip was *glowing*.

This was it!

STRANGE ANIMAL SIGHTING REPORTED.

The date was almost thirty years earlier. The day after Halloween.

Devon read:

> *Sheriff George Elcar today was investigating reports of a large animal in the vicinity of the village. According to Sam Pierce of Pierce Drug on Main Street, the animal was spotted around 3:00 a.m. last night, making a large growling sound. Pierce was awakened by the sound and saw the creature in his backyard. He described it as looking like a bear. Another local, Mrs. Fred Ingersoll of 16 Adkins Place, around the corner from Pierce, also reported seeing the animal, although she described it more as a cross between a wolf and a gorilla. "Sometimes it walked on all fours, sometimes upright," she told this reporter. "And it was howling at the moon." Sheriff Elcar assured citizens that his men are investigating.*

"So it *was* here before," Devon whispered.

He was drawn to the print on the back of the clipping. It was an obituary, cut off halfway, but it was still complete enough for Devon to see who the article memorialized.

Emily Muir.

It was a notice of her death. The day before the sighting of the strange animal, Emily had thrown herself to her death from Devil's Rock.

There was a connection between the beast and Emily's suicide.

Devon searched through the rest of the clippings, but none of the others in this batch were glowing. Devon turned to look at the filing cabinets behind him. Within one of them, he saw another glow, pulsing dimly through the black metal.

"May I look for myself?" he asked the librarian.

She nodded. "Just don't get them out of order."

He pulled open the drawer, his heart beating wildly. A ray of light rose in a steady stream. Devon saw that it emanated from the folder marked Murders.

Back at the table, it was easier to find what he's looking for, as the glow had only intensified. The glowing article stood out from among the other clippings. Devon made a sound as he read the headline.

GIRL FOUND MUTILATED ON THE BEACH

An unidentified young woman was found dead this morning at East Seaboard Beach, horribly mutilated and mangled. Police have roped off the area as a crime scene. Residents nearby reported hearing a confrontation during the night. At this point it is not clear if the girl's killer was human or animal.

Devon glanced up at the date. It was one day after the first sighting of the beast.

There were no follow-up stories about the killing. Apparently, it was never solved. But then Devon spotted another clipping that glowed toward the bottom of the folder, and he eagerly pushed aside the ones on top of it. And once again he gasped out loud.

It was a photograph of the ghost from the West Wing!

The headline read:

OGDEN MCNUTT SHOT TO DEATH

The date was two days after the first sighting of the beast, and one day after the girl was found dead on the beach. Devon read:

Mr. Ogden McNutt, a caretaker at Ravenscliff manor, was found this morning shot to death in the woods surrounding the estate. Sheriff Elcar has determined that he was killed with a single bullet through the heart. Mr. Randolph Muir has told deputies that he heard nothing unusual during the night, and did not know McNutt to have any enemies. The young man had worked on the estate for only a few months. Mr. McNutt leaves a wife and a three-year-old daughter.

An interesting detail to emerge from the autopsy is that McNutt was shot with a silver bullet. Sheriff Elcar hopes this will allow him to track down the killer.

A silver bullet.

I saw him change into the beast in my vision, Devon thought. Ogden McNutt was the beast that killed that poor girl on the beach. Then someone who knew what was happening shot and killed him with a silver bullet.

But why had McNutt returned now to terrorize Devon and his friends?

"Please may I see him?" Devon begged, standing on the front step of Marcus's house, his mother peering at him through a crack in the door.

"I told you he was sick. Just please go away, Devon."

Devon considered asking her about the beast she saw as a girl, but knew it would just upset her further. Her eyes were bloodshot with dark circles around them, as if she hadn't slept at all. She closed the door in Devon's face.

This is all my fault, Devon thought, trudging back down the steps toward the sidewalk. *I've put my friends in danger. I need to go away. I've got to find more of my own kind. Maybe I ought to leave Misery Point. They'd never find me if I didn't want to be found. I could go in search of those Native American Nightwing ...*

But the thought of leaving Misery Point staggered him. This was home. It was as if Dad's death, as hard as it had been for him, had opened Devon to a whole new way of seeing things, given him an opportunity to find his place in the world.

And Rolfe, and Marcus, and D.J., and Natalie, and even Cecily were all part of that. He couldn't imagine leaving them.

But he had to. He couldn't keep putting their lives at risk. All of this was because of him. Natalie could have been killed. D.J. and Cecily had been at risk of death several times. And who knew what had happened to Marcus?

"Psst, Devon."

He turned.

"Over here."

Behind a thicket of forsythia bushes, just starting to pop into bright yellow life, stood Marcus. In his pajamas. Trembling.

"Hey!" Devon called. "Your mom said—"

"I know. I heard you at the door. So I went through my window. I had to see you."

Devon approached him. Marcus was pretty scratched and bruised. His eyes were sunken, and his arms were wrapped around himself.

"Dude," Devon said, gripping his friend by his shoulders. He could feel Marcus's body shuddering. "You really *are* sick. What is going on?"

"I'm not sick, just scared," Marcus said. "It's just like last month. I have these horrible dreams, and then I wake up all scratched and bruised."

Devon looked at the wounds on Marcus's arms. "How do you get that way?"

"I don't know. But I'm apparently sleepwalking. Last month my parents were frantic because I'd disappear from my room. I must have gotten out the same way I just got out now, through the window. It happened just three nights, and then it stopped. We thought whatever it was, it was over. But last night it happened again. We weren't prepared. I disappeared, and my parents were out looking for me, but I didn't show up again until this morning, passed out in my backyard."

Devon gripped his friend's shoulders tighter, looking into his eyes. "It's the full moon."

"Yeah," he said. "The moon scares me. I admit it."

"There's some connection between you and the beast. I

don't know what it is, but I've found out who the beast is. It's a ghost from Ravenscliff's past." Devon made a little laugh. "Big surprise, huh?"

"But why me? And what happens to me during the night?"

"Maybe you're helping it somehow. Maybe you go to the beast, wherever it is. That's why you're so scratched up in the morning."

"My star pendant," Marcus said guiltily, looking at Devon. "I took it off to take a shower, and when I came out ..."

"I know. Alexander stole it."

"*Alexander*? Why?"

Devon closed his eyes and turned away from Marcus. "He's under some kind of possession again."

"Is it the Madman?"

"It can't be," Devon said, but his voice betrayed his own doubts. "He's trapped in the Hell Hole. He can't do anything to us while he's in there."

"But what if he's found a way? What if all this is because of him?"

Devon couldn't even begin to think about that. "We'll find out what's causing this, Marcus," he said. "I promise you." He looked over at the other boy again. "Man, you are really in bad shape. Did your parents call a doctor?"

"They did last month, and he said he could find nothing wrong with me." He made a face in puzzlement. "But they're acting so weird, my parents. Like how they don't want me talking to you, or anyone. They keep saying they'll handle this, that no one else should know about what's happening to me."

"They're just scared," Devon said.

"Maybe. But I can't go back in there, Devon. Let me come with you. I can't stay cooped up in my room any longer."

Devon smirked. "Then you should've gotten dressed first."

Marcus looked down at his pajamas. "Can you help me there, dude?"

"I'll try." Devon imagined Marcus dressed in jeans and a sweatshirt, and suddenly his friend was dressed accordingly, with a pair of brand new sneakers to boot. Devon grinned. "Awesome.

It worked. You never know with these types of things."

"Guess that means I'm *supposed* to go with you," Marcus said. "Um, where *are* we going, anyway?"

"Rolfe's. D.J. and the rest are meeting me there after school. We need to be prepared. There's another full moon tonight, and meanwhile Alexander has to be dealt with. The kid's already been through enough. I've got to find a way to break the hold over him."

Rolfe was at his restaurant when they arrived at his house, but Roxanne was there, and it was as if she'd been expecting them. There was a spread of food for their lunch, fresh fruit and cheeses and shrimp sautéed with Jamaican spices. They chowed down fast, both of them suddenly ravenously hungry. Once again Devon wondered just who this woman was, and what her powers are. All Devon knew was, whoever she was and whatever her abilities, he was glad she was on their side.

"You know," Marcus said, "my parents will come looking for me. Right now they think I'm sleeping, but when they look in my room and see I've disappeared again, they are going to freak."

"That's true," Devon said.

Roxanne sat opposite them in a big round wicker chair. She smiled slightly. "Why not put his doppelganger to work for him?"

Devon made a face. "His what?"

"His doppelganger." Her smile lengthened. "Everyone has one—a shadow self that accompanies every human being."

"I don't follow," Devon said.

"Doppelgangers look just like us," Roxanne explained, "but are usually invisible to human eyes. They almost always stand behind a person and cast no reflection in a mirror. Dogs and cats, however, have been known to see doppelgangers. Ever notice how a dog will bark for no apparent reason when someone comes into the room?"

"But what does a doppelganger do?" asked Marcus.

"Usually it offers sympathetic company. It listens and gives advice to its owners. We call it intuition."

Devon nodded. "So the Voice inside me … my intuition. It's really my doppelganger."

"It's a part of you. A doppelganger has all of your traits, good and bad. Usually a doppelganger is your ally, but sometimes it can turn mischievous or even malicious." Roxanne smiled. "But I suspect in this case Marcus's doppelganger will be glad to help."

"So you're suggesting we send my doppelganger back to my house," Marcus said.

She nodded. "Precisely. It can sleep soundly in your bed, and your parents won't be alarmed by your disappearance."

"Cool," Devon said, a thought suddenly occurring to him. "Can you also send your doppelganger to school instead of you?"

Roxanne smiled knowingly. "Ah, but we are grateful for the limitations on the power of the Nightwing. Otherwise young sorcerers like yourself would never receive an education." She stood. "Now do it. I sense a mother preparing to open a door and check on her son."

Devon looked over at Marcus. And sure enough, almost as if it were a double exposure on a roll of film, there was an exact copy of the teenager sitting right behind him. The contours of its body faded in and out of focus, but it was there all right, mimicking every movement, every facial expression Marcus made. Which made it even more uncanny when the doppelganger suddenly broke with that pattern and turned on its own to face Devon, as if to say it was ready to be put to work.

"Okay," Devon told it. "Get back to Marcus's room, and wear his pajamas."

The doppelganger disappeared.

"You think it will work?" Marcus asked.

"We'll find out," Devon said.

Rolfe arrived around the same time as D.J. pulled up in

Flo with Natalie and Cecily. Natalie was still shaken from her encounter with the beast last night, but she'd kept it a secret, even from her parents, until they could find out more information. Just how they were going to do that, however, remained the biggest mystery.

"It seems to me," Rolfe said, "given the information Devon discovered at the library, we are dealing with some malevolent spirit from the past. The return of the beast after all this time, the possession of Alexander—this suggests a restless entity has returned from the dead. For what purpose, however, is unclear."

"It's Ogden McNutt," Devon said. "He's the malevolent spirit."

"I don't know about that, Devon." Rolfe stood in front of the glass wall that overlooked the sea. Its waters, calm earlier, were starting to roil the way they always seemed to do whenever Devon was in this room. "My father knew McNutt," Rolfe said. "They both worked at Ravenscliff at the same time. My father liked him, always said he was a good man. I never learned the story of his death, but I never had the sense that he was evil, or that he would be likely to carry such malevolence to the grave."

"But if he was murdered," Cecily said, "he could be bitter, looking for revenge."

"It's possible," Rolfe admitted. "But McNutt has been helpful in Devon's visions, saving him from the Madman and offering warnings, not threats."

"It can't be Jackson Muir again, can it?" Natalie asked.

D.J. echoed her anxiety. "I hope not. I am *not* looking forward to tangling with the Madman again."

"He's in the Hell Hole," Devon insisted. "It *can't* be him."

"I wonder," Rolfe said. "I think your dream was real, Devon. Jackson has managed to find a way to contact you. As much as I don't want to believe it, I think there's a connection to Jackson Muir."

"But what about Clarissa?" Cecily asked. "We're all conveniently forgetting about her. A sorceress my mother kept locked away in secret rooms for the past ten years or more. *She'd* have cause for revenge."

"I haven't figured out what role Clarissa plays in any of this, if there's a role at all," Rolfe said. His face tightened. "Don't forget I knew her. Very well. And I can tell you there is not one malicious bone in her body."

"Not back when you knew her, maybe," Devon said. "But Cecily's right. Keeping her imprisoned all these years has made her crazy. I wouldn't count her out just yet."

Rolfe sighed, turning to gaze off across the sea. For years he'd thought Clarissa's body had washed out there somewhere. He'd thought she was dead, and that he might in some way have contributed to her death. Now she was alive—and with powers he never knew she had. Devon realized Rolfe felt responsible for her. It made all of this so much more personal for him.

"The answer," Rolfe said, his back still to all of them, "can be found in one place." He paused, looking over his shoulder. "Alexander."

"Yeah," Devon agreed. "If we can find out what's possessing him …"

"But you tried," Marcus reminded him. "You tried to see what it was, but you could discern nothing."

"This is true," Devon admitted.

"A séance," Roxanne offered. Her words took them all by surprise, as she was sitting across the room from them and up until now had not participated in their discussion. They all turned to look at her.

"A séance?" Rolfe asked her.

"It is a way of contacting spirits. I've conducted many. I think this is an obvious case that requires such a practice."

"This is totally cool," D.J. said, a grin stretching across his face. "I always wanted to be in a séance."

"A séance is not fun and games," Rolfe warned him. "I've witnessed several, and they can be terrifying."

"But if it's our only hope of finding out some answers," Devon said, "then we've *got* to do it."

Roxanne stood from her chair and approached the group. "We are missing one person, however," she said. "One who is vitally important."

"Who?" Devon asked.

"We need Alexander here."

Cecily laughed out loud. "My mother will *never* allow him out of the house without asking a gazillion questions. And she'd certainly never permit him to come *here*."

"Then Bjorn will have to smuggle him out," Devon said. "Cecily, let me use your cell phone."

It took some convincing, but Bjorn finally agreed to try. Whether Alexander, possessed by whatever spirit, would cooperate remained to be seen.

As it turned out, the boy was very happy to accompany Bjorn for a ride, asking no questions and agreeing without argument to keep their little jaunt a secret from Mrs. Crandall. As soon as Alexander walked into Rolfe's house, Devon suspected he was up to no good, that he couldn't be trusted. There was a canny, crafty look in his round button eyes, a fixed smile that seemed far too old and wise for a kid his age.

"A séance?" Alexander asked when he was told what he was there for. "Why, how fascinating. An attempt to contact the dead. How simply delicious."

"You are *weird*, kid," D.J. told him. "Can I just say that you've always creeped me out a little? Even when you're supposedly normal."

The boy just laughed that low, knowing, precocious chuckle.

"Oh, this is not good, not good at all," Bjorn fretted, rubbing his little hands together. "Mrs. Crandall would be so displeased if she knew what we were doing here, and involving the boy in it. But I did it for you, Master Devon. For you."

Devon smiled down at the gnome. "Duly noted and appreciated, Bjorn. Now join with us for the circle."

Rolfe had set up a large round table in the middle of the room. On its center Roxanne had placed a single lit candle. The lights were turned out, and each of them took a seat.

"Offer your hand to the person next to you," Roxanne told them.

Devon turned. Cecily sat beside him. Their eyes met, and she gave him her hand. Then the circle took shape, to Marcus to Natalie to Rolfe to D.J. to Bjorn to Roxanne to Alexander and back to Devon again. He recoiled from how cold the boy's hand was.

The sun had dropped lower in the sky, and the waves below them had only intensified in their fury. Far off on the horizon they heard rumblings of thunder.

"Close your mind to all thoughts," Roxanne commanded. "Close your senses to the physical world. Open your hearts to the world just beyond our grasp."

Devon concentrated. He felt the energy in the room begin to vibrate. He looked over at Alexander. The boy was staring at him, grinning crazily. Devon turned away quickly, so as not to be distracted, and closed his eyes.

"We are here looking for some answers," Roxanne intoned as the waves crashing against the moorings beneath the house took on an almost hypnotic rhythm. "Answers to questions we are not even sure how to formulate. Answers that we must know to keep those at this table safe."

Devon kept his eyes closed. He had the sensation that they were spinning, round and round.

"We are here because some of us are in danger," Roxanne said, her voice sounding increasingly distant to Devon. "We need to find out the cause of the danger, and stop it before any of us are hurt."

Devon tightened his grip on Alexander's hand. If the boy inside the possession could still sense anything, Devon wanted him to know that he was going to help him. After the Madman had taken Alexander into the Hell Hole, Devon had promised the boy he'd keep him safe, that he'd always be there for him.

"Give us answers!" Roxanne lifted her voice. "Speak to us!"

A sudden thud of wind slapped against the windows. Devon opened his eyes. The day had darkened. Trees were swaying fiercely. A storm looked ready to break.

"There is one at this table who is not himself," Roxanne said. "Speak to us, spirit within the body of Alexander Muir! Tell us who you are, and why you are here!"

Laughter.

Alexander had started to laugh again in that low, demented, obscene way.

"Share with us the humor," Roxanne said, addressing Alexander now directly. "Let us in on the joke."

"You expect me to be frightened of you, don't you, Island Witch Woman?" Alexander said, but the voice was deep, gravelly, not his own. "I know what you are, and from where you come, but still I am not frightened. I sit in your presence unafraid."

"I mean not to frighten you," Roxanne said, lapsing deeper into her Jamaican accent. "I mean only to get answers."

"Answers? Why would I give you answers?"

"Because we are commanding it. Because we have brought you out, made you speak. Because among us there is power far greater than any you possess."

"You think so?" It was Alexander's turn to squeeze Devon's hand. "Surely you do not mean this boy Nightwing to my left? He is terrified of me. Aren't you, Devon?"

"I don't know who you are," Devon answered, "but I can tell you that whoever you are, I am not afraid."

"Oh, no? Then why do you tremble in my presence? Why do you still wake up at night sweating in terror, remembering the time I brought you with me to my grave?"

"Oh my God!" Natalie blurted out. "It *is* the Madman!"

"Hush," Roxanne commanded. "We are not afraid of you here. Our circle is bound by commitment, by friendship, by strength. Not by fear. So tell us why you have returned, Jackson Muir."

"And *how*," Devon managed to say, desperately trying to stop his heart from racing in his chest. The Madman would be able to smell his fear. Surely he could already feel the sweat in Devon's palm.

"There is one who seeks me and has summoned me." Alexander's lips moved, but it was the Madman's voice. "I *will* live again. I will have my revenge on all of you, and I will control Ravenscliff and its portal into the world of the demons."

"Not if we have anything to say about it," Rolfe barked. "We've stopped you before, Jackson. We can do it again."

Laughter erupted from the boy's mouth. "Is that you, Montaigne? Would you like to say hello to your father? He's here, with me—in the Hell Hole!" Alexander threw his head back and laughed again.

Rolfe made a move to lunge at him, but Roxanne stopped him. "Do not break the circle!"

"All of you will die," the Madman rasped. "And the last to go will be our brave young sorcerer here, who will see all the others go before him."

"I wouldn't get cocky yet, Apostate," Devon snarled.

But the Madman had moved on to taunt someone else. "The sun is getting low, Marcus." Alexander's head had turned so that the eyes of Jackson Muir could gaze at the teenager. "Don't you have a rendezvous with the moon?"

"What do you mean?" Marcus asked, terrified.

Laughter again, hideous and gloating.

"What do I have to do with all this?" Marcus screamed, standing up, dropping the hands of Natalie and Cecily. It broke the power of the séance. The candle in the middle of the table snuffed itself out, and Alexander fell into an icy silence.

"I'm sorry," Marcus was saying, near tears. "It's just that—the sun is going down. And I'm starting to remember— remember what happens to me!"

Roxanne had put the lights back on. Rolfe took Marcus by the shoulders and led him over to a chair. The teen sat, his face in his hands.

"Tell us," Rolfe said. "What do you remember?"

"The beast," Marcus said. "It makes me—it makes me do things—"

Devon knelt in front of his friend. "What kinds of things?"

Marcus suddenly removed his hands from his face and looked at Devon wildly. "You've got to protect me, Devon! You can't let it happen again!"

"I will. I'll get you another star pendant ..."

"It won't work. I'll tear it off when the moon comes up. I know I will."

"Easy, man," Devon said.

He sat back on his haunches, completely at a loss. The full weight of the séance's revelations hit him. So they *were* dealing with the Madman again. The thought terrified Devon, as Jackson so rightly assumed. But he couldn't let that fear overwhelm him. He had to concentrate. The Madman said that someone was summoning him, trying to bring him back. Who? And why? And what did Jackson Muir have to do with the beast?

"Jackson knew McNutt," Rolfe said, as if reading Devon's mind. "Perhaps he had control over him. Might Jackson be using the beast to help him break out of the Hell Hole somehow?"

"Look," Cecily said, pushing her way to the front of the group. "We can't just stand around here wringing our hands over Jackson Muir." She pointed over at their friend, trembling his chair. "Marcus is clearly in a meltdown, and who knows what will happen to him when the moon comes out. And has anybody bothered to look over at Alexander?"

Their heads all turned. The boy hadn't moved from the table. He sat as if frozen, his eyes staring into nothingness.

"Oh dear, oh dear," muttered Bjorn, attending to the child. "What *will* Mrs. Crandall say? How do I explain *this* to her?"

"Better this state of unconsciousness than active possession," Roxanne said, feeling Alexander's forehead. "Take him back to Ravenscliff. He will sleep undisturbed through the night."

Bjorn was only too happy to comply.

"But what about me?" Marcus asked after they had gone. "The sun is setting."

Indeed it was, casting long, shimmering streaks of gold and red across the waves as it emerged from the dissipating storm clouds. Marcus had broken out into a sweat.

"The beast is going to come for me," he cried. "Just like last time!"

"What happens when the beast comes?" Rolfe asked him.

"What can you remember?"

"Just that it … appears," Marcus stammered.

"We have plenty of silver to protect you," Rolfe told him.

"You mean it appeared to you?" Devon asked.

"It overtakes me …" Marcus said.

"Not this time it won't," Devon told him, reaching into his pocket to withdraw a piece of white chalk that hadn't been there ten seconds before. "Sorry, Rolfe, but I'm going to have to write on your floor."

Rolfe made a quizzical face. "Write on my floor?"

"It's just chalk. It'll wash off." Devon got down on his hands and knees and began drawing a white line across the old dark wood. The line extended several feet, then Devon turned back to continue it at a forty-five-degree angle. He worked his way all around Marcus, who was still sitting, trembling in the chair.

"I get it, dude," D.J. said, watching intently as Devon drew on the floor. "You're making a star!"

"Yes, a pentagram," Devon said, "and Marcus will be contained within it."

"Brilliant," Rolfe observed, folding his arms across his chest and beaming down at Devon with obvious pride.

"The pentagram is a symbol of safety and protection," Devon said, his star diagram complete. He stood. "Marcus will be safe so long as he stays within it."

"But what about us?" Cecily asked. "If the beast is on its way here …"

"There go my windows again," Rolfe grumbled.

"We'll be okay," Devon assured them. "My intuition tells me it will be different this time. And I'll make us all silver armor if need be."

The sun was gone. The room fell into the stunned pink afterglow that followed sunsets. It lasted only a few moments, and then the shadows began to deepen into dark blues and grays. Roxanne switched on a lamp.

"I remember something else," Marcus said, calmer now.

"What's that?" Rolfe asked him.

"The pain. It's about to begin again. In fact—" He grimaced.

"It's here."

"What kind of pain?" Roxanne asked, rushing up suddenly.

But Marcus couldn't answer. He began to writhe in his chair, his body twisting first one way, then another. Outside, low and bright over the water, the full moon had appeared.

"May the angels watch over us," Roxanne breathed in horror. "Why did we not realize it sooner?"

"We've got to help him," Natalie called out, hurrying toward Marcus. "Look at him! It's like he's having a heart attack!"

Roxanne stopped her from crossing the boundary of the pentagram. "Keep back," she said, her voice small and terrified. "Keep back and pray."

Devon watched as Marcus continued to contort, his face expressing horrible, searing pain. He knocked over the chair he was sitting on but managed to stay on his feet, his hands covering his face—

His hands!

"No!" Devon screamed.

Marcus's hands were suddenly covered with hair.

His whole body was changing—twisting, growing, lengthening. His clothes tore away under his transformation. When he moved his hands—rather, his claws—from his face, Marcus was no longer a teenaged boy, but a snarling, savage creature with a snout full of fangs—

Cecily screamed.

"It's him!" D.J. shouted. "Marcus is the beast!"

THE STAIRCASE INTO TIME

The thing now stood before them, growling and salivating. It prepared to lunge but found it could not, contained by the pentagram on the floor. It let out a long and furious howl.

"Marcus," Devon said, stunned and horrified. "It was *you*. Not McNutt …"

It all made sense now: Marcus's scratches and bruises, his parents' horror. Had they witnessed such a transformation? Probably not, as Marcus would leave his room before anything happened. But they clearly knew *something* was happening to their son. Something terrible, something unspeakable …

"How? Why?" Devon stood as close to the pentagram as he dared. The beast lashed out him, its bear-like paw making an arc through the air but missing Devon's face by about six inches. Devon didn't flinch. He just kept staring at the creature. "I knew I saw something familiar in your eyes … Oh, Marcus, I'm so sorry. I promise I'll find out why this happening to you, and I'll put an end to it. I promise!"

Rolfe was clearly disturbed that the teens had witnessed such a thing. Natalie was sobbing uncontrollably. D.J. just stood there, staring blankly at the snarling, furious beast that once was his friend. Cecily was trying, absurdly, to soothe the creature, talking to it as if Marcus might be able to hear her somehow.

"Just be calm, sit tight," she said, her voice barely audible over the beast's roars. "It will be over soon enough when the sun comes up again …"

"Let's all go upstairs," Rolfe said. "You can't do anything for him now. The pentagram will keep him—and everyone else in Misery Point—safe for tonight."

"I'll stay and keep watch," Roxanne said. "Oh, that poor,

poor child trapped inside that brute's body …"

The beast tried again to jump free of the pentagram but could not. It hunched down, angry and frustrated, and howled at the ceiling. Yellow saliva spilled from its mouth.

Natalie allowed Rolfe to lead her upstairs. D.J. moved away gradually, walking backward as he kept his eyes on the snarling, snapping creature. Cecily placed her hand on Devon's shoulder.

"Rolfe's right," she said. "There's nothing more we can do for him right now. At least this time he's safe."

"I've got to find out why this is happening," Devon said. "I can't just stand here and wait for the sun to rise."

"But what can you do? If it's Jackson Muir who's behind this—"

"I beat him once, I can do it again." Devon pulled his eyes away from the beast to look at Cecily. "The room in the West Wing with all the books. Maybe there will be an answer there."

Cecily shuddered. "You mean the room with the portal into the Hell Hole? But you've never been able to get inside there, Devon. Some force won't allow you in."

"I suspect that's changed," Devon said. "When I physically broke through the secret room in the basement I seemed to have broken whatever mystical barriers your grandmother had set up within the house—barriers that were designed to keep me from discovering answers. I'll wager that if I wanted to, right now, I could disappear and reappear in that room in the West Wing."

Cecily smiled. "You know, I'm sure you could. You're one-hundredth generation from Sargon the Great, after all."

Devon returned the smile. How wonderful it was to smile at Cecily again.

"Tell the others I've gone," he said. He turned around to look at the beast once more. "If you can hear me, Marcus, I'm going to find out how to end whatever sorcery has done this to you. I'll find out and then change you back into yourself again. I promise you! I'll be back!"

"Godspeed, Devon March," whispered Roxanne.

"Be careful," Cecily echoed, looking up into his eyes.

With that, Devon disappeared from the room.

When he looked around, he saw he had been right; he was in West Wing, standing outside the door to the secret room. This wing of the old house had been abandoned and boarded up for more than thirty years—ever since Jackson Muir and his wife, Emily, had died, in fact. Devon was standing in what had been Emily's upstairs parlor. Here she received visitors who had come to welcome her to Ravenscliff. She had been an innocent young wife then, unaware of her husband's nefarious sorcery. No one had known what Jackson had planned. His brother Randolph, the Master of Ravenscliff, might have suspected, but when Jackson had come back to Ravenscliff after many years away, everyone had given him the benefit of the doubt. His dark days were over, he promised. He had repented.

How wrong they were to trust him—as poor Emily would find out.

The only remnant of the room's faded glory was the broken, dusty chandelier that hung overhead. Rusted picture wires scarred the walls. Dust an inch thick collected on the few antique tables strewn about. Devon could feel Emily's ghost here, somewhere in the dark, shuttered room, watching him. But it was not this room Devon had come to explore. It was the one that led off it, a small, windowless chamber that contained the great house's deepest secret.

The Hell Hole.

Devon expected the door to the inner room to be locked, but it wasn't. In fact, it wasn't even closed tightly. Someone had been here, he observed, and with his Nightwing eyes he could see the dust had been disturbed on the floor inside. Footprints.

So many books on the shelves within. Devon scanned their spines briefly, wondering if any of them contained the answer to Marcus's predicament. Rolfe had copies of some of them, but not nearly all; this was the sorcery library of the magnificent Horatio Muir. Aeons of Nightwing history and heritage were contained within this room.

Devon opened his palm to reveal his orb of magic light, shedding a helpful glow through the darkness. He turned it toward one wall, where a portrait hung—a portrait of a teenaged boy who looked identical to Devon, except that he was dressed in the clothes of an earlier time, perhaps fifty years earlier or more. "One more clue to my past," Devon whispered, "if only I could figure it out."

He turned, aiming the light toward the other end of the room. He made out the bolted metal door. The portal into the realm of the demons. The Hell Hole.

"The reason Ravenscliff was built," Devon whispered, finding comfort in the sound of his voice in this horrible yet fascinating place. "To contain the largest Hell Hole in the Western hemisphere. To seal it off forever."

That had been Horatio Muir's attempt, but his renegade son Jackson had succeeded in wresting it open, gaining mastery over the demons within for his power-hungry ambition. And he had taken Alexander down there with him, into the stinking bowels of hell—until Devon had plunged inside himself to rescue the boy and seal the Madman inside.

"But now he's struggling to get free," Devon said louder. "Someone is helping him ..."

"Hello, Devon."

He spun around.

"Clarissa!" he called out.

She stood there smiling. She looked less crazy than she had before.

"I knew you'd come here," she said. "I knew this was our destiny, to meet again, here, in this room."

"Why?" he asked, angry at himself for not being on high alert. He should have felt her arrival, sensed her presence. A well-trained sorcerer should never be taken by surprise. He pushed away his pique at himself and concentrated on the situation at hand. "What are you doing here, Clarissa? This isn't your first time here, is it?"

"No. I've come here several times to stare at that door."

Mrs. Crandall had predicted that she would try to open it.

"Don't you know the evil that lives behind that door?" Devon asked, approaching her. "You've got to stay away from here."

"I don't know about evil," Clarissa said, and she did seem more rational now. "I just sense the power that awaits me. Both of us, Devon. You and I. Our destiny lives behind that door."

"No. That's the Madman talking, Clarissa. He's influencing you. You're the one who's been summoning him, haven't you? Trying to bring him back!"

She looked over into Devon's eyes. "Our destiny, Devon …"

"No! Our destiny is to keep that door securely sealed! The Madman has gotten inside your head! That's why Greta Muir kept you safely behind the walls of her sorcery. She knew if you were set free Jackson Muir would get to you. And he *has*!"

Clarissa smiled indulgently, as if he were just a child. "Why do you take their side, Devon? Did Greta Muir or her children, Amanda or Edward, ever tell you the truth about anything? Haven't they, instead, stood in your way whenever you have attempted to discover your heritage?"

Devon didn't reply.

"Don't you *want* answers, Devon?" Clarissa asked. "Don't you *want* to know who you are?"

"Yes," he replied. "But that answer will have to wait. Tonight I'm looking for only one thing. The answer that will help my friend Marcus."

"The one who turns into the beast?"

"So you *know*! Tell me what you know!"

Clarissa smiled. "I can't give you any answers. The answers you seek are somewhere else."

"I suppose you mean behind that door," Devon said bitterly. "You're tempting me to open the Hell Hole and then promising me that I'll get all the answers I seek. Maybe I would learn the secrets of my past if I opened the portal. But I'd also unleash the demons onto the world—demons controlled by the power-mad Jackson Muir!"

"The Hell Hole can wait," Clarissa said, impatient with his attitude. "The answers you seek aren't there, Devon."

He eyed her suspiciously. "Then where are they?"

"They're in the past."

"The *past?*"

She smiled. "Come now, Devon. I've had even less training in my sorcery than you have, but surely you know about the past."

He studied her. She seemed to be enjoying this game with him. And what was it about her face? It changed, shifted, never looking quite the same. One moment she was worn and old, far older than she should be if indeed she was a contemporary of Rolfe and Mrs. Crandall. But then the next moment she was a young girl, no older than Devon. Sometimes Clarissa's eyes were blue, sometimes green, sometimes brown. Sometimes her skin seemed to glow, sometimes it seemed like faded parchment. But always her hair was white, long and luminescent.

"Which past?" Devon asked her. "Whose past?"

But she was fading away, dissolving into the dust that swirled through the room.

"The past, Devon," she said. "The answers are in the past …"

"Wait, you can't just say that and then just disappear!"

"The past, Devon," she said.

"Wait! What do you mean?"

But she was gone.

The answers were in the *past?* A lot of good they were doing there, since Devon was in the present. And what did Clarissa know anyway? She might have had powers, but by her own admission she was even more of a novice than Devon.

But she *had* been communicating with the Madman …

Devon glanced back at the Hell Hole and could feel the scurrying and scratching of the demons within. He could hear their pleas:

Let us out.

Set us free.

Oh, master, we could give you such power …

He turned away in disgust. There were no answers here.

And suddenly Devon knew Clarissa was right.

The answers are in the past.

The beast had existed in Misery Point more than thirty

years ago, on the same Halloween that also saw Jackson Muir's black magic engulfing Ravenscliff. There *was* a connection. That much was now obvious. But how could the knowledge of that past help Marcus now?

"The past has only raised more questions," Devon said out loud, striding out of the inner room into Emily Muir's old parlor.

He'd go downstairs. He'd confront Mrs. Crandall for the one-thousandth time. He'd tell her what had happened and demand she tell him what she knew—if anything. He'd ask her about the past. He'd scare her if he had to, by revealing Alexander's possession and the fact that their séance had revealed the Madman was trying to return …

He opened the door into the corridor, a corridor that he knew would lead to a secret passageway back into the main part of the house.

But there was no corridor when he opened the door.

There was only a staircase leading down.

Devon made a little sound in surprise. He knew what it was.

It was the Staircase Into Time!

One of the most ingenious manifestations of Horatio Muir's sorcery, the Staircase Into Time appeared and reappeared throughout the house, taking those who descended or ascended its steps into the past or the future. It had once taken Devon to fifteenth-century England so that he could uncover the origins of the demon witch who was threatening his friends. Where, he wondered, would it take him now?

The answers are in the past.

This is what Clarissa meant.

Devon started down the dark staircase. It descended for quite a way, so far down that Devon could not see the bottom of the stairs through the darkness. He was not frightened. Rather, he was pumped with excitement, certain that the lasting wisdom of Horatio Muir's great magic would protect him and take him where he needed to go. And then, after he had found what he needed, the staircase would bring him back here, armed with information that would help Marcus as well as ward off the Madman's attempts to break free of the Hell Hole.

But after about fifteen minutes, as the stairs continued to descend into the darkness with no end in sight, Devon began to have second thoughts.

"Either I'm going so far back in time that I'll end up with the dinosaurs," he whispered out loud, "or this is some kind of trick."

But he'd have sensed if it was a trick. Wouldn't he have? His intuition would have warned him. Wouldn't it have?

He felt heat suddenly. Not a good sign. Heat was the sign that demons were close by—or another sorcerer. Devon considered turning around and heading back up the stairs.

But now he could see light, finally, rising from below. The stairs became more recognizable. Instead of plain wood, they were carpeted. A familiar carpet.

It was the staircase leading down into the foyer of Ravenscliff. A staircase he used every day …

Music. He could hear music. Pop music.

Devon reached the final step. He was indeed in Ravenscliff's foyer. But it looked slightly different. The drapes were a different color. There were chairs placed against the far wall that had never been there before. And the phone on the center table had a *rotary dial*.

The music came from the parlor. Peering inside, Devon observed that the room looked pretty much the same as he'd always known it, with Horatio Muir's skulls and crystal balls wedged among the books on the shelves, the suit of armor standing in the same place it had always been. But the furniture was different. The sofa was low, with a floral print. Mrs. Crandall's wingback chair was nowhere in sight. And there was a dark-haired girl in the middle of the room, playing what looked like cassette tapes on a big black stereo, dancing and singing along with the music, which sounded like Madonna. Very early Madonna. Something about a lucky star...

Devon took a look at the girl singing along to the music. She was dressed in a green plaid skirt and pink leather boots that came up to her knees, swinging and swaying to the song. She was totally unaware that Devon was standing in the doorway watching her. The girl looked to be a few years older than Devon but no taller, and she wore a chunky, oversized crucifix around her neck. Her eyes were outlined with very dark mascara.

Suddenly she noticed Devon. "Well," she said, "it's about time."

"Uh, you were expecting me?"

"Of course I've been expecting you," the girl said testily. "I've been waiting all morning. We have a lot to do if we're going to prepare the house before they get here."

Devon was eyeing the room. The portrait of Horatio Muir hung over the mantel as it always had, but there was something missing from the opposite wall.

"Where's the portrait of Emily Muir?" he asked.

The girl made a face at him. "How can there be portrait of her before anyone has even met her?"

Devon turned to look at her. Suddenly he knew where—or *when*—he was. The rotary phone, the cassette player, the girl's clothes. He'd gone three decades into the past—to the year Emily Muir first came to Ravenscliff!

"It's she who's coming, isn't it?" Devon asked. "Emily Muir. She's the one we're supposed to prepare the house for, isn't she?"

The girl nodded. "She and her husband, yes. The prodigal son returned with his new bride after many years away in Europe."

"Jackson Muir," Devon breathed.

"Now what's your name? Montaigne promised a special boy, one with all the right training, so I expect I won't have to teach you anything."

Devon's intuition told him to play along as best he could. "My name's Teddy," he said, a picture of his father, Ted March, flickering through his mind.

"Okay, Teddy Bear, then we have a lot to do—"

"I would say so," came a familiar, arrogant voice.

Devon turned. Standing behind him, having arrived in that stealthy, cat-like way she had, was Mrs. Crandall . But it couldn't be. Not here, some thirty years in the past.

"We were just getting to work, Mrs. Muir," the girl assured her.

Devon looked closer at the newcomer. It wasn't Mrs. Crandall; it was Greta Muir, her mother—who, three decades from now, as an old, frail woman, would save Devon from the undead sorceress Isobel the Apostate, and die in the process. But here in this time she was young and vital—and the spitting image of her daughter Amanda Muir Crandall.

"Turn off that music, Miranda," she snapped. "What is the boy's name?"

She asked the question as if Devon wasn't even standing there, as if he were a nonperson. He could see where Mrs. Crandall got her imperious attitude.

"His name is Teddy," the girl, Miranda, replied, hitting the stop button on the stereo. "Montaigne assured me he'd have all the training we need."

"They will be here by six," Greta Muir said. It was all she needed to say. The command was there: everything needed to be ready by then.

"What do we have to do?" Devon asked after the great lady had departed.

"What do you mean, what do we have to do?" Miranda looked at him with distrust. "When a Sorcerer of the Nightwing returns to his family there is ceremony to be had. If you are going to be a Guardian, you had best know the basics."

She thinks I'm a Guardian-in-training. She must be, too. Montaigne—that would be Rolfe's father—must have sent for a young assistant to help with the ceremony marking Jackson's return to Ravenscliff. And Miranda thinks I'm him!

"Come on," she said. "I'm bringing you to Montaigne, and he can figure out whether you'll do."

She gestured for him to follow. They headed out the front door and across the grounds. It was the same time of year as it was when Devon had left the present. Spring was in the air, with the grass turning deep green and the buds on the trees starting to pop. The tangy scent of the sea rose up from the cliffs beyond. Out here, most everything looked the same; the woods and the paths would not much change in thirty-plus years.

As they walked, Devon studied this girl, this Miranda. He felt drawn to her, somehow. And her name—

Something clicked in Devon's mind.

When he first came to Ravenscliff, he and Cecily had pored through the old records at the Misery Point town hall to see if there was any mention of his birth, any clue as to his origins. Nothing—except one name.

"Miranda," he said, putting his hand on her shoulder. She stopped and looked around at him.

"What is it?" she asked.

"Your full name," he said. "What is it?"

"What should that matter to you? You are just a temporary ward here. Once your job is complete you will go back to the Guardian you were training under."

"Still," Devon said, "I'd like to know."

She smirked. "You've guessed it, haven't you? That I'm not just an ordinary girl training to be a Guardian. You've guessed that I'm part of quite an illustrious family, haven't you?"

"Yes," he said, flattering her. "Yes, I can see that."

"My name," she said, her dark eyes finding his, "is Miranda Devon."

He felt the shudder pass through him like an electrical charge. *Devon*—it couldn't be a mere coincidence. This woman was his kin—he was certain of it. The dark hair and eyes, the slight olive coloring to her skin.

Might she be—his mother?

No, his intuition told him immediately. He wouldn't be born for almost another twenty years, and sadly, the records of Misery Point had revealed to him that Miranda Devon would die before then. But there *was* a connection. He felt certain there was some kind of bond between them.

"The Devons are from the island of Martinique," Miranda told him. "We are an old family, originally from France. We are not mere Guardians. We have powers of our own. Nothing compared to the sorcery of the Nightwing, mind you. But powers still. Enchantments, really. Spells, incantations … My father was considered a great shaman on the island."

"But why are you working here, then, as a servant at Ravenscliff?"

She bristled. "They wanted a female to help train little Amanda, and naturally they wanted the best. Long ago my family came into contact with the Nightwing of the New World, and we have been allies ever since." Miranda lifted her chin. "We aren't just Guardians. We are *partners* with the Nightwing."

Devon suspected the girl had some delusions of grandeur; Greta Muir had certainly not treated her as any partner. Still, he indulged her; he was certain this history of the Devons of Martinique was his own heritage.

But she was through with background for now. "Come along," she insisted. "Montaigne is waiting."

Rolfe's father lived in the caretaker's cottage—a place that thirty years from now would be converted into a garage for Edward Muir's collection of sports cars. In the future it would smell of oil and grease, but now, as they pushed open the door and headed inside, it was the fragrance of incense and tobacco that greeted Devon.

"Here he is," Miranda announced. "His name is Teddy Bear."

A man looked up from a chair where he sat smoking a pipe. It was uncanny how much he resembled his son—or rather, how much his son would one day resemble him. Devon could swear it was Rolfe looking up at him with the same deep-set eyes.

"Younger than I expected," said Jean-Michel Montaigne, a Parisian accent to his voice. "Teddy Bear? I think it is a name given you by our feisty Miranda, and unfortunately, my friend, it will stick."

"It's okay," Devon said as he shook hands with the older man.

"Strange clothing," Montaigne observed, looking at Devon's Tommy Hilfiger jeans and long basketball shirt. "And you do not speak like an Englishman."

In an instant Devon intuited that the boy they had sent for was from England, probably a connection from the Muir family's history there. He quickly thought up an explanation.

"My mother was American," he said, "so I learned how to speak with an American accent."

"Pity," Montaigne said, standing from his chair.

For a moment, Devon considered what had happened to the real boy who'd been summoned—the actual English Guardian-in-training who had been sent to Ravenscliff for this special occasion. Would he still show up, ruining Devon's story? Would their paths ever cross?

But such speculation faded as Montaigne set them onto their tasks. Devon quickly absorbed the fundamentals of the Ravenscliff of this era. The master of the house was Randolph Muir, father to Amanda and Edward, and one day grandfather to Cecily and Alexander. Montaigne was Randolph's able right-hand man, the Guardian who had raised him, and who now oversaw the training of his children. Guardians lived to very advanced ages; though Montaigne looked to be no more than mid-thirties, he was certainly several decades older at least, if he'd already been an adult when Randolph was a boy.

From Montaigne, Devon learned more of the day's special significance. Jackson Muir, Randolph's elder brother, had been a rebel in his youth; his father, Horatio, had despaired of him and given Ravenscliff to the more obedient Randolph. Jackson had been consorting with all sorts of nefarious characters, using his sorcery for his own gain. He had made himself rich, carousing through Europe with a succession of petty witches and wizards—even (it was rumored) intelligent demons set free from their Hell Holes. Horatio had begun the proceedings to have the Witangemot—the governing body of the Nightwing—declare his son an Apostate, a renegade sorcerer. He had died, however, brokenhearted, before he could go through with it.

Now the family was celebrating—because Jackson had seen the error of his ways and repented, proving his sincerity by sealing off several Hell Holes throughout the easternmost reaches of Siberia and the Korean peninsula. He had proved a noble, trusted ally of the Nightwing there, and they had all written to Randolph attesting to Jackson's reformation. He had married a girl he'd met in Copenhagen who, by all accounts, was decent and kind. Now he was returning to Ravenscliff to ask his brother's forgiveness and to be reinstated within the family.

"But won't he expect to be Master of Ravenscliff?" Devon asked, surprising Montaigne with his question.

"Of course not," Montaigne replied. "That was an honor conferred onto Randolph Muir by his father."

"But Jackson will see it as his birthright," Devon insisted. It was knowledge he had gained in his own time, when he saw how the idea had became an obsession for the Madman. "After all, he's the eldest son."

Miranda was grinning at him. "Rather impertinent boy, aren't you? I like that."

"Don't be spreading such talk," Montaigne scolded him. "The brothers are reconciling, and nothing but harmony exists between them."

Devon sighed. How much should he give away? He could trust them, he felt; yet he felt certain he must keep his true identity a secret for now, if he wanted to learn what he needed to know.

Just then they were interrupted by a small voice. Devon looked down. Standing at Montaigne's side, tugging at his pants, was a small boy.

"Papa," the boy said. "I play?"

It was Rolfe. Devon stared down at him. He was not more than two, with big brown eyes and peanut butter on his cheeks.

"Have you finished your breakfast?"

The boy nodded. "I play outside?"

"Wash your face first," his father instructed him. "Then you can play outside, but don't go far."

The little boy toddled back into the other room. Devon watched him, staggered by the thought that someday this boy would be his friend, his mentor, his Guardian.

"He's the most precious child," Miranda cooed. "I hope someday to have one just like him." She smirked. "But not too soon. I want to keep the figure a while longer."

"Where is his mother?" Devon asked.

A look of sadness passed across Montaigne's face. "She died when the boy was born. Since then I have been blessed by the Muir family's kindness. Greta Muir has been as much a mother to him as she has to her own babies."

"All right," Miranda said, growing impatient. "Shall we bring down the crystals from the West Wing?"

"No need," Montaigne told her. "Mr. Muir wanted the ceremony held there, in the large upstairs parlor. He is giving Jackson and his wife that wing of the house."

"And all of the instructions are in the Book of Ritual, yes?"

Montaigne nodded. "Follow them precisely in setting up the room."

"And each of us will have a part to play," Miranda told Devon. "It's all spelled out in the Book of Ritual."

"It is the Ritual of Return," Montaigne explained. "It is held to welcome an errant Nightwing back into the embrace of the order. It is a joyous occasion when a renegade returns and repents."

Devon wanted to shout: *But he hasn't repented! It's a trick! He just wants control over the Hell Hole!*

But he couldn't warn them just yet. Maybe there would come a time, but he knew now to keep his tongue if he wanted to learn the answers that would enable him to save Marcus and keep Jackson from returning, yet again, more than thirty years from now.

They headed back across the estate to start their duties.

"He's very handsome, Jackson Muir," Miranda said. "I've seen his pictures."

Devon said nothing.

"I imagine he had quite the good time, carousing through the world," she mused. "I suppose if I were Nightwing I might go a little wild, too, then repent and everything would be fine. But at least I'd have had my fun."

"It's probably a good thing you aren't Nightwing then," Devon said.

She laughed. "Like you would be any better, Teddy Bear? Like you would be some great and noble sorcerer?" She laughed even harder.

How Devon ached to tell her a thing or two.

"Wait for me!" a little voice suddenly sounded from behind them.

They turned around. Little Rolfe came running through the grass.

"Now, Rolfe," Miranda said, "you go back to your father—"

That was when Devon felt it. The tingling sensation. The heat.

"Get back," he barked at Miranda.

"What?"

The little boy kept running toward them.

"I said, *get back*!" Devon ordered. "Get behind me!"

The girl lifted her chin obstinately. "Who do you think you are, ordering me—?"

Little Rolfe took a flying leap toward them.

Miranda's eyes followed him as he soared through the air.

And then she screamed.

The child had turned into a giant bat, with huge leathery wings and a mouth full of fangs.

"I was ready for you!" Devon shouted, springing into action himself, his feet out in front of him, making contact with the demon's furry midsection.

But the thing bit down onto his foot, sending Devon crashing to the ground.

The demon landed on top of him, emitting a long, chittering laugh as it prepared to sink its fangs into his face.

THE PRODIGAL SON

"Not so fast," Devon said, bringing up his arm to protect his face.

The demon screeched angrily.

That little temper tantrum gave Devon just enough time to ram his knees into the creature's gut, thrusting it off him. The demon flapped its giant wings as it tried to regain its balance.

"Don't even think about coming at me again," Devon said. "You've drawn blood, and that always makes me *really* mad!"

The demon's red eyes glowed.

"Back to your Hell Hole!" Devon ordered. "Back to your stinking pit!"

The thing screeched again, its wings spread wide—but then it was sucked into a vortex backward against its will, drawn up across the sky and disappearing on the horizon.

"Aw, geez," Devon said, letting out a long breath of relief and sitting down to examine his leg. "I sure wish I had Bjorn's potions to cure this. Demon infections can be really nasty."

Miranda was standing in stunned silence staring at him.

"Okay, so you know," Devon told her. "I'm no Guardian kid. I'm a sorcerer."

"And Nightwing to boot, it would appear," she said in a tiny voice.

Devon glanced around. "Do you think anybody saw?" The day seemed as calm as it had been before, and they were still a ways from the house.

"Who are *you*?" Miranda could barely speak. She took a step toward him, then fell back. "Why are you here? Why would they send a Nightwing to work as a Guardian?"

Devon wasn't listening, keeping all his attention on his leg.

His jeans were torn along his right calf and blood was seeping through. "Montaigne must have something for this," he said. "Maybe it won't be as good as the potions of the gnomes, but he must have *something*."

Miranda bent down to examine his wound. "Yes, the Guardians have their own medicine. We can treat injuries caused by demons." She went pale, almost as if she might have fainted. "A demon! I just saw a demon!"

Devon smirked up at her. "What kind of Guardian are you going to be if you get all freaked out by the sight of a demon?"

She looked at Devon with terror in her eyes. "I have never seen one in actuality. The Hell Hole is closed. At least, I've always believed it to be. Mr. Muir has told us all that he made it secure. We have never been threatened by demons here before."

"The Hell Hole under Ravenscliff is still secure," Devon assured her. "This demon came from somewhere else. I suspect it followed someone here. Someone it considered a friend."

"What do you mean?"

"It was one of Jackson's creatures, I'm sure of it. And it sensed who I was." Devon shuddered. "I'm just glad I was able to send it back to its Hell Hole before it had a chance to tell the Madman."

"The Madman? Is that what you call Jackson Muir?"

"It's what he'll come to be known as."

Miranda knelt beside Devon in the grass. "Who *are* you?" she asked again.

"I'm a sorcerer from the future," he told her, deciding that was enough information for now. "I've come back to find some answers—and maybe, in the process, to prevent some terrible things from happening to the Muir family."

"You frighten me, Teddy Bear," Miranda said, then she thought of something. "The child. Little Rolfe …"

"Don't worry. He's fine. Demons can take on the appearance of someone to throw us off." He grinned. "But it didn't fool me. I sensed it."

"You know quite a bit for someone so young," Miranda said.

"Yeah, well," Devon said, blushing a bit.

"And now I suppose you are going to erase my memory of what happened? So you can keep your identity a secret?"

I can do that? Devon wondered. But he said, "No, I think I can trust you, Miranda. And you may be helpful to me."

She smiled, some of her old attitude returning. "Of course. You must have heard of the Devons. My kin has always been eminently resourceful."

He smiled back at her. *Kin.* It was hard to believe, but he was convinced that Miranda was somehow family to him. Cousin? Aunt? It was an odd feeling, a sense Devon had never really experienced before. He'd never known anyone in his family— even when Dad was alive, it had always been just the two of them—and that had left a hole deep inside him. And now here was someone—*family*—sitting right beside him.

"Come on," Devon said, getting up off the grass. "We have work to do."

They hurried back into the great house, rushing quickly up the stairs and off toward the West Wing. In this era, the wing was not abandoned and closed off as it would be in the future. There were no cobwebs. The windows were not yet shuttered to keep out the sun. It was all rather mind-boggling, in fact. According to Devon's own time continuum, he'd stood in this same place just about an hour ago, and it had been covered in dust and shadows. Now it was bright and sunny, the windows open to let in the morning air. The chandelier that he remembered as broken and faded hung sparkling and new from the ceiling.

"Mrs. Muir fixed this room up so beautifully," Miranda observed, running her hand along a gold gilt table in the center of the room. "This is where we are to put the crystals."

But when Devon headed into the small chamber to retrieve the crystals, he stopped suddenly in his tracks. Where were the books of sorcery that were kept here? Even more startling: where was the door to the Hell Hole? In its place was just a normal wall, and instead of books there were just boxes. In the future this would be the chamber of the Muir family secrets; here in the past, it was just a storage room.

It made sense, Devon thought to himself. In the future,

the family would want to hide any relics of its sorcery, having repudiated their powers and Nightwing past. But here, in this time, they were proud and open (at least among the family) of their glorious heritage. There was no need to hide anything away.

But the Hell Hole? Where was it?

"In the far reaches of the basement," Miranda told him. "Why would there be a portal up here, dragging the demons up through the house?" She shuddered, obviously remembering their encounter in the yard. "Keep them sealed off down in the dark where they belong."

Devon smirked. "You can read thoughts."

She smirked back. "Sometimes they just jump out at me. At least the ones that are seeking some kind of response."

Devon looked back into the storage room. "At some point," he told her, "another portal will be created here, in this very room. *Why*?"

"I have no answer for that one, I'm afraid."

As he helped Miranda set out the crystals and drape the windows in the ceremonial Nightwing purple, Devon met the rest of the family, who had come upstairs to check on their progress. Accompanying Greta Muir were her two children: the toddler Amanda, her hair as fiery red as her daughter Cecily's would someday be; and the infant Edward, carried in his mother's arms. The uncanny family resemblance continued. When a tall, sturdy, fair-haired man followed them into the room, Devon knew him immediately to be Randolph Muir—because he was the exact image of what his son, the adult Edward Muir, would look like.

Except—and this was significant—he was what Edward Muir would look like if Edward had been noble and decent. In Devon's timeframe, Edward Muir was a good-for-nothing, globetrotting playboy, a coward, a man who shirked his responsibilities, especially where his son, Alexander, was concerned. Randolph Muir, by contrast, was clearly the opposite of his scalawag son: upstanding, solid, dependable.

Randolph's eyes caught Devon looking at him. They remained trained on him, watching the teenager precisely as he moved about the room. The sorcerer's eagle eye made Devon anxious, and he dropped a crystal.

"Careful there, young man," Randolph Muir called over to him, taking a few steps in Devon's direction. He picked the crystal up from the floor and set it on the table. "Montaigne told me you're from England. Whereabouts?"

"Um, Yorkshire," Devon said, recalling his time travel to the York of the fifteenth century.

The older man narrowed his eyes at him. "Yet no trace of a Yorkshire accent."

"Well, my mother—"

Randolph Muir was nodding. "Was American. Yes, Montaigne told me."

He doesn't believe me, Devon thought, as the master of the great house moved away.

It was only then that Devon realized that the heat he was feeling wasn't just his nerves. It was the heat of being in the presence of a fellow sorcerer—and a very good one at that. Randolph Muir.

At the designated time, a black limousine pulled up the long driveway outside Ravenscliff. From an upstairs window, Devon watched as the uniformed driver stepped out of the limo and opened the door to the backseat.

"It's him," Devon whispered, his eyes riveted to the Madman as he emerged from the automobile in his long black cape.

He looked different. Of course he did; he was *alive* in this time. He was an ordinary human being, albeit a sorcerer, flesh and blood instead of a disembodied spirit. Jackson was dark where his brother Randolph was fair. As he stepped out of the vehicle and looked up at the great house, he gave off a commanding presence. Yet he was the picture of gentility as he offered his hand to his wife, who alit now from the car herself.

She was beautiful. More beautiful than her portrait would reveal. Soft, delicate and blonde, Emily Muir looked up at the great house with wide, curious eyes. And in that second, she made eye contact with Devon as he stared down from above. With a start, he quickly let the curtain fall back over the window.

From the landing overlooking the foyer, Devon and Miranda watched the warm embraces. Greta, tall and robust, graciously welcomed Emily, so small and frail and ethereal. Little Amanda, in a long white lacy dress, curtsied to her uncle and aunt. Randolph shook his brother's hand heartily.

"Welcome to Ravenscliff," Randolph said.

"It is good to be home," Jackson replied, his eyes surveying the room. A chill ran down Devon's spine.

It was time for the Guardians to be presented. Montaigne took Jackson's hand in both of his, pumping it enthusiastically. "I always knew you would come back to us, Jackson," he said, his voice thick with emotion.

Jackson impulsively threw aside their handshake to embrace his Guardian, the man who had taught him so much of his sorcery. His black cape swirled around both of them, for a moment obliterating the sight of Montaigne.

"Your son?" Jackson asked, noticing the little boy standing timidly behind his father.

"Yes. This is Rolfe."

Jackson stooped down so that he was eye level with the child. "May we always be friends," he said, offering his hand to the little boy.

You'd almost think he's sincere, Devon thought, watching him. *You'd almost think he's truly repentant.*

But that demon attack earlier today put any such notions to rest.

Now it was Devon's turn. He was nudged forward by Montaigne. "This is Teddy, our apprentice from England."

Devon braced himself. But instead of the look of malevolence he was accustomed to seeing in the Madman's eyes, Devon saw nothing there. Just weariness. Jackson Muir shook Devon's hand politely but with disinterest.

I'm just an apprentice, Devon realized. *No one to concern himself with.*

Suddenly he flashed on a lesson that had been taught to him by the great Nightwing instructor Wiglaf. *Our time continuums are different*, he remembered Wiglaf telling him. *Here, in this time, Jackson has never met me, though I have met him. I have defeated him, cast him into the Hell Hole, but he does not yet know that. When I met him for the first time at Ravenscliff, he had the advantage; he knew who I was. No wonder he had known so much about me, for he had met me here, in the past.*

But now I hold the upper hand …

Much more interest was expressed by Jackson in meeting Miranda: he was gallant, kissing her hand, charming the girl and the whole room. But not Devon. Devon was not fooled by his gestures of civility.

He is here to destroy this family.

Devon knew the heartbreaking history of what was to come. So many of the people who were standing in that room at that very moment would die because of the Madman's evil ambitions. And the rest would live with the terrible memory of what would come to be called the Cataclysm.

The ceremony, conducted in the parlor, was simple and went according to plan. Randolph read from the Book of Return: "And I say to you, the errors of judgment are forgotten and the ties of family are restored. We welcome you back unto our bosom and restore to you your place in the noble Order of the Nightwing."

Emily, dressed all in white, began to cry with joy.

Jackson stepped forward, bending down on one knee in front of his brother. As he had practiced, Devon stepped forward with the sword of Quentin Muir, a shiny golden weapon laid upon a purple velvet pillow.

Randolph lifted the sword and brought it down gently upon Jackson's shoulder, as if he were knighting him. "Herewith you are restored," Randolph intoned.

Jackson then took the sword from his brother and rose to his feet. Devon braced himself. Was he going to attack? Was this the moment he revealed his true colors?

But Jackson turned the sword on himself, slicing his left

wrist. Devon was ready to cry out, but since no one else reacted, he kept quiet and assumed this was part of the ceremony. It was, for Montaigne was ready with a small golden plate to catch the droplets of the Madman's blood.

"I let my blood," Jackson said. "I cleanse myself of my apostasy. I drain my spirit of all aberrance. I heal now with your good will."

Miranda was right there to wrap his wrist in a golden cloth.

He looked down at her with such peace and joy in his eyes. She smiled up at him.

"Then let us rejoice!" Randolph said, louder now. "Apostate no more! You are my brother, Jackson Muir! You are Nightwing!"

All but Randolph fell to their knees, Devon with great reluctance. His hesitation did not go unnoticed by Randolph, however, who cast him a glance before calling them all to rise and join him and Jackson in the feasting downstairs.

Two days went by, and Devon began to get really worried.

How long was he to remain in the past? All of this was interesting and filled gaps in his knowledge of the Muirs and his own Nightwing heritage. But how did it help him stop the Madman from returning in his own time? How did it help him find a way to save Marcus from the curse of the beast, or to rescue Alexander from the Madman's possession? If only he'd been wearing his father's ring when he came back through time. That might have given him some answers.

Devon was terribly anxious to get back home to his friends. Sleeping in a small room in the servants' quarters, he couldn't help but worry about what was happening to them … but then he reminded himself that none of them—Marcus, Cecily, Natalie, D.J., Alexander—were even *born* yet. He just hoped that when he went back to his own time, he wouldn't have missed too much. The image of the beast howling within its pentagram in the middle of Rolfe's study was never far from his mind.

Neither were the faces of Cecily and Natalie. Neither girl even existed in this time and place, but Devon surprised himself by still feeling all the confusing emotions he had for them whenever their faces popped into his mind.

The celebrations continued. Feasting, games of swordplay, tournaments of sorcery. It was extremely cool to watch the brothers don suits of armor and mount their horses and joust with invisible rods. For a moment Devon found that he could forget his fears of the Madman and instead just marvel at his magical agility—though, whether out of lack of skill or deference to his brother, Jackson always lost to Randolph. It must have been humiliating for him, Devon thought, being the elder of the two brothers.

But he always lost graciously, bowing to his brother and saluting him.

Jackson did manage to shine on his own, however, when he regaled the children with his magic show. Boys and girls from the village were brought up to the estate to watch as Jackson, dressed as a clown, emerged from behind a black velvet curtain set up in the parlor. Devon had to grip the edges of his chair tightly to keep from falling over. This was how he first met the ghost of Jackson Muir: dressed as an infernal clown in cakey white makeup and a bulbous red nose. He called himself Major Musick, and he played a strange-looking horn. Watching him, Devon felt the same terror he'd felt in those earlier days; this was no happy-go-lucky clown but a demonic creature with a croaky voice and malice gleaming from its eyes.

And he wanted to send all those children into the Hell Hole!

Are they crazy? Devon thought, as the village kids laughed and clapped at Major Musick's antics. That funny-looking dragon the clown just pulled out of his hat? That was no Muppet. It was, Devon was certain, a demon straight from hell.

He suddenly noticed that little Amanda, sitting up front, was afraid of her uncle in his clown disguise. The little girl started to cry, and Miranda had to rush in and pick her up and carry her out of the show.

Major Musick seemed amused by her fright. He rubbed his

hands together. "Do we have a volunteer?" he rasped.

Devon was about to raise his hand, but another boy, some blue-eyed kid about ten years old, had beat him to it. They all thought this was just sleight of hand; Randolph probably thought it was all just good fun, his brother reviving his magic show for kids. But Devon knew better: it was actual sorcery, and none of them were safe.

The blue-eyed kid took his place on the makeshift stage. Jackson lumbered toward him in his floppy white pants with the red polka dots. "Do you believe in other worlds?" he asked the boy. "Do you believe in other realms beyond our own?"

The boy turned out to be a bit of a wise guy. "You mean like Canada or somethin'?"

The other kids laughed. Major Musick didn't seem to like being upstaged. He smiled wickedly. At least his smile looked wicked to Devon.

"Oh, the realms I'm thinking of are much farther away than that."

The kid scoffed. "You know, I don't buy this magic act."

The clown laughed. "Let's see if I can change your mind!"

He suddenly waved a large sheet of red satin in front of the boy, and when he folded it back into his hands, the boy was gone.

The children in the audience gasped.

Then, all at once, from the velvet backdrop burst the face of a demon. No silly-looking dragon this time, it resembled a T. rex, snapping and snarling as it loomed over the audience. Screams fill the air, but before pandemonium could break out, the red-eyed thing with the dripping fangs disappeared, and the clown was laughing.

"Look behind you, boys and girls," he said, pointing.

There, at the back of the room, stood the little boy who had disappeared. He was stunned, shaken, no longer so cocky. Emily Muir gently helped him to a chair.

"For one moment I switched them," the clown said, to the thunderous applause of the children. "The youngster went back in time and the Tyrannosaurus rex came forward!"

"Wow! That was cool!"

"Groovy, man!"

"Do it again!"

But the show was over. Randolph Muir had appeared in the doorway of the parlor, and from the look on his face, Devon didn't think he approved. The children were ushered out, as well as Devon, Miranda and Emily, and Randolph closed the doors to speak with his brother alone.

"I do hope Randolph isn't angry with Jackson," Emily murmured, looking at the doors of the parlor. "My husband just wanted to entertain the children."

Devon wanted to grip her by her small, frail shoulders and tell her the truth. But he couldn't—not yet, anyway. He had to bide his time if he was to learn whatever it was the Staircase Into Time brought him here to discover. But looking at Emily's sweet, innocent face, Devon knew he was going to have to try to help her, too. He knew how Emily Muir would die—jumping to her death from Devil's Rock once she discovered her husband's evil ways. Devon was going to have to try to prevent that. He couldn't just let her die.

"Someday," she said, turning to him, "I will be given the powers of the Nightwing, too, just as Randolph has given them to his wife. What a glorious day that will be."

Devon couldn't picture this delicate lamb as a sorceress. "It's a great honor," he said, knowing all too well himself, "to become Nightwing."

"Oh, yes," Emily said. "I remember when Jackson first told me the truth about himself. We were in Copenhagen, walking along the banks of the Stadsgraven, watching the swans. And he opened his hand and produced a diamond. For me!" She held out her hand to display the ring on her finger. "No one had ever bothered with me before. I was a scared, nervous little girl, but Jackson saw something in me. Now here I am, in this great house, with such a great future ahead of all of us."

Devon felt terrible. All Emily's future held was a mangled corpse at the bottom of the cliffs and decades as a weeping ghost wandering the halls of Ravenscliff.

Whether Randolph reprimanded Jackson for such an ostentatious display of powers, Devon didn't find out, but he suspected that he did so, further fueling his elder brother's resentment of him. After all, this house was supposed to have been Jackson's—until he messed up and went bad, forcing his father to change the will and leave Ravenscliff—and control of its Hell Hole—to Randolph.

But now Jackson's come back to claim what he believes is his rightful heritage, Devon thought, *and all hell is going to break loose.*

Literally.

Would he still be here to see it? Or would he be safely back in his own time by then?

Two more days went by.

Devon fell into a routine. First thing every day, he helped the cooks prepare breakfast. In this era, the great house had several servants, rather than just the one—Bjorn—in his own time. Part of a Guardian's job is devotion—or *varshan*—so each of them had to perform some small duty of servitude to symbolically show their allegiance to the Nightwing. Devon was given the task of gathering eggs from the chickens that were kept in a coop out back—another feature of life at Ravenscliff that would disappear thirty years from now. They were special hens, Devon could plainly see: big, bold birds that laid enormous eggs. Their eyes gleamed an odd intelligence at Devon as he reached gently under them, into their beds of straw, to retrieve their eggs. The chickens were treated very well, given free range to walk about throughout the coop and out into the barnyard. Several ravens perched on the rafters, like sentinels watching over them.

Back inside the house, Devon set out the plates in the grand dining room. He stood to the side as first Randolph, then Greta, then Jackson and Emily each took their seats. They were followed by the two children, Edward carried by a nanny, and then the entire family feasted on the eggs, as well as large mounds of cinnamon pancakes and homemade raisin bread. Devon couldn't help but think of the more health-conscious breakfasts that would be served at this table in his own time, spurred by Cecily's latest concerns over too many calories and carbohydrates. After the meal was complete, Devon helped Miranda clear the plates away, and only then did he have anything to eat on his own.

It was after breakfast, however, that his days really got interesting. He and Miranda headed down to Montaigne's cottage, where they were given instruction in the Guardianship of little Amanda and Edward. Devon, of course, was only there temporarily, and at some point everyone expected him to return "home" to England. But while he was here, he was expected to do his part in helping to train the Muir children. Montaigne demonstrated exercises to help the children adjust to their powers—making just a finger disappear, for example, before trying the whole body. "It can be rather disconcerting for a child to suddenly vanish completely," Montaigne said. "Better to take them through it with baby steps."

Don't I know it? Devon thought. As a boy, stumbling across his abilities terrified him. And he had had no one to explain why or how. All Dad had ever been able to tell him was that he was stronger than anything that might frighten him, and that he must always use his powers for good. How Devon wished he'd had Guardians like Montaigne and Miranda to help teach him the ways of the Nightwing, as Amanda and Edward Muir had. And to think someday they would give it all up, renounce their sorcery and their Nightwing heritage!

Devon liked Montaigne, probably because he reminded him so much of Rolfe. He had the same intensity as his son would have, the same deep-set green eyes, the same carefully modulated voice, even if Montaigne *père*'s was accented in French.

The best part of his day, however, was the early afternoon, when he and Miranda got to apply what Montaigne had shown them. Taking the children out onto the grass, they would try various tricks to acclimate the youngsters to their powers. Devon found it ironic that little Amanda took to him immediately. Thirty years in the future, she would be the ice queen of all time, distant and often hostile to him—but now she laughed at Devon's funny faces and responded well to his encouragements to try some magic.

"Let's open one of those beautiful flowers for your mama," Devon said, pointing to a daffodil still closed tightly in its bud. "Concentrate, Amanda. Imagine it unfolding and opening into a brilliant yellow flower."

The little girl laughed, stumbling through the grass to stand over the daffodil. After a couple of minutes, however, apparently frustrated, she reached down and tried to peel open the petals with her hand. The flower just ripped apart, and the child started to cry.

"It's okay," Devon said, coming to her aid. He decided to cheat a little. "Just do it like this."

He concentrated on the next flower over. Slowly its petals begin to unfold, with Devon guiding it with his mind to full expression. Miranda, observing, made a face in disapproval—a Guardian wasn't supposed to have such powers—but little Amanda watched Devon's example in wonder.

"Now you try," Devon said.

With some effort and a wrinkled forehead, the girl managed to open a third flower. She was elated and threw her little arms around Devon's neck.

Is it possible this child will someday be my mother? Devon wondered. *Is that really what Clarissa meant?*

Looking into the child's eyes now, Devon tried to see the answer. *Was this why I came back? Will I finally learn who my real parents are?*

Miranda, meanwhile, was busy with baby Edward, holding him in her arms, allowing him to play with a magical crystal in his hands. Montaigne told them that children even as young as Edward could absorb knowledge through the Guardians' crystals. Devon watched as the boy gurgled his wonder, fascinated by the small glowing orb in his pudgy hands.

"You are good with babies," came a voice.

Devon looked up. It was Jackson Muir, and he was speaking to Miranda.

He was strolling across the grass with his brother Randolph. Both sorcerers were dressed all in black, with red ascot ties.

Miranda blushed as she looked up at Jackson. "It is my

privilege, sir," she said.

Devon noticed the look that passed between them. He'd warned Miranda about Jackson, but apparently, she'd paid no attention. Devon had watched her as she fluttered around the dark-eyed sorcerer. She was easily swayed by his flattery, and especially his excessive praise of her family, the Devons. She seemed to have totally forgotten Devon's warnings and been seduced by the wily charm of the Madman.

But Devon couldn't think too long about any of that, for Randolph Muir had approached him. He stood now looking down at Devon and little Amanda.

"Flower, Papa," Amanda said, showing him the daffodil. "I opened it."

"Very clever of you, sweetheart," her father said, but his eyes remained fixed on Devon. "Why don't you run along into the house and give your flower to Mama? I would like to talk with our young Guardian here."

Amanda happily obeyed. Devon watched her totter off through the grass, then noticed Miranda, still carrying Edward, wandering off toward the stables with Jackson. Randolph seemed to take no notice of them, however. His only interest was Devon.

"My daughter seemed to like you a good deal," the Master of Ravenscliff said.

"Yes, sir. She's a great kid."

"With all the good instincts of a true Nightwing." His eyes revealed more than he was saying. "Tell me, Teddy. Any more battles out here in the garden? Any demons you've had to send back to their Hell Holes?"

Devon was stunned. Randolph *knew*.

The great sorcerer smiled. "Did you think, Teddy, that I would not recognize another Nightwing in my own house? That I would not sense your presence? Surely you might have done a better job of disguising yourself, of obscuring your energy, had you wanted to remain undetected."

"I'm—I'm not hundred percent sure how to do that," Devon admitted.

Randolph looked surprised. "It's one of the first lessons a Guardian teaches. Why was yours so lax?"

"I—I never had one, sir."

"Never had one?" Randolph folded his arms across his chest. "Well, well, well. I suspected there was something odd about you. Not threatening, but odd. That's why I enveloped you in a cloak of obscurity myself, so that my wife and my brother wouldn't notice you. At least not until I found out your story. Care to divulge it?"

Devon hesitated. "I'm not sure if I should, sir."

Randolph lifted his eyebrows in surprise. "You stand on my estate and in my presence and defer an answer to a direct question?"

"Look, I'm not trying to be disrespectful. But I was sent here to find out some things—"

"Sent by *whom*?" Now Randolph's brow furrowed with concern.

"I came down the Staircase Into Time," Devon told him.

Randolph smiled. "Ah, my father's most brilliant bit of sorcery. Now tell me, Teddy. I demand to know. From *what* time did you come, and from what place?"

Devon gulped, trusting his intuition that it was okay to reveal more details. "I came from about thirty years in the future," he said. "And from ... *here*."

"From *Ravenscliff*?" Randolph dropped his arms to his sides and his face took on an expression of great interest. "You are from the future of Ravenscliff?"

"Yes, sir. And I have to say, sir, that your brother—"

"Don't continue." Randolph Muir raised his hand to silence Devon. "You are about to say that you do not trust him. That you have come to this time to warn me of his apostasy."

"Well, sir ..."

"Say no more. It is a rule of time travel that information not be given before its time. You can corrupt the flow of days. Tell me nothing of what will come."

"But sir!"

Randolph Muir made a face of terrible sadness. "I am not

an ostrich with my head in the sand, young Teddy. Do you think I have not had my doubts about my brother? Do you think I am not watching his every move?"

"If you had doubts about him, why would you allow him to return?"

"What was I to do? Continue to permit him roaming the world? Better to have him here, so I might watch him." Randolph sighed, looking off in the direction where Jackson had walked. "I lost two brothers, you know. Gideon is forever gone. But Jackson …"

Randolph's voice trailed off.

"I must believe that he is being honest with me," the sorcerer continued. "Perhaps you are here to tell me otherwise. Perhaps your presence means that I am wrong to hope that he has changed. But for now I must continue to hope, to believe." He closed his eyes and then with great effort opened them again. "His love for his wife, so pure, so honest—that is what has changed him. I must believe it will keep him true."

"Do you want to know what happens, sir? If I tell you, maybe we can prevent—"

Again he was silenced. "History cannot be changed, Teddy. You will see that. If it could be changed, everything would be constantly unraveling. Change one little fact here in our time and then you yourself might not be born. Time would collapse in on itself."

"But Jackson will try to—"

"I want no further details, my good young man. I insist!"

Devon was silent.

Randolph smiled. "You may be here simply to set into motion my own process by which I can truly change Jackson for good. At least, that is what I must try to do. It is the only way I have."

"Yes, sir," Devon said.

"Whether that happens or not depends on the fates." Randolph looked sadly back toward the house. "I admit your presence here does unnerve me. I must protect my children if indeed Jackson means any harm. They will be sent away when the time comes. I have no right to ask—it is against the laws of time travel—but I am a father. Tell me, Teddy. Do I have time at least to keep my children from harm?"

"Yes, sir. Your children will remain safe."

Randolph Muir let out a sigh of relief. "Tell me no more, Teddy. I want neither to be discouraged nor complacent. But you can be assured I shall remain vigilant in watching my brother."

He said nothing more, just strode off through the grass.

The next couple of days were terribly frustrating for Devon. He felt gagged. Being prevented from speaking the truth—giving these people warnings about the danger they faced—was really eating away at Devon.

And it wasn't like he could divert himself with other things. Montaigne watched him like a hawk. Mostly Devon just performed menial tasks, like polishing silver or washing floors. Was this really the way a Guardian was trained? Where was all the instruction in magic, alchemy, and Nightwing history? And never could Devon use his sorcery to finish his chores. That would have given away his secret.

And forget about texting or tweeting or checking Facebook on his phone. Though he hadn't brought his phone with him, he knew he'd have no service here in the past. Cell phones hadn't even been dreamed up yet. All they had in this time period were big, clunky landlines, some of them attached to walls.

Television was also another waste of time. There were only like three channels. Devon thought cable TV existed, but clearly Randolph Muir didn't put much stock in it.

"Yes, it can be boring here," Miranda agreed as the two of them carried armloads of children's books up to Amanda's playroom. Devon recognized some of them as the ones he'd find, thirty years from now, in the Ravenscliff cellar. "I wish we'd have more ritual here. But Mr. Muir doesn't like to attract much attention from the village. They already suspect too much."

Devon knew that the people of Misery Point whispered about the legends.

"The parents of those kids at Jackson's magic show are all aflutter, thinking he caused a real dinosaur to appear with his magical powers," Miranda said.

"He did," Devon told her. "But not a dinosaur. A demon. And it was kind of a dangerous thing to do."

Miranda was sliding the books onto Amanda's shelf. "I know. Mr. Muir was angry."

"I tell you, Jackson is up to no good."

She smirked. "At least he livens things up around here."

"You need to watch out for him."

Her dark eyes danced. "I came here to learn about the Nightwing. I'm tired of playing housemaid."

"Yes, but Jackson—"

Miranda shook her head. "There's a time for apprenticeship, and a time for action." She looked over at Devon. "Maybe you're just too young, sorcerer or not, to understand what I'm talking about."

With that she huffed out of the room.

Devon fumed as he watched her go. Miranda was only a few years older than he was. He didn't appreciate her superior attitude.

She had no idea how dangerous the Madman was.

If only Randolph would hear him out—if only he'd let Devon tell him what he knew. That Emily would die. That Jackson would try to open the Hell Hole. That a battle would ensue—but that Randolph would win. Jackson was marked by history for defeat.

But such information, given out of time's proper sequence, would make Randolph complacent. That was the reason he gave, anyway, the reason he insisted he didn't want to know what the future held. Yet something about that reasoning bothered Devon. If history couldn't be changed, then what need was there to worry? Complacent or not, Randolph would still be victorious over Jackson.

Unless history *could* be changed. Unless Randolph was

handing him a line.

Devon began to wonder if it was indeed possible to alter the course of history. Maybe Randolph wasn't being fully honest with him. Maybe he had his own reasons to want Devon to believe in history's immutability. Maybe he feared the possibility of time collapsing in on itself far more than he feared Jackson's apostasy.

Change one little fact here in our time and then you might not be born.

If time could be changed, I'd cease to exist, Devon thought. *And maybe Cecily and Alexander would cease to exist too. And who knew who else?*

That night, Devon felt the heat.

Randolph had left earlier in the day on a mysterious errand. Off he had driven in his long black car, which had magically disappeared at the end of the driveway. With Randolph out of the house, Devon felt vulnerable and alone, especially when he awakened in the middle of the night, sweating into his sheets.

The Hell Hole. Someone is at the Hell Hole.

He knew not to head to the West Wing. In this time the Hell Hole wasn't there. It was in the basement. Devon disappeared from his bed and reappeared in the very spot where, thirty-some years later, a room would contain the crazy Clarissa.

Looking through the darkness of the basement, he could discern, set into a far wall, a bolted metal portal, about three feet wide and four feet tall. The same sort of door that would one day be in the West Wing.

Devon approached the portal carefully, feeling the heat around him shooting up dramatically. Placing his hand against the door, his hand was nearly scalded by the blazing hot metal. His presence awakened the things that live behind it. The demons began to scratch.

Is that you, master?

Set us free, master!

From somewhere farther off in the basement Devon heard the soft echo of a footfall. He hurried away from the portal, trying to take refuge in the shadows. He looked from side to side, trying to discern who was down there with him. He walked through a cobweb, its sticky fingers clinging to his face.

And then a hand dropped onto his shoulder.

"What are you doing down here?"

Devon looked up into the face of Jackson Muir.

For a moment, he couldn't speak.

The Madman's eyes were black, burning into Devon's own. His grip on the teenager's shoulder tightened.

Devon remembered that Randolph had hidden his sorcery from Jackson's senses. He would not be able to feel the heat standing beside the teenager.

"I was just looking," Devon said, concentrating on keeping his voice steady, "for some picture books for Amanda." He was able to swallow his fear, carefully modulating his heartbeat to keep the Madman from detecting any anxiety. "Miranda and I brought her up some earlier today and she enjoyed them very much."

Jackson studied him. Devon took some comfort in the fact that he was protected by Randolph's cloak of obscurity, but the suspicious glare in the Madman's eyes couldn't be denied. Devon could barely manage to hold his gaze, remembering their battles in the future. How the Madman had taunted him, laughed at him, pulled him down into his stinking, rotting grave …

"It's awfully late to be looking for picture books," Jackson finally said, still not releasing his grip on Devon's shoulder.

The teen sorcerer looked defiantly into the Madman's shining black eyes. "I had forgotten to get them earlier, and I wanted to be ready first thing in the morning. We're going to read all about the great Nightwing of China in the tenth century."

Jackson Muir still did not break his gaze or his grip. He continued to stare into Devon's eyes for several more moments, and Devon stared right back.

At last he turned away. "Get along with you. Go to bed, little boy."

He let Devon go and moved off through the shadows of the basement. Devon made a sound with his feet to suggest he was departing, but in truth he simply turned invisible. *If Jackson can't detect anything about me when he can see me*, Devon thought, *I'll really be free of any danger when he can't.*

He waited several long minutes. Then, ever so quietly, he moved back toward the Hell Hole.

Jackson stood facing the bolted metal door. His face was contorted in a weird kind of ecstasy, and his teeth were bared like an animal's, sharp and yellow. Even from a few yards away Devon could feel the staggering heat emitted by the sorcerer, and the tremors made by the demons as they scuttled and shoved from behind the portal.

Let us out, master!

Set us free to do your bidding!

"All in good time," Jackson told the creatures. "All in good time."

Just then, from the shadows, there was movement beside the Madman. He was not alone.

Devon covered his mouth to keep from gasping.

It was Miranda!

And she was looking right at him.

Somehow, she could see Devon despite his invisibility.

"We have company," she told Jackson calmly, and the Madman turned his face, filled with rage, to gaze in Devon's direction.

A Terrible Discovery

"A raven," Miranda said. "That is all."

From a rafter, one of the big black birds fluttered its wings, its shining eyes observing their every move.

"Accursed things," Jackson said, and with one wave of his hand caused the bird to fall over dead onto the floor.

"Oh," Miranda said, stooping to examine the bird. "Did you have to kill it?"

"It is my brother's eyes. Do you think I'd allow it to live and tell what it has seen?"

Miranda stood, looking again directly at Devon. He was sure she could see him, but she had not given him away to the Madman. What was she doing down here? Why was she with Jackson Muir?

The portal into the world of the demons remained secure for tonight. The Madman and Miranda looked upon it, saying nothing. The hammering and pleading from the other side eventually died down. The Madman placed his massive arm around Miranda's slender shoulders, guiding her as they returned upstairs.

Devon thought about following them, but he was afraid of what he might witness. He'd seen a lot of nasty things, but if what he thought was happening between those two was, in fact, happening, he couldn't bear to see.

So, instead, Devon reappeared in his own room and finally allowed his heart to start racing in his chest.

Sleep didn't come easily. He tossed and turned most of the night. The next morning, he dressed quickly and confronted Miranda in the hen house.

"Why were you with Jackson Muir? I saw you—and I know

you saw me!"

The young woman tossed back her black hair and flashed Devon with her dark eyes. "Of course I saw you, Teddy Bear! The island magic of the Devons is not blinded by the same tricks that can deceive the Nightwing. I saw you plain as day, you little fool!" She snarled at him. "Do you know how dangerous it was for you to be there? Oh, why must you interfere?"

"He's evil, Miranda! You could see that yourself. He plans to open the Hell Hole!"

She lifted her chin in haughty defiance. "Only to reclaim what is rightfully his. This house!"

Devon was thunderstruck. "You don't care that he'll unleash the demons onto the world?"

"It is not Jackson who is evil, Teddy Bear." She leaned in close to stare directly into his eyes. "It is Randolph. Jackson has shown me the truth. It is *Randolph* who has dreams of conquering the world. Why do you think he is so jealous of the portal? Why won't he allow Jackson to share in its guardianship? Randolph has fooled you, like everyone else. It is Randolph who will unleash the demons!"

Devon couldn't speak for a moment. "He's brainwashed you," he finally said.

Miranda took great offense. "I am no ordinary Guardian, or have you forgotten that? Yes, you might be Nightwing, so great and noble. But I have powers and intuition, too, and I can see the truth for myself. I can read thoughts, remember? My gifts may not be so wondrous as yours, Teddy Bear, but they are not blinded by the pomp and arrogance of the Nightwing. I could see you standing there last night, just as clearly as I can see Jackson as the good man he is, wrongly disinherited, kept down from achieving his greatness by an envious brother."

"What has he promised you?" Devon asked. "What do you get for going along with him?"

"Join us, Teddy Bear," Miranda said, suddenly gripping Devon by his hands. "From the moment you first arrived here, I have felt drawn to you. I do not know why, but I have. And so I have not exposed you. I have not told Jackson of your powers.

He suspects nothing."

"But you *will* tell him," Devon said, "if I oppose you."

Miranda dropped his hands and averted her eyes.

"I can't stand by and see anyone in this house hurt," Devon told her.

"No one will be hurt." Miranda looked over at Devon with wide eyes, and it was clear she truly believed what she said. "Jackson may have to threaten Randolph. That arrogant man will not surrender easily. But he knows it is Jackson who has the knowledge of the demons. If Randolph unleashes them as he plans, they will not rally to him. They will look to Jackson for leadership, and Randolph knows this. He will eventually see the wisdom of stepping aside and letting Jackson take his true place as Master of Ravenscliff and overlord of its Hell Hole."

"You're crazy," Devon told her, dropping the last of the morning's eggs into the basket and heading back toward the house.

"Jackson will make sure Randolph and his family live safely and comfortably. It will all work out. You will see!"

"You're crazy," Devin said again, not looking back at her.

"The Devons are a wise and knowing clan!" Miranda called after him. "We know with whom to ally! You will see! You will join us eventually!"

Walking back across the estate, Devon considered whether he should tell Randolph of Miranda's treachery. Or whether he should march down right now to Montaigne's cottage and reveal all to him. He had to *do* something.

But Devon was no squealer. For now, this was between the two of them. Miranda was right: there *was* some kind of bond connecting the two of them, and Devon knew what it was. It was *family*, and he couldn't rat out the only blood family he'd ever known. Miranda was misguided, brainwashed. She wasn't evil. If he revealed her involvement with the Madman, who knew what Randolph or Montaigne might do to her? Devon felt protective of Miranda. He would save her on his own from whatever Jackson had in store for her.

Yet as the days went by, Devon was lulled into a false sense of security, believing that all of the portentous evil he feared might never show its horrible face. Randolph returned and there was nothing but good will between the two brothers.

It was a happy season. Spring warmed into summer, and Devon watched as the village filled up with people, with seasonal homeowners opening up their cottages, tourists flocking in to bronze their bodies on the beaches, and college kids arriving to work in the shops and the restaurants. In his own time, he'd been waiting for the arrival of summer for so long; Misery Point had been cold and blustery ever since Devon had first arrived, and he'd been looking forward to warm weather. Who knew he'd be experiencing it some thirty years in the past?

The music that floated up from the beaches came from boom boxes and radios. Not an iPod to be seen. Instead of rap and hip-hop and Katy Perry, it was punk and Cyndi Lauper and Prince. Devon took a liking to some of the music, especially The Smiths, and The Pretenders, and Depeche Mode, and Sade. Miranda, of course, was a huge Madonna fan, with her short skirts and crucifixes and dangling earrings.

For Devon, it was also a crash course in history. On the television in the study, whenever the newscast mentioned "the President," it was Ronald Reagan who came onto the screen. When they mentioned "the Princess," it wasn't Kate they were talking about, but Diana, who was pregnant with a baby Devon knew would be Prince Harry. But mostly watching the news left Devon utterly lost. None of the world leaders matched those he'd been learning about in his current events class in school. In Canada, it was Pierre Trudeau; in France, Francois Mitterand; in the Netherlands, Ruud Lubbers; in Poland, some guy named Jaruzelski; and in Britain, one very tough-sounding lady named Margaret Thatcher. And Russia wasn't even Russia. It was still the Soviet Union.

Since he'd arrived in the past with only the shirt on his back, Devon had had to conjure up some clothes, and he did his best to match the fashions he saw in the village. He wore button-down shirts and skinny leather ties, grew his sideburns long, and slipped Ray-Ban Wayfarers over his eyes. On his feet he wore big black Doc Martens boots. *Gotta keep up with the times*, he told himself with a smile.

But he was homesick for his own time. He'd been gone long enough now that he had missed his final exams and all the end-of-the-year parties at school. He'd missed the trip to Florida D.J. had promised them all. How he longed to be piling into D.J.'s Camaro with the rest of the gang and heading over to Gio's Pizza—which, in this era, hadn't even been built yet. The whole shopping plaza was just a field of daisies and dandelions. Devon caught himself wondering what his friends were all doing, and then remembered, with a horrible shudder, Marcus as the beast howling in the middle of Rolfe's study.

He's not born yet, Devon consoled himself. *None of them are.*

How long did he have he stay here? Devon asked himself that question every day, hoping his sorcerer's intuition would give him an answer. But it never did.

Every once in a while, whether he was at Ravenscliff or walking around the village, Devon would spot a staircase going up—maybe to the second floor of Snow's department store or to a deck wrapped around a seasonal beach house. One never knew where the Staircase Into Time might appear, so when he spotted these sets of stairs, Devon would stop whatever he was doing and rush at them, taking them two at a time, hoping at the end he'd return home. But every time the staircase turned out to be just ordinary wood, and he knew his time in the past was not yet complete.

That was a bummer. He wasn't eager to witness what he knew would soon occur: Emily's death, Jackson's struggle for the Hell Hole, the battle of the demons. He was eager to get home so he could help Marcus and Alexander—but nothing he'd learned here in the past so far had given him any clue as to how to do that. Devon wondered again: *How long will I have to stay here?*

Emily's death occurred on Halloween—four long months from now! Surely he wouldn't be here that long.

Would he?

But then Randolph Muir, knowing Devon's Nightwing

identity, concocted a story that he'd been asked to keep "Teddy" at Ravenscliff longer than originally expected. It was announced that he would apprentice for several months with the Muirs. Devon therefore settled in, figuring he was here for the duration, at least through Halloween—though every morning he still woke up hoping this might be the day he learned what he needed to know and got to go home.

He and Miranda came to an unspoken truce. No further mention of Jackson or the Hell Hole passed between them. But they watched each other. Devon felt the girl's eyes whenever he walked into the room, and he observed her just as closely. He rarely saw her any more with Jackson, but he did catch the occasional knowing glance they would exchange, sometimes with poor, clueless Emily standing right there.

Of all of them, Devon liked Emily best. Greta Muir was proud and officious, but Emily was modest and friendly.

"You must miss your mother and your father," she said to Devon one day, sitting in the upstairs parlor.

He smiled. "I would miss them, if I knew who they were."

"You poor boy. You don't know your parents?"

"No. I was raised by an adopted father who was very good to me, but he's dead now." Actually, Devon knew, Ted March was still alive somewhere in this time—but since Devon had yet to be born, Ted would have no clue as to who he was. So there was no use in trying to find him. "So," Devon added with a sigh, "I'm alone."

Emily put down the embroidery she had been doing in her lap. "You poor child. I know the sorrow of losing one's parents early. I was alone, too, until Jackson married me and gave me this wonderful home and beautiful family."

Her eyes looked sadly off into the distance. Her mouth twitched as if she might cry.

"Are you all right, Mrs. Muir?" Devon asked.

"Oh, yes. It's just—"

"Just what?" Devon approached her. His intuition told him this might be important information. "You can confide in me, ma'am. That's what Guardians are here for."

"But you are so young," she said, smiling down at him.

"You would be doing me a great honor to share your sorrow with me, as well as offering me a valuable lesson in learning how to support."

She sighed. "The Nightwing have great powers. At times, when I first married Jackson, I thought the powers of the Nightwing were limitless."

"But they aren't," Devon said.

"No. There are indeed limits on what a Nightwing can do." She stood, moving across the room. Her blond hair caught a ray of sunlight, and suddenly she was suffused with a golden glow. "No sorcerer can make a barren woman conceive a child."

A barren woman …?

At first Devon didn't know what she meant. Barren … he didn't know the word. He'd heard it, but wasn't sure what it was. It seemed old-fashioned. So he concentrated, and it was as if dictionary pages started flipping through his mind.

> Barren
> (of land) too poor to produce much or any vegetation.
> (of a tree or plant) not producing fruit or seed.
> archaic (of a woman) unable to have children.

That's it, Devon suddenly realized.

Emily couldn't have kids.

Wow. That dictionary in his head was cool. But somehow he just knew it wouldn't work when he was taking a test in school.

But the information it had just given him was significant. Emily was unable to give Jackson a child—a son and heir, who might have inherited Ravenscliff from him one day. If she had been, Jackson never would have betrayed her by fooling around with another woman. And so Emily wouldn't have jumped off the cliff. And possibly Jackson's own evil might not have risen to such heights.

But Jackson was already involved with another woman. Miranda. And it was almost certainly Miranda who Emily would discover with her husband on Halloween night, causing her to take her final, fatal swan dive off Devil's Rock.

"Look," Devon said, trying to find the right words. "There are ways of having children even if you can't have them yourself. You can adopt ..."

"But the child wouldn't be of Nightwing blood ..."

"Jackson could bestow powers onto the kid, just like he's going to give them to you."

Emily smiled sadly. "For a man as proud as my husband, there would always be that difference ... between being *born* Nightwing and being *made* Nightwing." She sighed. "I was always a disappointment to my father. He said I was too shy, too timid, to amount to anything. Now I'll be a disappointment to my husband, too."

Devon suddenly had a glimpse of her as a young girl. It was as if a layer of time had just peeled away and Devon could see through space and time. There was Emily, maybe twelve years old, wearing glasses, sitting in a junior high classroom. It must have been the last day of school, because everyone around her was getting commendations. Everyone but her. All the other kids got up and walked to the front of the class to accept their award. Emily just sat there. Her name was never called. She looked utterly bereft.

And there, to the side, among the gathering of parents, was a man that Devon was certain was Emily's father. He was glowering.

Devon felt really, really bad for Emily. She was way too nice to have such a bad-luck life.

"You know," he said, an idea forming in his mind, "what if there was some Nightwing orphan who needed adoption?"

Emily looked over at him. "A Nightwing orphan?"

"Yeah. I know there are. I've, er, met one myself. He grew up not knowing who his parents were or anything about his Nightwing heritage. And I know he'd give anything if some cool Nightwing couple had adopted him and raised him and trained him."

Emily's face brightened. "Why, I'd never thought of that. Teddy, you may be on to something. Where is this boy?"

"Well, he's kind of gotten too old for adoption now. But

I'm sure there are others. I'm sure Mr. Muir would know."

Emily was smiling. "It is definitely an idea worth checking out. How good you are to think of it." She withdrew something from the pocket of the jacket she was wearing. It was a small book, and she handed it to Devon. "Please, accept this as my thanks."

He looked down at the title. *Prayers and Meditations.*

He suppressed a gasp. It was the same book he'd found in Clarissa's room.

"Often I have found comfort in the words inside this book. I've practically memorized them all by now, so it's time to pass it on."

"Wow," Devon said. "Thank you."

Now how does this book get from me to Clarissa? How did I end up getting it before she did, but after I'd already seen her with it? These time paradoxes really gave Devon a headache.

Emily was looking very sweetly at him. Devon felt more rotten than he could ever remember feeling, knowing what he knew about her. He had to look away.

"Do you have a girlfriend, Teddy?" Emily asked.

"Well, sort of, back home," he said, still keeping his eyes averted.

"You mean in England?"

He nodded.

"Does she know you're a Guardian?"

"Um, no, not really," he said, not liking the fact that he had to lie to her. Sometimes, not being sincere with someone as truly nice as Emily felt really, really wrong. "Actually," Devon said, "she and I aren't really seeing each other any more."

Emily smiled. "Well, then, how about I fix you up with Miranda? I think the two of you would be so cute together."

Finally Devon looked at her. "Um, well, I think Miranda is a little old for me ..."

"You're very mature for your age," Emily said. "Let me know if you'd like me to put a bug in her ear. I like playing Cupid."

"Yeah, well, thanks, but I'm good for now."

Emily smiled and moved off across the room. Watching

her walk through the sunlight, Devon knew he couldn't just stand back and let history take its course.

He couldn't let her die.

I'm the one-hundredth generation from Sargon the Great, he thought. *I am destined to be the greatest of all Nightwing. If anyone can change history, it's me.*

He couldn't just be a silent witness to all the horrible events that would reverberate for decades in the Muir family. He would have to stop them from happening.

And he'd just have to take the chance that time wouldn't collapse in the process.

It was at the height of a thunderstorm a few nights later that the evil reasserted itself.

The glass in the window of Devon's room shattered inward, causing him to sit up in bed with a shout.

He'd been sound asleep. That was why he hadn't sensed it coming.

No excuse, he scolded himself. *Even asleep, I need to be aware.*

Because a sorcerer never knew when he'd have a visitor.

A demon.

It stood amid the shattered glass snarling up at him. It was in the shape of a giant lizard—perhaps the same that had masqueraded as the dinosaur at Jackson's magic show. Opening its maw to screech at Devon, it made a sound like an exhaust belching from the back of a bus. Devon swung his legs off the bed and slammed his bare feet into the creature's cold, scaly belly. It belched again.

Devon managed to roll off the bed and position himself better to fight. "Come on," he called to the thing, his heart still thudding. "Come on at me one more time!"

He was angry at himself; even asleep he had to be on guard. The calmness of the past couple of weeks had lulled him into a false security. One-hundredth generation he might be, but he still had a lot of work to do if he was going to ever be a great sorcerer.

The thing hissed at him but didn't lunge.

"What's the matter?" Devon taunted. "Give me your best shot. You afraid of me?"

"No," the demon said. "It is *you* who are afraid."

It *spoke*. Devon had heard demons speak before, but it was rare, and it always creeped him out. The thing's voice was grating, like fingernails on a chalkboard. But it was *right*: being caught unawares, Devon's heart was still racing, and until the shock of surprise died down in his system, he was powerless to send it back to its Hell Hole.

"I'm not afraid of you," Devon told it. "You know as soon as I calm down just a bit, you're a goner."

"Perhaps," the demon said, its breath escaping its mouth like fumes. "But there are more of us. We can see what you are even if our master cannot."

"Where did you come from? What Hell Hole in what part of the world?"

"I think you call it Siberia. Even now the great Russian Nightwing are working to seal it shut. But our master tore it open when he was there and set enough of us free that we will keep coming after you until you are dead."

"Well, it won't be you to kill me," Devon said.

"Oh, no?"

The demon sprung at him, its great jaw opening to reveal its many sharp fangs and a long, forked tongue. It got mighty close to Devon, too, and some of its stinking saliva dripped onto the teen sorcerer's face.

"You're starting to bore me," Devon told the creature, punching it in the jaw and sending it sprawling against the far wall. "Now get out of here. Back to your Hell Hole."

The demon had time enough only to curse its fate before being sucked back out the broken window into the storm.

Lightning crashed, illuminating the mess the fight had left in the room. Bookshelves had been knocked over, the wall was scraped, glass and rainwater had spread across the floor.

And Greta Muir was banging on his door.

"What is going on in there? Teddy, open this door!"

When he did, the room and the window had all been repaired with a blink of his eye.

"I'm sorry, Mrs. Muir," Devon said. "The storm blew open my window—"

She pushed her way in to look around. Clearly she had felt the heat of the demon, but everything was back to normal now. She looked at him oddly.

"My husband said there was nothing to be concerned about," she said, more to herself than to Devon. "But I'm not so sure."

"I'm sorry it disturbed you," Devon said.

Greta Muir just eyed him suspiciously and walked out of the room.

Devon slept the rest of the night with his guard on alert.

As startling as the demon attack was, however, it was the following morning that brought a far greater surprise.

Devon was with Montaigne at his cottage, cataloguing crystals, learning about their various storehouses of knowledge, when he heard a knock.

"Hullo," came a voice when Montaigne opened the door. "Please forgive my tardiness, but I have had a most curious delay."

The voice was that of an Englishman. Devon strained to get a good look, but Montaigne stood in the way of the visitor.

"Delay?" Montaigne asked. "I'm sorry, but I don't know who you are."

"Of course not." The man began again. "I was sent here to help preside over the return of an errant Nightwing, to participate in the Ritual of Return."

"Oh?" Montaigne's head turned slowly to look at Devon.

Oh, great, Devon thought. *Now my cover is blown. The real guy finally shows up.*

"A most unusual occurrence happened on my way here," the Englishman was saying. "I am quite eager to speak with a Nightwing expert about it. For, you see, I seemed to travel through time—"

"Come in," Montaigne said, stepping aside so the young man could enter. "What is your name?"

"Oh, forgive me, I should have introduced myself directly."

Montaigne stepped aside and the visitor's face was revealed. Devon gasped.

"My name is Ogden McNutt."

Sure enough, it was he: the young man in tee shirt and blue jeans whose ghost would one day haunt Ravenscliff. The man who was, in reality, the beast.

"I was on my way here," McNutt said, "but on the ship traveling across the Atlantic, I took a staircase up to my room only to emerge in a time some thirty years in the future." He shivered. "And what a strange place it was. I must say, sir, you have an exact duplicate in the future. He called himself Rolfe."

"Rolfe?" Montaigne reacted. "That's my son."

"If you met Rolfe," Devon said, suddenly approaching McNutt to look him directly in the eyes, "you must have met others, too."

"This is Teddy," Montaigne said, raising a suspicious eyebrow at Devon. "Who claimed he was here to do your job."

"Um, I'll get to that in a minute," Devon said. "First, Ogden, tell me who else you met in the future."

McNutt's face saddened. "Several people. A lovely dark-skinned woman by the name of Roxanne. And a boy named Marcus, who was plagued by the curse of the beast."

Devon's heart dropped. He wasn't sure at what exact point McNutt landed in the future, but if Devon had been hoping for evidence of Marcus's cure, those hopes were now dashed.

But it was clear that McNutt did not suffer from the same affliction—at least not yet. The curse of the beast was something alien to him. Sitting down over a pot of steaming hot coffee, the newcomer told his tale: how after an evening spent in Rolfe's study he had headed up the staircase only to emerge in a shop just outside Misery Point. Quickly determining he was back in his own time, he had hurried to Ravenscliff, realizing that while he'd only spent a few hours in the future, *weeks* had elapsed in the past.

"I so regret my delay," McNutt said. "But I must conclude that my timeslip served some purpose …"

"It did." The voice was a new one. They all looked up. Standing in the center of the room was Randolph Muir.

"It allowed the arrival of young Teddy here," Randolph said, approaching them. "I'm sorry to have deceived you, Montaigne, but it was necessary at the time. You see, Teddy is not a Guardian. He is Nightwing."

Montaigne looked at Devon with astonished eyes. "I must not sit, then, in your presence," he said, standing quickly from the table where the three of them had been sitting.

"Oh, no, man, it's cool," Devon said. "Don't start treating me any differently …"

"I must," Montaigne told him. "You are Nightwing. I am a Guardian. My job is to serve you."

McNutt likewise stood. Devon groaned, but Randolph smiled.

"If all of this is true," Montaigne said, "then I would advise McNutt not to reveal too much of the future then. Isn't that right, Randolph?"

The great sorcerer nodded. "We must honor the boundaries of time."

"Are you so certain history can't be changed?" Devon asked. "I mean, I know things—I know what is going to happen—I could help you all prevent—"

"No!" Randolph Muir raised his hand to silence him. "I have told you, Teddy! You must not try to alter the course of history. It is futile to try."

"If it's futile," Devon persisted, "why are you so insistent that I not even *try*?"

"Heed my words, young novice," Randolph said, cleverly reminding Devon of their positions relative to each other. "Do not go against my warning."

"Well, sir," McNutt said, "if I may … I suppose I am no longer needed here. I have missed the Ritual of Return, and I do regret that, because I was so looking forward to working with you, sir, the heir to the great Horatio Muir."

Randolph smiled. "We could still use you, McNutt. My brother's wife will need training for her eventual Gifting. She has no powers as yet, but they will be bestowed upon her, as I bestowed them upon my wife. We could use another Guardian to train her."

"I am greatly honored, sir," McNutt told him. "But the assignment was to be temporary. You see, I am newly married, with a child—"

"If we brought them here to Ravenscliff to live," Randolph said, "would you be interested in the position?"

"Sir!" McNutt stood, beaming a grin from ear to ear. "Would I ever!"

"Then it's done. Send for them." He gripped McNutt's hand and shook it heartily. "Welcome to Ravenscliff, Ogden McNutt."

Devon couldn't help but feel an overriding sadness as he watched the scene. Part of him wanted to warn McNutt against the idea, to tell him to hurry back to his home in England. If he remained here at Ravenscliff, only one destiny awaited him.

The beast.

But for now Devon did heed Randolph's order to not make any attempts to change the flow of history. For the rest of the day he felt heavy and discouraged—for he had begun to believe that this whole trip back into time would be for nothing. Marcus would still be afflicted by his curse. The Madman would be allowed to return.

And maybe—Devon fought the idea, but it was gaining on him—maybe he was never to go home.

Maybe the future would be destroyed, and the Nightwing fates had sent him back in time to live out his life and avert the tragedy.

No, Devon thought. *I won't accept that.*

If he did, it meant accepting that all his friends would die.

And it would mean accepting the fact that he'd never learn who his real parents were.

I've got to start looking harder for answers, Devon thought. *I've got to find out why the Staircase brought me to this time.*

As usual, he turned to the books of the Nightwing for the

answers he sought. In this time, they were not kept hidden under lock and key in the West Wing. Here they were proudly displayed in the parlor and in Randolph's study. Once his chores were done for the day, Devon hurried to peruse the titles of the books. A slim purple volume on the top shelf in the study jumped out at him right away. Enchanters of the Islands. The book seemed to *glow*—always a good sign that something awaited within for Devon to learn.

"Miranda's family," he whispered to himself as he opened the book and looked upon the frontispiece. It was an engraving of a map of the Caribbean islands, with Martinique circled in red pen. "*My* family," Devon added significantly.

The book revealed there were many island families who practiced magic. Nothing so powerful as the elemental sorcery of the Nightwing, but some of the families had achieved reputations of note. Devon flipped through the pages, letting them fall open to reveal what he needed to learn. There, under a drawing of an obelisk—like the one in the cemetery that would bear the name—was an account of the Devons.

Andres Devon, at the cusp of the twentieth century, allied himself with the great Nightwing sorcerer Quentin Muir.

Below these words was a sepia-tinted photograph of the two men. Quentin Muir was fair and tall. Andres Devon was dark and stocky. Quentin boasted a beard and muttonchop sideburns. Andres was clean-shaven.

Does he look like me? Devon wondered, studying the picture. *Is Andres Devon my ancestor?*

But then his eye dropped to the paragraph beneath the photograph.

After a successful alliance of several years, Andres Devon challenged Quentin Muir's decision to send his son to the Americas. Like many of the lesser wizards, Andres had grown envious of the Nightwing's exalted position, and he had staked out his own power base in the Western hemisphere. But his power was nothing compared to the Nightwing, and eventually Andres was forced to back down, welcoming young Horatio Muir to the Americas. Still, the alliance between the Nightwing and the Devons was severed, and neither trusted the other again.

"That's it," Devon whispered to himself. "That's what drove Miranda. She is proud like her clan. She cannot face her family's subordinate status to the Nightwing. By allying with Jackson, she's hoping to restore her family's greatness the way Andres Devon once allied with Quentin Muir."

As he slid the book back onto the shelf, Devon realized that in his veins ran not only the blood of the Nightwing but also the lesser wizards of the islands. Somehow, apparently, a Devon had gotten together with a Nightwing. Perhaps in England? There were no other Nightwing in the Americas except for the Muirs—

No, wait. Devon realized that wasn't true. There were Native American Nightwing! A rush of excitement suddenly pulsed through his body. Could his real father have been a Native American Nightwing? Could one of them have had a kid with a Devon on the island of Martinique?

It was an idea that fascinated him, and he thought about it the rest of the day, rolling it around in his mind. *Maybe I'm Cherokee. Or Hopi. Or Sioux.*

Whatever his origins, it did seem less and less likely that his mother was Amanda Muir Crandall.

Why had he thought it so? Why had that idea been so compelling? Clarissa had never precisely said so; Devon had simply taken it as her meaning. Cecily pointed out that he was jumping to conclusions. Why had he been so willing to accept the idea as truth—and in the course of doing so, utterly derail his relationship with Cecily?

Wandering through the great house, Devon couldn't deny how much he missed Cecily. He couldn't forget the way she had looked at him right before he left Rolfe's study. Yes, getting to know Natalie had been wonderful, and she had certainly claimed a piece of his heart. But it was *Cecily* he missed most of anybody.

He'd come to realize that more and more. He missed Cecily like mad. Her laugh, her sparkling eyes, the way she tossed her red hair. The way they used to hang out, and talk, and listen to music. The way she kissed him.

Devon scolded himself for feeling like a stupid lovesick puppy. But he really *did* miss her more than he thought could be possible. Maybe it was because there had been so much hostility between them during the last few weeks he'd been there, so many things left unsaid.

And now he might never get home to make it up to her.

The next several days went by in a blur. There was a lot to do, as Devon helped Montaigne and McNutt set up a schedule of lessons that the children would begin in the autumn. With Amanda they would practice levitation, disappearance and mind-over-matter. With Edward it would be mostly exposure to various crystals, allowing the baby to absorb as much fundamental knowledge as possible. Once again, Devon lamented the lack of such instruction in his own childhood, but he realized this teaching process was benefiting him as much as the children.

Sitting with Amanda on the grass, reading the children's storybooks that related the adventures of the great Nightwing of history—Brutus and Diana and Wilhelm of Holland and Vladmir of Moscow, to name just a few—Devon absorbed their exploits for his own enjoyment and education as well.

Meanwhile, summer finally reached its peak in August, with the crowds of tourists never so great as they were in the last three weeks of the month. Devon found time to occasionally head into the village and sit with a plate of fried clams and a Coke—in its commemorative Olympics bottle—overlooking the beach. He was alone, watching the crowds, the kids his age having fun playing volleyball or tanning on blankets. From boom boxes floated the sounds of Michael Jackson's *Thriller*.

But for Devon, it was just a reminder of the things he missed from his own time, like his own music, downloaded onto his iPod. He missed his computer games and Instagram and Twitter and texting.

But most of all he missed Cecily.

Heading back up to Ravenscliff from the village, Devon took the steep cliffside staircase that was built into the rocks at Eagle Hill. It wasn't as crumbling or in as much disrepair as it would be in his own time, but it was still pretty treacherous. At its top the staircase offered a sweeping view of the village below and the sparkling blue-green sea beyond. That always made the climb worthwhile.

The smell of salt water was heavy in the air as Devon trudged through the grass into the Muir family cemetery. Three decades from now the cemetery would be overgrown with weeds and tall grass, but in this time it was still well maintained, fresh and new. The windswept stones that would unnerve him so much in the future were not yet built. There was no monument to Jackson with its broken-winged angel. There was no sad memorial to Emily, proclaiming how she was "lost to the sea." There was also no obelisk that would bear the name Devon.

In fact, the only monuments in the cemetery were those dedicated to Horatio Muir and his wife, as well as a few other stones marking friends and faithful servants.

The last time I was in this place, Devon recalled, *I had a vision of a dead man.* It unnerved him to remember it, so he quickened his pace to get back to Ravenscliff.

He heard a sound. A snap of a branch.

Oh, man, not another zombie, please…

No, not a zombie.

He looked up. The sky had suddenly gone dark. But not a storm …

Birds—ravens!

Hundreds of them! Maybe thousands! The familiars of the Nightwing alit everywhere—in the trees, on the grass, on the stones of the cemetery. They cawed, they cried out, they flapped their wings. One landed on Devon's shoulder.

"What's going on?" Devon asked as the ravens continued to descend from the sky.

He made eye contact with the bird on his shoulder. In its glassy black eye he could see his reflection.

"It's beginning," he whispered, understanding the message of the birds.

The raven flew from his shoulder up into the sky to join the flock. They were heading to Ravenscliff, preparing for the battle. Devon took a long breath to steady himself, and then followed the birds to the great house.

A Month of Omens

The hundreds of new ravens that had taken up roost at Ravenscliff elicited quite the reaction from the townspeople, of course.

"Ayup, I've never seen so many," said old Mr. Parsons, in typical Maine accent, who worked at the cannery. "Not since my Granddaddy took me up the hill to see the place back in the nineteen twenties, and that was when Mr. Horatio Muir was a young man."

The board of selectmen even trudged up the hill to visit, worried that the birds might pose a health hazard for the village. But they quickly observed that the big black birds left very few droppings, a fact that surprised the bespectacled ornithologist who accompanied the selectmen. One bird was actually noticed scraping its residue from a perch with its beak—seeming to clean up after itself!

"Truly remarkable," said the ornithologist, while Randolph and the rest of them simply laughed.

Even Jackson.

Yet the birds' presence kept Devon on high alert all through the month of September. He knew the final conflict wouldn't take place until Halloween, but the arrival of the ravens indicated that mystical forces were roiling. How Jackson could think his plotting would go unnoticed by his brother puzzled Devon. Perhaps it was a sign of his arrogance, Devon surmised, or his madness for power.

"There is still hope, always hope," Randolph told Devon one morning as both walked along the edge of the cliffs overlooking the sea. They were near Devil's Rock, and Devon couldn't help but imagine Emily out there, ready to jump. The summer season was over; the sun, still warm upon their faces, could not obscure the hint of autumn chill in the air. Randolph pulled his cloak around himself tighter and said, "My brother may yet validate my belief in him."

Devon didn't reply. His silence was not unnoticed by Randolph.

"I have not ended my vigilance," the older man assured him. "I have read in my father's books that often a visitor from the future arrives to play devil's advocate, and perhaps that is your role now. To force me to fully consider my relationship with my brother, and ultimately to affirm my faith in him." He smiled. "And I have reason to believe I am justified. For Emily is pregnant now, and surely that will keep Jackson on the path of truth and light."

Devon had stopped in his tracks. "Emily? She's going to have a baby?"

"Yes. It has brought me such hope ..."

"But it's impossible. She can't! She's—"

"Barren? Yes, she thought so, too. Jackson was terribly disappointed when he thought she couldn't give him a child. But she was wrong. For next year there *will* be a child born to them, and I believe that single miracle is enough to keep my brother on the side of the angels."

It couldn't be true. Devon knew history would record Emily as never having a child. But ... was history changing? Had his very presence in this time meant the course of history was going to be different?

And if so, what did that mean for his friends in the future?

From that point on, Devon watched Emily carefully, especially on the day that Ogden McNutt's wife and little daughter arrived from England. How kind Emily was to them, baking them bread and cupcakes, carrying her welcoming gifts to the servants' quarters wrapped in a large basket with a red bow.

"Mrs. Muir," said McNutt's wife, "you are very sweet."

Never would Greta Muir have condescended to carry baked goods to the servants' quarters. But Emily embraced McNutt's wife and stooped down to look into the eyes of the young girl.

"What is your name, my little darling?"

"Georgette," replied the girl.

"What a lovely name." Emily stood. "How precious she is." And she hugged the girl to her. "I hope to have a child just as sweet and good as she is."

How had it happened? Devon was absolutely bewildered. How had Emily become pregnant if she'd been unable to conceive? The Nightwing power did indeed have limits. Jackson couldn't have made such a thing happen with sorcery. How then? How?

In the village, enjoying a few hours off, Devon watched as the local kids headed off to school on their bright yellow school buses, and once more he felt a terrible pang of homesickness. Randolph had warned him that if the local authorities discovered him living on the estate they'd insist he enroll at school. *It might happen*, Devon realized. *If I'm stuck here in the past for much longer, sooner or later I'll have to go back to school ...*

It had now been more than four months that he'd been in the past. *Four months!* Had that much time elapsed in the future too? Had Marcus and Rolfe and Natalie and Cecily and D.J. given up on him?

But then he remembered how relative time was: he hadn't yet been born, so no one was waiting for him, no one was wondering where he was. He could only hope that when he *did* go back home that he arrived not long after he left, so he wouldn't have missed much. That was what had happened the last time he went to the past. But that trip had been brief compared to this ...

The days continued to go by. By the end of September, Devon was finding himself becoming a true youth of his era, dressing in bolo ties and pirate's shirts and even, sometimes, a touch of mascara like Adam Ant. It kind of made him feel more like a sorcerer in some ways—but less and less like Devon March, a kid of the twenty-first century.

"So come with me to a rave tonight, will you?" Miranda asked him, just as September shivered into October.

"A rave?"

"A party at a club in the next town over," she said. "They play a lot of acid house and techno music. You'll love it."

"Can I get in? I mean, I don't have an ID ..."

She smirked. "I should think getting in would be very easy for you."

Devon shrugged. "Only if I'm supposed to. My powers don't work just for fun."

Apparently, he was supposed to. Miranda drove them up to a huge warehouse that was vibrating from the music inside. "See you in a bit?" she asked.

Devon said he'd try. And sure enough, he turned invisible and walked right past the big brute at the door.

Wonder what I'm supposed to learn here? he thought to himself as he rematerialized inside. Some girl with really big teased blond hair saw him and did a double take. She walked away, apparently thinking she'd done too many drugs.

Devon hoped Miranda wasn't into the drug scene. She was related to him somehow, and he felt protective of her. Like a sister.

He found her off to the side, eyes closed, nodding her head along to The Clash.

"Pretty cool, huh?" she asked, opening her eyes to look at him.

Devon glanced around. The place was packed with young people, some teenagers but mostly early twenties. Guys wore big blue mohawks, girls wore skintight black Lycra. He'd been to hell and back, but he'd never been to a place like this before.

"I guess if I'm going to be in this era, I ought to really see it," Devon said.

"Do you want to dance?"

He shrugged. "Why not?"

Devon felt awkward, but Miranda seemed to get into it. She slithered around the dance floor, closing her eyes, tossing her head back. She really was quite pretty, Devon admitted to himself. But he cautioned himself against thinking any more about her. He'd already experienced the agony of liking a girl who might be related to him.

It took a few minutes for Devon to realize that Miranda was high. On what, he wasn't sure. But the way she was moving, the way she was talking, she was definitely on something. It worried him.

"Look," he said, "I think we ought to go ..."

"Go? Teddy Bear, you're no fun."

"I don't want anything to happen to you, Miranda."

She scowled at him. "Nothing can happen to me. Don't you understand?"

"No, I don't. Explain it to me, why don't you?"

She laughed. "Jackson takes good care of me."

Devon turned around and stalked off the dance floor. Miranda followed.

"I don't care if you *are* Nightwing," she seethed. "No one walks away from me!"

He spun on her. "Don't you get it? In a few weeks, you're toast. You're gone. The Madman will see to that. There's going to be a stone for you out there in the cliffside cemetery!"

Even as the words came out of his mouth, Devon realized his blunder. He was forbidden from telling anyone what the future held.

But his words seemed to have no effect. The music continued on. The walls continued to vibrate, the smell of smoke—cigarette and marijuana—still hung in the air.

Miranda was glaring at him. "I was warned that I'd hear such lies," she said, her voice barely audible over the thumping music.

"Believe what you want," Devon said. "But I can't go on pretending the Madman isn't going to attack. I'm going to stop him! If I have to change history to do so, I will."

"You're so infuriating, Teddy Bear! You just refuse to see Jackson for how he really is!"

Devon knew arguing with her was pointless, so he pushed through the crowd and left the hot, stinking club. The night air was cool and smelled fragrant. He walked back to Miranda's car and leaned against it, staring up at the purple sky.

"When the time comes and Jackson regains his rightful place at Ravenscliff," Miranda whispered, coming up behind him, "you'll be sorry you were on the other side."

Devon turned his eyes to her. "You really think he'd settle just for Ravenscliff? You really think, if Jackson had his way, Misery Point would go on like it always has? You think kids will still be able to come to this warehouse and smoke pot and dance? Listen, Miranda, I've seen a village terrorized by demons. It was in England in the fifteenth century. People lived in fear. Demons smashed into their homes and bit off their legs and stole their children. That's what will happen to Misery Point if Jackson Muir gets control of the Hell Hole."

She scrunched up her face. "You are *such* a downer, Teddy Bear."

"Well, I don't know how you can carry on with him."

Miranda smiled. "When you're a little older, you'll understand. When I was your age, I didn't understand love either. But Jackson and I love each other."

Devon pulled away from her. "How can you say that? Especially now that his wife is going to have a baby!"

Miranda smirked. "You don't really believe that, do you?"

Devon said nothing. He just looked at her.

"Emily can't have children." Miranda sighed. "Poor sad Emily! Don't you see, Teddy Bear? Jackson's only made her *think* she's going to have a baby."

"Why would he do that?"

"Because there *will* be a baby born next year," Miranda said. "Except that Emily won't be its mother."

Devon stared at her. "You?" he managed to say.

Miranda nodded. "Of course, I understand the necessity of making Emily *think* it's her child. The baby must not be born in scandal. I'll have the baby, but Emily will believe it's hers. I am willing to make that sacrifice so that my beloved can claim his rightful place as Master of Ravenscliff."

"Your *beloved?*" Devon was disgusted. "You're pathetic! So clueless! He doesn't love you! He's just using you. He loves *Emily!*"

Miranda frowned. "Teddy Bear, my patience with you is growing thin. You need to decide to come over to our side, and you need to decide *soon*."

Devon faced her. "And if I don't, you'll tell Jackson all about me?"

"I should. You're threatening to fight him." She narrowed her eyes at him. "You have the ability to erase my memory of your Nightwing powers. So why don't you?"

"Because I have faith in you, Miranda. I know you will see the Madman for what he is and come around. I know you will!"

She just made a sound in exasperation and stormed off back into the club.

Really smart choice for a pregnant woman.

So that was it. That was how he had it planned. Emily would be mesmerized into thinking Miranda's baby was her own. So would everyone else at Ravenscliff.

But history had already recorded that Jackson never had a child. At least not one that was ever known …

Once again Devon feared for Miranda. Once again he vowed he would change history. He couldn't let the only blood family he'd ever known die at the hands of the Madman.

He dematerialized in the parking lot and intended to reappear in his room at Ravenscliff.

But, in fact, he ended up someplace else.

Someplace he didn't recognize.

It was dark. Very dark. And all he could hear was breathing.

The breathing of an animal.

Or a beast.

The thing's yellow eyes opened in the darkness and then roared.

Lights came on. Devon was back inside the club, and the rave was still going strong, and the beast was suddenly in the midst of the dance floor. It let out a howl and the kids all around it went scattering in terror. It leapt after them, grabbing one by the shoulders.

Devon realized it was Miranda.

"Let her go!" he shouted, lunging for the creature.

But it was too late.

The thing ripped Miranda's head off her shoulders as easily as he might behead a daisy.

Devon screamed.

And sat up in his bed.

He still stunk of the cigarette smoke from the rave. His heart was thudding in his chest. Devon concentrated and was able to see in his mind a glimpse of the rave. There was no beast there. It went on as ever. He saw Miranda, dancing by herself, more spaced out than ever.

He'd had a vision. It wasn't real, but it was telling him something.

I shouldn't have left her there alone.

Devon disappeared from his bed, reappeared beside Miranda on the smoky dance floor, took her by the shoulders, and disappeared again. When he rematerialized, he was in Miranda's room with her. He eased her down onto the bed, and she was asleep as soon as her head hit the pillow. He kissed her on the forehead then faded away.

She was safe. For now.

They'd worry about her car in the morning.

The leaves on the trees began to change color, turning from green to yellow with tinges of red. Watching the metamorphosis sent Devon into a depression. It had been in the autumn that he'd first come to Ravenscliff in his own time. A year had passed since then, but now instead of living in the great house in the twenty-first century, he was stuck in the past, gearing up to watch the destruction of people he had come to care about deeply.

"You there, boy," came a voice.

Devon was walking down the stairs into the foyer when he looked around to see Jackson Muir in the doorway of the parlor, beckoning to him.

"I'll have a word with you," Jackson said.

Devon's heart began to race but he steadied it. He followed the Madman, who was dressed in his sorcerer's cape and boots, into the parlor.

Sitting in a chair beside the fireplace was Emily, her chin lifted, her hands clasped in her lap. Across from her, Ogden McNutt's wife was painting her portrait, the one that would hang on the far wall in Devon's own time.

"We didn't know what talents she had," Emily said, smiling as she looked over at Devon. She returned her head to the proper position. "I've never had my portrait painted before."

"I'm sure it's going to be very beautiful," Devon said, his voice thick with emotion. He knew she wouldn't live to see it hanging there very long.

Jackson stared at his wife with obvious pride and affection. "The portrait is in honor of Emily being Gifted with powers," he said, turning his eyes to Devon. "I want you to bring up the books on the Gifting ritual. We must start preparations. I want her to have her powers before the arrival of the child."

Devon looked over at Emily. How she beamed, thinking she really was carrying Jackson's child. The teenager's heart broke.

"Now, listen, boy," Jackson said, leaning down to bring his eyes close to Devon's. "There can be no mistakes, no errors, no glitches. I want the ritual to be perfect. Do you understand?"

Devon held his gaze. "Of course. I understand."

Their eyes locked onto each other's for several seconds longer than necessary. *He suspects me of something*, Devon thought. *Ever since that night in the basement, he's been watching me. He's not sure what threat I pose, if any—but he's watching me nonetheless.*

Finally Jackson moved his black eyes away. "Go on with you," he said, and with a wave of his hand he dismissed Devon from his sight.

In the basement, Devon searched for the books.

A small furry spider dropped onto his hand.

A spider that burned.

The heat.

Devon tried to shake the spider from his hand, but the tenacious little thing clung on. Peering down at it, Devon could see the spider had a tiny head, like a human's, and it was chomping down with sharp little teeth on the skin on the back of his hand.

"Oh, this is the best you can do?" Devon said out loud. "Is this the most ferocious demon the Hell Hole has to cough up?"

He whacked his hand against the concrete wall, splattering the demon spider.

He pulled his hand away. Yellow and green spider guts dripped down the wall, stinking like rotten eggs. Devon looked down at his hand. The bite wasn't too large or sore. But it was very red and starting to swell.

I'll have to ask Montaigne for a remedy, Devon thought.

But for the moment he continued searching for the books on Gifting. He supposed the spider was another demon who'd recognized Devon and was fighting its master's battle, even if Jackson wasn't clued in to Devon's identity yet. But, really, a demon spider? The size of a nickel? Like such a thing represented any kind of danger ...

Devon laughed.

But then his hand started to itch.

"Oh, great," he mumbled. "An allergic reaction to a demon spider bite."

Now his wrist was itching too. And now his arm.

Devon pushed up his shirtsleeve and looked at his skin.

A dozen raised lines, like swollen veins, stretched from his hand, from the spot where he'd been bitten, all the way up to his shoulder.

And as Devon stared, the lines began to vibrate.

Things were moving up and down his arm!

Devon gasped out loud.

All at once, the lines burst. His skin tore open in long, painful slits, and out crawled tens of thousands of baby demon spiders, no bigger than commas on a printed page. They swarmed all over his arm and up his neck and into his hair.

Devon screamed.

"Take it easy!" came a voice.

It was Montaigne.

"I had a premonition you needed me," the Guardian said. "Hold on. Don't move. And close your eyes!"

Devon obeyed. But just before he did, he saw that Montaigne had in his hand what looked like a giant can of Raid.

He sprayed Devon with it. It smelled like mothballs. The spray settled all over Devon, and he could feel the spiders dropping off his body.

"This will just numb them," Montaigne explained. "You'll still have to send them back yourself."

Devon was completely grossed out. "Back to your Hell Holes," he said under his breath, and suddenly all the little spiders just popped into nothingness.

Montaigne was wrapping his wounded arm. "The bandages will facilitate the healing. The wounds should be mostly gone by morning."

In that moment, it seemed to Devon that it was Rolfe tending to him. His father resembled him so uncannily. They sounded alike. Even smelled alike. Devon missed his friend and mentor.

"I know I'm not supposed to reveal anything about the future," Devon said. "But I need to tell you that your kid grows up to be one very cool guy."

Montaigne smiled. "That is not revealing anything I had not already surmised. But merci beaucoup, Devon. It is good to hear."

Devon just wished Montaigne would be around to see Rolfe grow up. He was sure going to do what he could to make sure that happened.

The whole of the next week was spent in preparation of Emily's Gifting. It would take place on November 1, the day after Halloween. But the closer they got to that date, the more anxious Devon became.

How will I stop what is about to happen? I've got to keep Emily from discovering the truth about Jackson and Miranda. But if I can't do that, then I've got to get Miranda to admit it ahead of time, to renounce Jackson and leave Ravenscliff.

But knowing how ambitious Miranda was, how prideful she was about her heritage, Devon couldn't imagine her willingly walking away from what she saw as a chance at greatness.

"I've got to tell someone what I know," Devon said out loud to himself, suddenly looking up from the book he was reading in Randolph's study. "I'm going to need help if I'm to prevent the tragedies. I've got to reveal what I know from the future."

"And what might that be?"

Devon looked around. It was Ogden McNutt, coming up behind him with another stack of books in his arms.

"Ogden," Devon said. "I was just—just talking to myself."

"I have been to the future of which you speak," McNutt reminded him. "The man Rolfe mentioned a boy about your age who disappeared. A boy by the name of Devon."

"Oh yeah? What did he tell you about this Devon?"

"That he had gone off in search of a way to end the curse of the beast."

Devon nodded, looking back down at the book. "Yeah, he did. But he hasn't been very successful."

"You are this Devon, are you not?"

Devon nodded.

"But what does the boy Marcus some thirty years from now have to do with all of us here?" Ogden asked. "What is it that you need to tell?"

Devon looked back up at him. Perhaps McNutt was the confidante he needed. After all, it would be McNutt's ghost who would warn him in the future.

"All right," Devon said. "I am here, I think, to prevent some terrible tragedies from happening. I thought at first the Staircase Into Time had brought me here simply to teach me something, to give me the opportunity to learn ways to help my friends in the future. But now I think, given how long I've been stuck here, that my fate is to save the people of this time."

"Save us from what?"

"That much I'm not sure I can reveal."

"But you must."

"No. You see, I don't know if by trying to change history I will change the events of the future beyond all recognition. If I can end Marcus's curse, I will be glad, of course. But I may also end up changing other things." He looked significantly into McNutt's eyes. "Perhaps my own existence."

"Randolph Muir told us we cannot change history."

Devon suddenly felt desperate. "I've got to try! No matter what it might mean for me! Look, McNutt, you trust me, don't you?"

"You are Nightwing. I am here to serve you."

Devon smiled. "You have kept my secret, and I am grateful. So listen to me when I tell you that one of the greatest lessons I have learned is that with my great abilities come great responsibilities and all that sort of stuff."

It was Ogden's turn to smile. "Yes, and all that sort of stuff."

"So I wouldn't be very noble if I just looked away when I knew people in this house were going to die, would I?"

McNutt's face betrayed fear. "People will die in this house? Who, Devon? Who will die?"

Devon hesitated. "Will you help me, Ogden? Help me prevent the tragedies?"

"Yes, of course! Tell me what you know!"

Devon looked around to make sure they were alone. "Randolph has forbidden me to tell of future events. He said it is against the order of time travel. But I will tell you. You are not Nightwing. Perhaps you can do what he can't."

"Tell me!" Ogden was growing insistent. "I have a wife and baby daughter in this house! Please tell me they will be safe."

"I don't know about their fate," Devon admitted. "All I know is … on the night of Halloween, Emily Muir will discover Jackson with another woman and jump to her death from Devil's Rock."

"No!"

"And her death will set into motion great evil in this house. You see, Jackson has not repented. He is planning to open the Hell Hole. He is planning to use the demons to achieve the kind of power and wealth he's always dreamed of having."

McNutt glanced behind him, suddenly terrified. "We must stop it from happening. That must be why you came back in time. To save us!"

"And you," Devon said gently, resting his hand on McNutt's shoulder. "You, too, are in danger, Ogden."

But he couldn't tell him what kind of danger. He just couldn't bring himself to describe the future that awaited poor McNutt. Maybe later but ... not now.

"I do not fear for myself," Ogden said.

"Still," Devon added, "if we can prevent the other tragedies, we can hopefully save you as well."

"I do not fear for myself," Ogden repeated, a premonition of doom settling into his eyes. "I fear for my dear wife ... and my precious little Gigi."

Devon reacted to the name.

"Your daughter?" he asked. "What did you call her?"

Ogden McNutt gave him a weak smile. "Her name is Georgette, of course, but we call her Gigi. Our little Gigi."

Gigi.

Of course.

That was the name of Marcus's mother! Devon had heard Marcus's father call her by that name.

So Ogden McNutt's daughter would grow up to be Marcus's mother! Which made Ogden McNutt Marcus's grandfather! That was how Marcus got the curse of the beast! It was passed down through the generations and must have emerged at a certain age—like sixteen, which Marcus had just turned. And it must have only included boys, because Marcus was Ogden's next male descendant!

The question now was: how would that curse begin, and how could it be stopped?

Devon realized the only way to free Marcus of the curse of the beast in the future was to prevent Ogden from ever being cursed in the first place.

One more bit of history he was determined to change.

Devon had now been in the past for almost as long as he had lived in Ravenscliff in the future. It was a strange realization. His life here had become normalized.

He no longer woke up expecting to see Cecily, or Alexander, or Bjorn. He no longer automatically reached for his phone to send a text or check Facebook. He no longer jumped when the telephone on the kitchen wall rang, or thought it was odd to use a rotary dial to make a call. He no longer missed his old television shows, or his favorite music, or felt surprised when he saw old-fashioned cars on the road. In fact, they no longer looked old-fashioned to him.

I've become part of this time, Devon thought.

I'm never going back to the future.

But no. He wouldn't accept that yet. Not until after Halloween. He was here until then. After that, he would go home.

He was here for a reason, he believed.

I'm here to change history.

But to do that, he needed people to do things differently than they had in the original course of events.

He decided to tell Miranda everything.

She sat there, listening to him with wide, shocked eyes. He told her everything that would happen. He told her how Emily would die—and how he would end up fighting the Madman in his own time.

But Miranda would hear nothing bad about Jackson.

Her face darkened. "I know how cunning you Nightwing can be," she seethed. "My father and my grandfather warned me about it when I came here. How you sorcerers play tricks with people's minds to get them to bend to your will."

"No, Miranda, no true Nightwing would do such a thing.

But a renegade like Jackson might …"

"It is *you*, Teddy Bear, who walks the path of the renegade! You who flirt with apostasy!"

Devon made a face. "You're even beginning to talk like him now!" He leaned in close. "How does he plan on doing it? Tell me! How does he plan to convince Emily that your child is hers? Will you be sent away? Will she be hypnotized even further?"

"I'll tell you nothing." She folded her arms across her chest and glared at him with her dark eyes. "Our friendship is over, Teddy Bear. Sad but true, but this is the place where we must part. Do nothing to interfere, I warn you—or else I will tell Jackson about you. You will have forced me into it."

"If it gets to that point, I *will* erase your memories of me," Devon threatened right back. "It will be *you* who will have forced *me* into taking action."

She spun on her heel, her black hair swinging behind her, and stomped off. Devon let out a long sigh.

If Miranda wouldn't budge, then he would have to approach someone else. Someone else who might be persuaded to stop the tragedy before it occurred.

Jackson Muir himself.

Devon spied on him, protected by his invisibility. The Madman stood once again at the Hell Hole in the middle of the night, saying nothing, simply staring at the portal and resting his palms against its metal door. When he made a move to turn and head upstairs, Devon leapt ahead and met the renegade sorcerer as he walked up the basement stairs.

"Sir," Devon said.

Jackson's eyes met his, annoyed as he might be by a pesky fly. That was all Devon was to him in this time. An annoying little insect.

"What *is* it, boy?"

"I just wanted to go over the plans for the Gifting ritual with you."

Jackson sighed. "It is late. I am tired. Talk to me tomorrow."

"But, sir, I plan to meet with Mrs. Muir first thing. If I could just ask you a question …"

Jackson stopped, leaning against the wall and closing his eyes. He looked so human, so vulnerable, that in that moment Devon couldn't fear him. He was just a man, a weary, and perhaps even frightened, man—frightened of what he was about to do. He was taking a great risk. If he'd ever cared about his brother before, the idea of putting Randolph and his family in such danger must have troubled him, even a little bit.

Devon stepped forward and cleared his throat.

"Well, sir, what I want to know is how I should to talk with her about the responsibility that comes with great power."

The Madman opened his black eyes and fixed them on Devon.

Devon continued speaking. "A Nightwing pledges himself or herself to the light, to the pursuit of good, forsaking all personal gain. Isn't that right, sir?"

Jackson Muir just continued to stare at him with eyes as black and glassy as a raven's.

"This is what the Guardians have always taught," Devon said, astonished that he was actually standing there lecturing the Madman about good and evil, right and wrong. "Good is its own reward," he said, and his voice was steady, calm, and cool, "and the path of greed and desire can lead only to apostasy. These are the truths that have been affirmed by all great Nightwing, from Sargon to your father, Horatio Muir."

Jackson's eyes narrowed as he studied Devon.

Is he hearing me? Might I be able to reach him? Might I touch the conscience I know exists within him? Might I be able to stop him even now, to change his plans, to forever change the course of history?

What would happen if Jackson Muir truly repented his evil ways? Emily would live. The cataclysm that would one day descend upon Ravenscliff would be averted, and the Muirs would not have to renounce their sorcery. Instead of bitterness and denial, the great house of the future would be filled with welcome when Devon arrived there—welcome and eagerness to train him in his powers and teach him his heritage …

Or else, time would collapse in on itself.

That's what Randolph warned would happen if I tried to

change history.

But Devon couldn't help but make the attempt. Halloween was getting closer and closer ...

"With Nightwing power comes responsibility," he said again, remembering the lessons taught him by both Montaigne *père* and *fils*. "And accountability ..."

"Do you think I do not know the lessons, little Guardian?"

Jackson spoke in a soft, calm, unemotional voice, but there was emotion in his eyes. Devon could see it. Anger, sadness, regret, guilt, fear. And he could feel the heat now being put off by Jackson. A staggering, damp, sorcerer's heat ...

Devon swallowed. "I'm just going over what I will teach your wife."

"My wife has all good qualities. You need not teach her anything she already knows."

"But that is our role, sir. We Guardians teach ..."

Suddenly the Madman's arm thrust out and grabbed Devon by the shirt collar.

"I need no lessons," he snarled, "from a boy such as you."

Devon choked back his fear. Jackson loomed over him now, bearing down at him with his black eyes and twisted mouth.

"There's something about you, boy," he said. "Something I don't like. You've been an inconsequential little gnat to me up until now. But suddenly I don't like the way you *smell*. I don't like the curve of your lip or the light in your eyes." He moved in even closer, his whisky breath in Devon's face. "I don't think I want you around here any more."

"I serve at your brother's pleasure," Devon reminded him.

"Ah, yes. My brother." Jackson snorted. "The Master of Ravenscliff."

He let Devon go.

"Be gone out of my sight, little gnat," the Madman growled. "Cross not my path from here on. And know that I will be watching you."

Devon knew it was time to make a hasty retreat.

All he'd managed to do, he realized, was harden Miranda's resolve and further Jackson's suspicions. If he'd been trying to prevent what was destined to occur, he'd made a major muck of it. He'd probably made it *more* likely to happen now, not less.

History cannot be changed.

"I won't accept that," Devon said out loud, alone in his room. "Not while there's still time. Still hope. If Randolph can still have hope, then so can I."

But things began to happen that tested that hope. As the leaves began to change into a deep rusty bronze, then fall from their branches under the cold northern wind, noises were heard emanating from the Hell Hole in the basement. Concerned over the reason for the demons' restlessness, Randolph built a room around the portal, sealing off the entrance to anyone but himself.

"No one," he assured Devon, "will now have access to that portal except for me."

Yet a few days later a demon was detected perched on one of the eaves of the house, pretending to be a stone gargoyle. Randolph sent it promptly back to its Hell Hole, but talk in the great house centered around where the creature came from, and why it was here. "I am beginning to question," Greta Muir said to her husband, "exactly how much apostasy Jackson left behind."

Devon was eavesdropping from his room.

"I am watching him," Randolph assured his wife. "I still want to believe he is reformed, but I am prepared for him if he is not."

But on a crisp late October morning Amanda woke up screaming.

There was a snake in her bed.

A long, green, shiny snake with the head of a cat. It hissed as Randolph approached, followed by Greta and Devon.

"Back to your Hell Hole!" Randolph shouted.

The snake was gone. The girl was safe.

But Randolph turned to Devon, a deep sadness in his eyes, and asked simply, "It's beginning, isn't it?"

"Yes, sir, I think it is. I think—"

Randolph lifted a hand to silence Devon. "I will have Greta take the children away today. I do not want to risk their safety."

So Greta Muir, pretending a visit with her family in the Midwest, bundled the two children into the long black car and drove off.

Later that same day, Ogden McNutt sought out Devon. "Jackson is doing something in the room off the upstairs parlor," the English Guardian informed him. "He won't let anyone in, not even Emily. The servants have told me how they hear him in there, struggling, grunting, crying out, as if exerting some huge effort."

"Randolph should know about this," Devon said.

"I told him. He said he'd given the West Wing to Jackson to live in. He is bound by a sorcerer's honor not to move in and take it back from him."

Devon slammed his right fist into his left palm. "You know, all this noble Nightwing crap is making me want to puke!"

"Sir—?"

"The Madman is planning to take down this house and Randolph sticks to this ridiculous code of honor!"

McNutt looked aghast. "It is clear, Devon, you are *not* a Guardian. For if you were, you would never call the Nightwing honor code ridiculous. It has been what has kept us all on the path of light. It has been what has kept us allied with the angels instead of the demons, what separates us from the petty wizards and witches—what keeps true Nightwing from the Apostates. You can be sure that Randolph will not be caught unawares. He is too clever for that. But neither will he trample on our sacred, cherished beliefs. He is a true and noble Nightwing."

Devon felt suitably chagrined.

There was no mistaking that the energy in the house had changed. The servants avoided Jackson as much as possible as he stalked through the house, rarely dressed in anything other than his ceremonial sorcerer's costume of black cape, red shirt and trousers, and tall black boots. "He's a madman," Devon heard one of them whisper.

It was a phrase repeated in the village as sightings of strange creatures among the trees suddenly became widespread. Schoolchildren reported seeing flying monkeys and two-headed tigers. A huge flying creature was spotted soaring over the cliffs. "If I didn't know better," said the farmer who'd seen it, "I'd'a said it was a pterodactyl."

The old legends about ghosts and demons at Ravenscliff resurfaced.

Blame was placed on the strange Muir brother who had returned from his world travels amid stories of dalliance with black magic. Once again, as they had during the days of Horatio Muir, the villagers began to suspect supernatural activity taking place in the great house on the hill.

And so, at last, Halloween arrived.

Devon awoke early and turned on the TV. It was times like these that he suddenly remembered things like a weather app on his phone. How long ago that seemed. How easy it had been to see if it was going to be sunny or going to rain. Instead, he sat there in front of the TV waiting for a news update before he learned what the weather was supposed to be that day.

And, of course. Thunderstorms were threatening.

He also saw that the moon would be full tonight.

Devon's research in the future had revealed that the beast would make its first appearance on Halloween night, the same date as Emily's death.

Could he prevent both?

If he could somehow stop the curse of the beast in this time, he could divert Marcus from it as well. If Ogden was never cursed, then he'd never pass it on to Marcus.

Of course, he knew he might never see Marcus again. As much as he hoped he'd be going back to his own time after today, he had no idea if that would really happen.

But even if it didn't, at least he'd know he'd saved his friend from that horrible curse in the future.

Ogden McNutt entered the room.

"The Gifting ritual is slated for tomorrow, November the first," he said. "I am preparing the ceremonial robes ..."

"It will never occur," Devon said, "unless I can prevent what's destined to happen tonight."

McNutt looked frightened. "Do you have a plan?"

Devon smirked. "Do I look like I have a plan?"

"I don't know, sir."

His smirk turned to a scowl. "Don't call me sir. I'm just a kid."

"You're a sorcerer of the ancient rod—"

Devon raised his hand to silence him. "Yeah, yeah, I know. But right now I just feel like a kid." He sighed. "I have no idea what to do. I've been trying to think of something but ... I don't know when or where things will happen."

"What set the events into motion?" McNutt asked.

"Well, Emily found Jackson with Miranda ... and then she ran to the cliffs and jumped, and then Jackson got so upset that he destroyed everything."

"Well, then, it seems to me ..." McNutt began.

Devon had the same idea at the same time.

"That we've got to keep Emily from ever seeing Jackson with Miranda," he said, finishing McNutt's sentence.

The Guardian nodded.

"That's it!" Devon exclaimed. "If we can get through the night without Emily ever seeing the two of them together, then everything can be avoided. Emily will live—and I will have changed history!"

"Oh, good luck, sir—I mean, Devon."

Devon gave him a little salute and hurried out into the corridor. Miranda's room was at the far end of the house, where Jackson could easily slip in and out. Devon stood outside her door. He sensed she was inside. He took a deep breath, then knocked.

"Come in," she said.

He opened the door. Miranda was sitting on her bed, caressing her belly. That was the Madman's child she carried. For a second Devon wondered what would become of that child if he managed to change history tonight.

"Well, I suppose you've come to wish me a happy Halloween," Miranda said, giving him a sarcastic face. Devon had told her this was the day he was dreading. "Is that why you've come barging into my room?"

"No," he said. "That's not why."

Her face turned defiant and suspicious as she stood up to face him. "Then what *do* you want, Teddy Bear?"

"Just a moment of your time," Devon replied. "Literally."

In that moment he froze her. Miranda stood there unmoving, unblinking, not breathing, in the middle of her room.

"You'll be fine when you wake up," Devon promised her. "I'm doing this for your own good. For the good of all of us."

With one nod of his head, he then caused her to shrink to the size of a small doll.

He walked over to her and picked her up. "Forgive me, Miranda," Devon whispered, settling her inside the pocket of his jacket. "You're going to pretty angry with me, I'm sure, but I'll deal with that tomorrow."

He looked off through the window.

"Tomorrow," he echoed. "When the whole world will be a different place."

Outside the sun had begun to rise up into the sky.

All during the day, Devon noticed Jackson stalking around the house, clearly looking for Miranda. But he never asked about her. He seemed to suspect that something was wrong, but he did not voice a word.

At one point, Devon saw Randolph take Jackson into the parlor and close the doors. He tried to eavesdrop but Randolph's own sorcery prevented it. All he could hear were angry, muffled voices. Before too long, Jackson bolted out of the room and across the foyer and out onto the estate.

Maybe he was leaving. Maybe Devon had already changed history!

Montaigne approached him and asked what was happening. Devon replied that for now, he'd just have to trust him. Something told him that he needed to keep secret what he held in his pocket, even from Montaigne.

"I've drawn a pentagram around Rolfe's room," Montaigne told him, "and I've asked McNutt to keep him in there all day. His wife and daughter are in there, too. I hope that will protect them, if something is going to happen."

Devon knew all three would survive what was coming, so he felt confident telling Montaigne that the pentagram would keep them safe.

The day dragged out. Devon had never felt so anxious in his life. Every once in a while he'd reach down into his pocket to check on the little doll he kept there. She was there, hard and cold as ceramic.

And then, late in the afternoon, the sun began to set over the horizon, just as a thunderstorm rolled in off the sea. Thunder crashed.

Halloween night had arrived.

THE BIRTH OF THE BEAST

"Too bad little Amanda is not here," said Emily Muir as she helped paint whiskers on young Rolfe Montaigne's cheeks. He was dressed as a lion. "She could go trick-or-treating with you as a lioness."

Devon considered the irony of her statement, knowing the history those two would have. But he didn't really have the time or the heart to think about anything else except what was supposed to happen this night.

For Rolfe, his trick-or-treating would be confined to his room in Montaigne's cottage. Randolph had come by to give him a small, glowing, candy jack-o-lantern that spoke to him, wishing him "Happy Halloween." Rolfe promptly took a bite.

Emily, totally unaware of what the night might bring, had baked gingerbread cookies in the shapes of witches and ghosts and—another irony, Devon thought—moons. She dropped several into the little boy's paper sack.

"I don't know why he couldn't have come up to Ravenscliff," Emily said. "I had hoped to decorate the parlor for the occasion."

"Too many roiling forces on Halloween, especially in a place like this," Montaigne said. "That's why I prefer the boy to stay within the pentagram tonight." He paused. "In fact, ma'am, why don't you stay here with us?"

At the moment, the door to Montaigne's cottage was thrown open. Jackson stood silhouetted against the night sky in the doorway.

Devon's heart leapt into his throat. He coaxed it back down to his chest.

"Emily!" the Madman barked. "I have been looking for you."

"I'm here bringing Halloween treats," she said.

Her husband took a few steps into the cottage but paused on the other side of the pentagram that was drawn upon the floor around Rolfe's room. He did not step across it.

"Come back with me to Ravenscliff," the Madman told his wife, his voice softer now.

"Yes, of course, Jackson," Emily said.

Her husband eyed his brother. "I expected dinner waiting for me at Ravenscliff, but there was none. Where is that servant girl? Miranda?"

Randolph stared icily back at him. "I would prefer that you not call her, or *any* of our Guardians, servants. They may reside with the cooks and the housemaids, but they are our teachers, our partners, our friends."

Jackson smiled in mock repentance. "Of course, Randolph. As ever, you are right, and I am out of line." He looked over at his wife. "Shall we go back to the house, my dear?"

"Yes, of course."

Jackson turned and strode off into the night. Emily followed.

Devon grinned to himself, reaching into his pocket to pat Miranda again.

It's going to be okay, he thought. *He'll never find Miranda, so Emily will never see them together.*

Outside, the storm rose in intensity. The electric lights flickered, then went off.

"We should go back," Randolph announced to Devon.

"I'll go with you," Montaigne said.

"As will I," McNutt added.

Devon watched as each man turned and kissed the head of the child they were leaving behind. "We will be safe here," McNutt's wife said.

Devon agreed they would be. He knew the power of the pentagram.

But as he trudged back up to Ravenscliff behind Randolph, thunder and lightning crashing overhead, he had to wonder if he would be.

When they got to the great house, the power was off.

Randolph waved his hand and the dozens of candles, which always stood ready, were suddenly lit. The soft amber glow of candlelight suffused the foyer.

Emily came out of the parlor to greet them. "I like candlelight better, actually," she said. Behind her, Jackson was holding a snifter of brandy.

"Certainly more appropriate for Halloween," Randolph said with a laugh as he moved into the parlor to pour some brandy for himself.

Devon entered the room as well. He felt eyes on him. He glanced over at Jackson. The Madman might have been lifting the brandy snifter to his lips, but his black eyes were trained on Devon.

"A toast," Randolph proposed, lifting his brandy. "To Emily. Tomorrow you will join us as a Sorceress of the Nightwing."

She looked near tears. "I could never have imagined such a glorious life. Thank you, Randolph, for welcoming me to Ravenscliff." She turned, lifting her glass to Ogden McNutt, who stood off to the side of the room with Montaigne. "Thank you, Ogden, for teaching me so much of the Nightwing tradition." Finally she turned and faced her husband. "And thank you, most of all, my beloved Jackson, for making me your wife."

The anger and suspicion in his eyes faded away as the Madman turned his gaze to Emily. Devon could see how much he loved her, even if he cheated on her, even if he lied to her, even if he planned a future for her that she would detest.

"You are my entire world," he said to Emily, taking her hand and bringing it to his lips.

"No," came a tiny voice.

Only Devon heard it. There was movement in his pocket.

Miranda had broken free of her immobilization. Even now the little creature was attempting to crawl out of Devon's pocket.

Devon hurried out of the room as she crawled up his sleeve. He plucked her off his jacket between his thumb and forefinger as if she were cricket. In the safety of a dark corridor, he held her in front of his face.

"Let me go!" Miranda called out in a tiny voice, thrashing

and kicking between Devon's fingers. "Undo whatever you've done to me!"

"I can't," he told her, "not until tomorrow." He looked in at her more closely. "How did you break free anyway?"

"You've never given much credit to the magic of my family, have you? Well, I'm not just some girl you can freeze up and shrink down, Teddy Bear! I am a *Devon*!"

"Shh," he cautioned her.

"Jackson!" she screamed, but her little voice was too weak to be heard.

Still, taking no chances, Devon dropped her back into his pocket. This time he zipped it shut.

Of course, now he was worried she'd suffocate. So he rushed down the hallway to the kitchen, where he grabbed the first jar he could find. It was a nearly empty container of peanut butter. He took a knife and punctured several holes in the lid. Then he hurried upstairs to his room.

Once safely behind closed doors, he unscrewed the lid, scooped Miranda out of his pocket, and plopped her inside. She was ankle-deep in peanut butter.

"Gross!" she screamed in her tiny doll voice.

Devon screwed the lid back on the jar.

"Sorry," he said. "You'll understand one day. I hope."

"You'll pay for this!" Miranda screeched. "When Jackson finds out, he'll have no mercy on you! And I won't save you! I'll let him do whatever he wants to you!"

There was a knock at his door.

"Who is it?" Devon asked.

"It's Ogden."

Devon let McNutt inside.

"Are we safe?" the Englishman asked. "Have we diverted the course of history?"

"We won't know until the end of the night. But I think we have a good shot. We have to keep them apart until morning."

McNutt looked around the room. "But where is Miranda? What have you done with her?"

Devon grinned, pleased with himself. He lifted the peanut

butter jar from the side of his bed and showed McNutt. Inside, Miranda was pouting, sitting on a mound of peanut butter, her tiny arms wrapped around her tiny knees pulled up close to her tiny body.

"Very clever," McNutt said. "And at least she won't starve."

Devon tried not to laugh.

But the seriousness of the situation once again hit him. He set the jar down on the table and moved over to the window to look out into the night. "There's one other danger we have to avoid tonight," he said. "Behind those storm clouds there lurks a full moon. At some point those clouds will go away, and the moon will be revealed."

"But what do we need to fear from the moon?"

"A curse." Devon leveled his eyes at him just as an extremely loud thunderclap reverberated through the house. "A curse that will be passed down through the generations. You need to go to back to your wife and daughter now, Ogden, and stay there. Do not come out of the cottage for anyone or anything. Do you hear me? Stay there until this night over!"

McNutt smiled. "You need not fear for me, young master."

"But I do."

"I have protection," McNutt said.

"Protection from whom?"

Again McNutt smiled as he backed out of Devon's room. "Just put all your fears to rest, young sir. Everything is going to be fine."

Devon watched him as he left, puzzled by his change in attitude. McNutt had been as frightened as he was. Why was he now so calm and reassured?

That was when Devon looked back at the table and noticed the lid was off the jar of peanut butter, and Miranda was gone.

"Stop him!" Devon shouted as he ran after McNutt, but the young man was nowhere to be found in the house. Neither was Randolph or Jackson, for that matter. In the parlor stood only Emily, looking out at the storm, candlelight dancing across her face.

"Teddy, what has gotten you so aroused?" she asked.

"I've got to find Ogden. Or Randolph—"

"I haven't seen them since they left the parlor …"

Devon turned to dash out of the room and ran straight into Montaigne. "What's going on?" the Guardian asked.

"I've got to talk to you!"

They hurried down the hall into the study and Devon told him everything.

"You talk madness," Montaigne said.

"No, no, it's true! Jackson must have put McNutt under his power! I shouldn't have trusted him! I shouldn't have trusted anyone but myself! I got cocky and showed him the jar! He must have taken Miranda out and brought her to Jackson. Now—if we don't stop things from happening—Emily will die!"

Montaigne's face had gone pale. "I'll talk with Randolph," he said.

"No need," came a voice behind them. "I've heard it all."

It was Randolph Muir. The master of Ravenscliff stood in the doorway behind them with a terrible, defeated look on his face.

"It goes against all the rules of time," he said hoarsely, "but I had to listen. I had to hear what the boy had to say."

Devon rushed up to him and grabbed his coat. "We still have time," he said.

Randolph looked down at him significantly. "Do we?" he asked.

In that instant, Devon's Nightwing vision allowed him to see what was happening upstairs in the West Wing.

Emily was heading down the corridor to her husband's study.

"We've got to stop her!" Devon shouted. "We've got to stop Emily from going into that room!"

They all started to run.

Devon could see Emily getting closer to the study.

He tried to disappear and reappear in the corridor but was

unable to do so. He didn't have time to wonder why. He just ran up the steps as fast as he could, Randolph and Montaigne fast on his heels.

Clearly concerned by Devon's anxious state, Emily had gone off in search of her husband. She must not find him!

Devon could see her hand on the knob of the door to the study.

"Emily!" he shouted.

He saw in his mind's eye the way she turned when she heard her name echoing down the corridor, but she did not pause. She opened the door and walked inside.

Devon cleared the top of the stairs and booked down the hallway, desperate to get there in time.

But he was too late. Emily stood in the doorway. There, a smelly, messy, but normal-sized Miranda was in Jackson's arms.

"Choose, Jackson!" Miranda was demanding. "Choose her or me!"

Devon could see it all clearly even though he was still some yards away from the study.

Jackson's black eyes saw Emily in the doorway. He thrust the peanut-butter-smeared Miranda away from him. "I love my wife!" he roared.

Devon could see the rage that suddenly distorted Miranda's face. He saw the magic of the islands fill her eyes.

"Is that so?" she seethed, making a sound like a pot of tea reaching a boil. She spun on Emily.

"Is this what you want, Emily Muir?" Miranda snarled. "Is this the life you would gratefully accept as your own?"

And just as Devon arrived at the door he saw what Miranda conjured. As if projected onto a screen, terrible images filled the room. Slimy green hands crept out of the Hell Hole. Randolph lay dead in a shimmering pool of blood. Little Amanda and Edward were crumpled by his side. The vision of Jackson Muir grew into monstrous size until he loomed over the black spires of Ravenscliff.

Emily screamed.

The scene continued to unfold: the demons got down on

their knees, slobbering and gnashing their teeth.

"All hail our new master!" they chanted. "All hail the child of our destiny!"

"My child," Miranda taunted, her eyes flashing as she patted her belly. "Not yours, Emily! Not yours!"

Emily screamed again.

Then she turned and fled, pushing past Devon with such a force that he nearly fell off his feet.

"Stop her!" Devon shouted as Emily headed for the stairs.

But for all his sorcery—for all of Randolph's—they could not stop her. She sailed down the stairs, hair and tears flying.

Jackson bolted from the study, intending to follow her, but Miranda was all at once on his back like a she-cat, snarling and clawing his face.

"You promised me, you filthy, lying Nightwing!" she screamed.

They were all stunned as they witnessed her assault.

"You lied to me, just as your ancestors lied to mine! I should have known never to trust a Nightwing! Now taste the fury of the Devons!"

Her nails gouged into his eyes as she clung to his back. Blood streamed down his face. He screamed in pain. He was trying to shake her off his back, but the great Nightwing found he was powerless against her. He was at the mercy of this second-rate witch, one whose powers should never have been able to get this far. He had underestimated her. They had all underestimated her.

Underestimated all of the Devons and the enchanters of the islands.

From the shadows staggered McNutt. Devon could see from his eyes that his will was once again his own.

"What have I done?" McNutt cried. "Oh, what have I done?"

"Go after her," Montaigne told him, pointing behind them in the direction Emily had fled. "The three of us need to try to contain Jackson. But you can go after Emily and bring her back here!"

"No," Devon told him. "What matters right now is Emily. If we can stop her from jumping off Devil's Rock, we will be able to deal with Jackson. I suspect he won't carry out his plan to open the Hell Hole if we can bring Emily back to him." He looked around at the three men. "But if she dies, he will be out of control."

"The boy's right," Randolph said. "I fear it is futile, but we must try."

"We must prevent Emily from reaching the cliffs," Devon said.

They raced down the stairs, leaving Jackson to struggle with Miranda, and flew out the front door.

Through the driving rain and the gusts of wind they ran. Ahead of them was Emily, just a barely glimpsed figure in white. It was like a dream to Devon; it was just as the legends would tell of it, just as the villagers would someday whisper in the taverns of Misery Point. Devon was living the story he had been told on his very first day at Ravenscliff: the night Emily Muir jumped from Devil's Rock.

As the fog thickened near the cliffs, the sensation of a dream increased. Time slowed down; sound grew dim. Devon became separated from the other three. He tried to find them, to spot them in the mist, but he was alone now. He moved through the fog in a kind of slow motion, utterly by himself.

"Montaigne!" he tried to call. "Randolph!"

But his voice came back at him like a sound underwater. He realized he was no longer on the grounds of Ravenscliff. He was in the air above. His feet didn't touch the earth.

Devon felt his spirit detach from his body. It was the sensation of a piece of tape, or a Band-Aid, being pulled away from skin. What was happening suddenly became clear to him. He was an observer in this time, that was all. A witness. He was not a participant, and never was.

And then the despair set in.

Randolph Muir was right: history could not be changed. If it could, then time itself would have collapsed. It would have become meaningless. That was why the elemental gods had decreed that it could never happen. What had Devon been thinking? How had he dared to imagine—dared to *presume*—that he could alter the course of history? Arrogant and dangerous dreams, not worthy of a true Nightwing.

Devon became part of the mist. Just a witnessing spirit, as ethereal and disembodied as the wind. But from slightly above he watched as McNutt dashed after Emily. Of the three, McNutt ran the fastest and caught up with her first. Devon watched as he pleaded desperately with her, and he recognized the frantic fear on Emily's face, the terror of the life Jackson had in store for them. He witnessed what he now understood was inevitable if time—and all of the lives intertwined within it—should be allowed to proceed.

From his vantage point above the scene, Devon watched as Emily jumped. She was like a gazelle leaping into the air, a ballerina in the midst of a grand jeté. He saw her slender form twist in the wind and then corkscrew gracefully down toward the rocks. He watched her plunge. He heard her final scream. Devon watched as Emily's body sliced into the surface of the roiling water.

He might be only a spirit at the moment, but he felt the tears dropping from his eyes.

And then the storm dissipated. The moon came out above.

Jackson arrived, too late. He stood on the cliff, his grief and rage overwhelming. He turned his bloody eyes to McNutt.

Devon witnessed the poor man's flight through the woods, his battle with the Madman, and then, finally and most awfully, his transformation into the beast.

McNutt howled up at the moon.

So it was the Madman who turned McNutt into the beast, the Madman who was behind the curse that would afflict Marcus three decades from now. Devon wasn't surprised. So much of the pain and tragedy of Ravenscliff could be traced to Jackson Muir's lust for power. Poor McNutt—how terrible was his transformation, twisting and contorting into that horrible creature. Devon watched from the mist as the beast howled at the moon, then lumbered off into the night.

And suddenly the teenager was himself again, standing in the wet grass, breathing heavily, his heart thudding.

"Return to the house." A comforting hand was placed on his shoulder. It was Montaigne. "There is nothing more we can do here."

"But what about Jackson?" Devon asked as they began to walk. "Where is he?"

"Everywhere and anywhere," Montaigne said. "Now the battle begins."

"Look," Randolph said, motioning for them to join him in the small room off the upstairs parlor in the West Wing. Devon and Montaigne had just arrived. The house was eerily quiet. Neither Jackson nor Miranda was anywhere to be seen. "Now we can see what my brother was doing in here."

Devon gasped. Built into the far wall was a door into the world of the demons—the very same portal Devon would know in his own time.

"Jackson tore open another Hell Hole once I prevented access to the one in the basement," Randolph said. "He reached down through space and matter and ripped open a passageway right through the house."

"Have you sealed it?" Montaigne asked.

"Of course." Randolph rested his hand against the iron door. "It was why I did not continue on to the cliffs. This had to be done." He shook his head sadly. "Not that I would have been able to prevent a tragedy that has already been foretold."

The master of the house dropped down into a chair and held his face in his hands.

"I called my brother an Apostate," he said thickly, "for that is what he is."

Montaigne, too, dropped his eyes in regret. He had known both these men as young boys, when they had their entire futures spread out ahead of them, when both were shining stars of promise in their father's eyes. The sadness of these two men was palpable.

Devon, too, fought off his own grief—not for Jackson, but for Emily. He'd come to like Emily a great deal. Just a few hours ago, she'd been downstairs, sharing a toast for a joyous future. Tomorrow she was to have been Gifted with the power of the Nightwing. How happy she was. She had believed herself pregnant. She had believed in her husband's goodness and fidelity. Now she was a rapidly bloating corpse, tossed about and claimed by the unrelenting sea.

All because of the Madman.

No, not all because of him.

Miranda—Devon's friend—who'd first befriended him in this time—bore responsibility for Emily's death as well. How had such a sweet, fun-loving girl become such a destructive monster?

"Where is Miranda?" Devon asked.

"Somewhere in the night, I assume, planning her next move." Randolph looked up at them both. "Just as Jackson is. My friends, prepare yourselves for a long night. And perhaps a long several days before a victor in this battle emerges."

Devon didn't try to offer what he knew to be the course of history: that the Madman *would* be defeated, although Randolph and Montaigne would die in the process. Devon had given up hoping he could change history. All he could do was witness it.

Yet there was one big unknown still left.

Would Devon survive the night?

Or was it his fate to die here, in the past, never to return to his friends and his own time? After all, McNutt had not seen Devon during his trip to the future. Devon had not returned, Rolfe had told him. He had left to seek a cure for Marcus, but he had not come back. That was the last Devon's friends would apparently know of him.

Plus—and this fact startled Devon even more—Amanda and Edward Muir would grow up with no memory of Devon from their childhood. Neither would know him when he first showed up at Ravenscliff. That fact fit with the idea that he would die here in this time, and *soon*—while they were still too young to retain a memory of him.

Then Devon's fate had also been foretold, and there was no way to change it.

Had that been the meaning behind the Madman's taunts when Devon fought him in his own time? Jackson had said then that he—Jackson Muir—was Devon's destiny. Would Jackson carry a memory with him of killing Devon in the past? Devon might have defeated Jackson in the future, but perhaps the ultimate irony was that Jackson would get to kill him here, in this time.

It was all so confusing. The time paradoxes left Devon reeling.

I've got to concentrate, he told himself. *I cannot become discouraged. I cannot give in to my fear.*

"First," Randolph said, standing from the chair and steeling himself for war, "we must remove Rolfe, the servants, and McNutt's wife and daughter from the house. They must be given safe haven." He placed his hand on Montaigne's shoulder. "I'll have a car take them to where I've secured Greta and the children."

"Where *is* that, sir?" Devon asked.

"Never mind, Teddy. The fewer who know the better. Even you, my friend."

"But we may need Mrs. Muir's help," Montaigne said. "Two Nightwing against one would give us the upper hand."

"No." Randolph was adamant. "Jackson will be gunning for her. My brother has lost his wife tonight. He'll make mine his particular target." The master of Ravenscliff smiled, turning to Devon. "Besides, we already have two Nightwing."

He placed his arm around Devon's shoulder.

"I've beaten him before, sir," the teenaged sorcerer said, careful not to reveal more details than that. "I can do it again."

"Good boy." Randolph looked over at Montaigne. "Break the news gently to Mrs. McNutt. We may yet be able to save poor Ogden. Tell her not to give up hope."

Once again Devon stayed silent about what he knew from the future.

From somewhere near the cliffs, the beast howled, sending shivers through Devon's entire body.

A short time later, the McNutts, little Rolfe, and the servants filed into Randolph's long black car. The chauffeur drove off down the driveway, and once again the car disappeared before it rounded the bend. Devon wondered just where Randolph sent them, where anyone could find refuge from the Madman's wrath.

Outside the windows of the parlor, the cries of the beast grew ever louder and closer. Devon stared up at the moon, a cruel, unblinking eye.

"There will be no reasoning with my brother," Randolph said. "There is only one outcome that can result from our battle."

"Jackson's death," Montaigne said, his voice choking with emotion.

"Or mine," Randolph said.

Or mine, Devon told himself.

"But as for McNutt," Randolph added, "my hope is if we capture the beast—"

As if on cue, the thing howled. It was on the grounds of Ravenscliff now.

"We have no power over it," Devon told them. "Its only weakness is silver."

"Like the werewolf," Montaigne said.

Randolph nodded. "It makes sense. It is a creature of the moon."

"In my own time, I made silver armor for myself—"

But there was no time. Devon barely knew what happened. The large French doors overlooking the terrace were suddenly blown inward, glass shattering everywhere. The roar of the beast filled the room.

"Montaigne!" Devon shouted.

The beast had the Guardian in its hairy paw, lifting the man up by his shoulder. Too fast for anyone to interfere, it flung Montaigne across the room, sending him crashing into the far wall. A table and lamp were knocked over as Montaigne slid to the floor.

"Silver armor!" Devon called out.

Instantly he was protected in a suit of shining silver. Just as the beast was about to pounce on Randolph, he, too, was shielded by his own armor. The creature recoiled, hissing.

"Remember it is McNutt," Randolph said. "We mustn't kill it. We must simply contain it. Get behind it now, Teddy. Block it from leaving the way it came."

The beast stood between them, hissing and spitting. Its wolf-like mouth of teeth dripped saliva as its bearish arms swung wildly but futilely through the air. From Devon back to Randolph it looked, the silver of their armor hurting its eyes.

Montaigne was dragging himself slowly to his feet.

"In the drawer of my desk, Montaigne," Randolph said, not removing his eyes from the beast, "there is a pistol equipped for just such an emergency."

"Silver bullets?" Devon asked.

"Yes. I will only disable it, not fatally wound it. A shot to the leg to keep it from walking."

Montaigne staggered toward the desk, his hand outstretched—

—when suddenly a yellow column of light seared across the room, scalding his hand. Montaigne pulled back in pain, grasping his burned hand with his other.

"You weren't thinking of shooting my little pet, now were you?"

It was the voice of the Madman. Suddenly Jackson Muir was in the room, in every corner, his essence filling the parlor from floor to ceiling. No matter where Devon looked he saw the face of the renegade sorcerer. It obliterated everything else.

"First you kill my wife," the Madman growled, "then you would kill my beast!"

"You cannot win, Jackson," Randolph's voice boomed out, though Devon could not see him. All he could see now were the Madman's bloodshot, swollen eyes, filling every inch of Devon's vision.

"My dear brother," Jackson said, his voice icy and brittle, "I won the moment you welcomed me back into this house. You with your noble code of honor! You wouldn't listen to the boy, would you? You wouldn't listen to his tales of the future. See where it's gotten you now!"

The terrible, enormous eyes turned their bloodshot gaze to Devon.

"I know all about you now, little sorcerer," Jackson said. "I know all about your warnings and your pathetic little attempts to change history."

"Miranda told you!" Devon shouted. "What have you done to her?"

"The time for questioning is over," Jackson said in a singsong voice not unlike that of the clown he played, pretending to entertain the children. "And the letter for the day is Kayyyyy!"

The Madman now appeared as the clown, his white face and red nose filling the room.

"K for Killing!" He laughed maniacally. "The time for killing has begun!"

Suddenly Devon felt the sting of hot metal.

He looked down at his body. His silver armor was melting.

The beast growled, sensing an opportunity.

I'll be boiled alive in molten silver if I don't get out of this thing, Devon thought, jumping out of his melting armor. He ended up on the ceiling, holding on by his hands and the soles of his feet, as if they were suction coups, as if he were Spider-Man.

In the precious few seconds he had, Devon surveyed the room. He could see Randolph's armor was also melting, and the older man had likewise jumped out of it. Montaigne had been knocked unconscious by Jackson's laser, and the Madman stood in the doorway, projecting his image and essence through the room.

Devon leapt.

Jackson didn't have time to react. Devon's feet crashed into the sorcerer's face, sending him sprawling onto his back. When he immediately sat back up—like some terrible, unbeatable, mechanical doll—his face was even bloodier than before.

And he was mad.

Really mad.

"Bring them on," he whispered through clenched teeth.

For a second all Devon could hear was the rush of wind. Then came the crashing of wood and glass.

Then the high-pitched cries and shrieks of the demons.

The Madman's minions.

The demons came smashing through the walls of the house. There were dozens of them. Scaly, reptilian things and hairy, lumbering brutes. Some half man, some half animal. Some whose flesh decayed even as they flew through the air.

And if the Madman had his way, if he could make it back to the West Wing and open that Hell Hole, there would soon be hundreds—*thousands*—more of the vile, stinking, filthy things.

In the pandemonium that ensued, in the chaos of claws and reek of decay, Devon lost all sense of where he was or where Randolph might be. He was on his own. Completely and utterly on his own.

"Back to your Hell Hole!" he commanded as first one, then another, and then still another demon lunged at him. They disappeared, one by one, sucked by an invisible vortex back to their otherworldly realm by the power of the sorcerer's command. But there were so many... and they kept on coming...

The smell in the room threatened to overpower him. The stink of death—like rotten eggs, like raw sewage—made Devon choke. Why did these things have to *smell* so bad on top of *looking* so nasty?

But even as the next one—a skeletal soldier with six arms and the face of a walrus—snarled its way toward him, Devon realized this was just a diversion. Where was Jackson? Where had he gone?

The demons can wreck the house, Devon realized, *but we can put all that back together again.*

If the Madman gets to the Hell Hole, however, there will be nothing we can do to make things right again.

Just as the walrus opened its mouth to chomp down on him, Devon disappeared.

He hoped Randolph wouldn't feel he was running out on him. But there was a more important place he needed to be at the moment.

The West Wing.

The Hell Hole.

It was quiet when Devon reappeared in Emily's parlor. Her embroidery still sat in the chair where she had left it.

Devon made his way into the little room where Jackson had constructed the new Hell Hole. The teenager sighed in relief. The portal was still bolted, still secure.

He turned around, ready to rejoin the battle downstairs, the sounds of which echoed up through the floorboards.

"So, alone at last," came a voice.

The door to the small chamber slammed shut, and the Madman materialized in front of Devon, glaring down at him with his black eyes, wearing his black cape. His face was still bloody.

"Who are you, boy?" Jackson asked. "Who sent you here?"

"I came on my own."

Jackson grabbed him by the front of his shirt. "Look behind me, boy. Look at that portrait. It looks exactly like you. It's been there since I was a child. *Who are you?*"

Devon remained defiant. "My name is Teddy."

"Are you from the future as you claim," the Madman asked, "or the past? What manner of time traveler are you?"

"The time for questioning is over," Devon replied calmly, pulling back and out of Jackson's grip. "Didn't you say the time for killing had begun?"

With one nod of his head, he catapulted Jackson Muir backwards into the wall.

"That's for what you did to Montaigne," Devon shouted. "But this will be for what you did to Emily!"

He lunged, preparing to land his feet on the Apostate's neck, hoping to snap his spinal cord. The only outcome, Randolph had said, would be death. *Better the Madman's*, Devon thought, *than my own.*

But Jackson was too quick. His hand darted up, grabbing Devon's ankle and toppling the teenager to the floor. He was quickly on top of him, his crazed, bloody face not an inch above Devon's own.

"You dare to mention my wife's name? You dare to pretend to avenge her honor when it is all of *you* who bear responsibility for her death?"

He laughed as Devon struggled beneath him.

"So noble," the Madman hissed. "You and my brother are so upstanding and proud. Never would you think of departing from the Nightwing code of honor."

He grinned horribly.

"I'll bet your good Guardian never told you about *this* little trick," Jackson said, pinning Devon down now by both of his hands, his knees on the teenager's thighs. "Prepare to welcome me, boy, into your very *mind*."

The Madman's face overpowered him. Jackson's essence—the same that had filled the parlor downstairs—now forced its way within Devon's very consciousness. The Madman entered his body, smashing its way into the sanctuary of Devon's mind—

And Devon screamed.

DESCENT INTO HELL

It was the most horrible, excruciating sensation that Devon could possibly ever imagine, the sense of another spirit, another intelligence, invading into the private thoughts and memories of his mind.

No! I won't let you enter!

But I am here already! You have lost!

You cannot have access to my thoughts!

How you fear exposure! But of course! If I know where you come from, I can see how you can be beaten!

It was as if they were no longer on the floor of the inner chamber, but rather disembodied spirits dueling in a realm that had neither time nor space. Here they had no physical bodies, yet Devon could "see" his nemesis quite clearly. He could see the blackness, the void where there should have been a soul.

That was when he understood how the Madman could be defeated.

I am stronger than anything that comes for me, Devon remembered.

Invade my thoughts if you will, Jackson, but you cannot take my soul!

Even in their spirit states, Devon could "hear" the Madman's laughter.

I'll take your soul, boy, and I'll eat it for breakfast!

Go ahead and try! Devon suddenly felt triumphant and unafraid. *And while you're at it, look around among my memories. See one of them in particular, Jackson! This one I give freely to you. Take it, Jackson! Here it is!*

He felt the Madman's sudden wariness.

Are you looking, Jackson? Are you experiencing it? Do you see how, in my own time, I cast you into the Hell Hole? Made you a prisoner among the very creatures you now want to set free!

No!

Devon felt the Madman's essence pull back, unwilling to be exposed to such an experience. It made Devon feel even bolder and more confident.

You will spend eternity in there, Jackson! And I sent you there!

Devon could feel the Madman shudder.

Go ahead, look around, Jackson. What else might you find among my thoughts? Go ahead and see if, instead of my defeat, you find your own!

Devon's newfound strength allowed him to return to his body and shove the dormant sorcerer off of him, sending Jackson tumbling onto his back. Instantly the Madman's essence was withdrawn from his mind as well—a horrible ripping sensation, like an ear being torn off the side of his head. Devon stood, victorious.

The Madman opened his bloody eyes and looked up at Devon. He snarled once, then disappeared from the room.

Devon shivered. Had the Madman looked around longer in his mind, he might indeed have found ways to combat Devon, maybe even to defeat him. But Devon had wisely thrown at him the one memory that would demoralize him and cause him to withdraw. He had managed to fight him just in time.

For he wasn't sure he could have survived the Madman's wholesale plunder of his mind.

He'd have to learn how to prevent such a violation of his thoughts in the future. He could see why mind invasion went against the Nightwing code of honor. There had to be ways to keep renegades from doing so.

When he reappeared downstairs, Devon found that the demons were all gone. Randolph had sent them all back to their Hell Holes, wherever they might be across the globe.

"We can't be sure if that was the last of Jackson's army," the sorcerer said, breathing heavily. "More demons could be lurking in the bushes outside, for feel how hot and sticky the room remains."

Randolph let out a long sigh and sank into his chair beneath his father's portrait.

The parlor was in shambles. The western wall had collapsed,

and large chunks of the ceiling had fallen to the floor, exposing the rafters above. The windows were all smashed, the French doors torn off their hinges, glass everywhere. Much of the furniture was broken and overturned, and blood and lizard scales were ground into the carpet.

"Want me to clean up this mess?" Devon asked.

"I'd appreciate it, Teddy," Randolph said. "I'm exhausted, and Greta would have a fit if she got back and saw we'd left it this way."

Devon waved his hand, willing the room to look the way it did before the demon attack. It took almost a full minute, such was the damage, but when he was done no one would be able to tell what had just happened in this place.

Having finished that task, Devon sat down to tell Randolph about his encounter with Jackson.

"We've got to make sure he doesn't open the Hell Hole," Devon concluded.

Randolph was shaking his head. "He cannot open the portal," he explained, "without either forcing me to do so or killing me first. For I am the sorcerer who sealed it shut, and only through my will or my death can it be opened again."

"So he'll be back," Devon said.

Randolph gave him a rueful smile. "Oh, he's never left. He's somewhere in the house right now. You must remember that he believes this is rightly *his* house, and that *we* are the trespassers."

The sorcerer stood.

"Come," he said, "we need to help Montaigne."

They helped him walk over to his cottage and got him to lie down. Montaigne insisted he'd be all right, that nothing was broken. But Randolph could see he'd lost some blood and was pretty badly bruised. He told the Guardian he would send someone to tend to his injuries.

Walking back across the grass to Ravenscliff, Devon watched the sun edge the horizon, turning the sky a fiery red. The night was over.

Ahead of them they spied a figure in the grass.

"It's McNutt!" Randolph shouted.

Ogden lay sprawled on his back, battered and bloody. The sunrise had transformed him back into his human self.

Devon ran to him. The young man groaned as he stirred awake.

"What—what happened to me?" he murmured.

How could Devon tell him? How could he possibly begin to explain what his life had become?

They helped him back to Ravenscliff, where Randolph made a mysterious phone call. Within an hour there arrived a small, blunt, white-haired man knocking at the front door—a gnome, Devon realized, summoned for his medicinal skills.

Just as Bjorn would do in Devon's own time, this gnome, named Magnus, produced a bag of potions and powders. The bruises and scrapes suffered by McNutt were magically healed within a few minutes. Then he headed down to Montaigne's cottage to tend to him as well.

If only the rest of it were that easy.

For the moon would be full again tonight, and Ogden McNutt would again transform into the beast. And, according to the newspaper accounts, tonight he would kill someone—and then he would die himself.

How can I live with such knowledge? Devon asked himself. *Knowing that I can't prevent it, that I can't warn anyone?*

He was exhausted. A night with no sleep battling demons and crazed renegade sorcerers was bound to leave one a little wasted. Devon closed his eyes sitting in a chair in the parlor, though he never fully went to sleep. By mid-morning he'd gotten a second wind. He'd need it, he knew, for the Madman would strike again. And soon.

Randolph sat in his great chair in a meditation pose: alert yet also conserving his energies for the next battle. He didn't speak. He sat with his legs folded beneath him, staring straight ahead. Devon tried it for a while but was too anxious. He slipped out of the room, one thought on his mind.

Miranda.

Randolph hadn't attempted to find her. He'd apparently decided she wasn't worth pursuing, that her powers were nothing to fear. But Devon wondered. Was she on their side now, or had she returned to Jackson? Better to be prepared, Devon believed, for anything she might spring at them.

He closed his eyes, willing himself to join her wherever she was. He disappeared, then reappeared outside the door to the room at the top of the tower. The same place where someday Clarissa would be held prisoner.

He rapped on the door. "Miranda!" he called. "I know you're in there!"

"Go away," came her voice.

"Let me in! I need to talk with you."

"It's too late for talking," she said, opening the door a crack. Her dark eyes made contact with Devon's own. "The Madman will destroy us all."

"I've told you that's not what happens," Devon insisted. "Now let me in."

She stepped aside, allowing Devon to push his way into the room. She looked behind him. After determining no one had followed him, she closed the door.

"I have shamed the name of Devon," Miranda said, tears rolling down her lovely face. "I caused the death of an innocent woman."

"You played a part, Miranda, I can't deny that. But it's the Madman who is ultimately responsible for Emily's death."

She moved over to the window and looked over the estate. The day was foggy and damp. The smell of seawater wafted through the air.

"I should never have come here," Miranda said. "I had hoped it would mean the restoration of my family. I had hoped that the Devons might once again become trusted partners of the Nightwing. That is what my father wanted when he came to this country. That is why I accepted the role of Guardian to little Amanda."

She turned from the window to look at Devon.

"I had such dreams, such hopes! But he lied! He seduced me, Teddy! I have had enough of Nightwing lies!"

Devon approached her. "I may be Nightwing, Miranda,

but I am Devon as well. Look at me. Can't you see it? That's the bond between us, Miranda. I am your family. In my own time, my name is Devon—given to me, I'm sure, in honor of my family."

She blinked a couple of times, as if finally seeing him as he really was.

"You … are a Devon?"

"Yes. As much as I am Nightwing."

She began to cry again. "But I can do nothing now, Teddy Bear. My will is gone. He took it from me. He invaded my mind—" She cried harder, cringing at the memory. "It was horrible. He forced his way inside my mind, reading all my thoughts, all my secret hopes and dreams and fears—"

Devon took her in his arms. How his heart broke for her. She was so young, only a few years older than he was. She was still just a girl, a girl who once laughed and danced, a girl who had been used and hurt by a cruel older man. Now Miranda felt as weary and dispirited as an old, old woman.

"He tried to do it to me, too," Devon told her. "I know how awful it feels."

"He took everything from me. All my memories. My dreams. All my energy and passion. I am just a shell now. Just a shell." Miranda flopped down in a chair, seemingly too weak to stand for long. She lifted her dark eyes to Devon's. "That's how he found out about you. He read my mind. I didn't tell him. I kept your secret to the end."

Devon smiled. It made him glad to know that. He stooped down beside her. "Then will you help us, Miranda? Help us defeat the Madman?"

She shook her head. "I cannot. I've told you. He took everything. I am now just an empty body. My soul is gone."

"No," Devon protested. "You can win back that soul."

She closed her eyes, as if the exertion of keeping them open was too much.

"You carry his child," Devon argued. "He'll need you—"

Miranda laughed weakly. "On top of everything else, Jackson is a male chauvinist pig. He saw in my mind that my child would be a girl, and he has no use for girls as his heirs. He told me so. He said he will find another woman who will give him a son."

"He lies," Devon said. "He's trying to demoralize you, to neutralize you against him. He fears you, Miranda! He fears the Devon power!"

"It is no use, Teddy Bear. My spirit is broken. I cannot help you."

With great effort, she pulled her legs up to her chest and wrapped her arms around them.

"It is no use," she repeated. "Randolph may win as you claim he will. Jackson may yet be defeated, but I am forever lost. All that is left to me is to give birth to my daughter, and then my life is over. He has taken it from me." She began to cry. "Which is perhaps my punishment for disgracing the name of Devon."

Devon left the tower with a heavy heart.

The day moved slowly, as every tick of the grandfather's clock in the foyer seemed to foretell the next strike of the Madman. How long would they have to wait? Was Jackson replenishing his army of demons? How would he attack next?

In the parlor Randolph still sat, deep in meditation.

When the front door opened, Devon jumped.

"Montaigne!" he cried as he recognized the figure entering the house. "I thought you were still recovering."

"The gnome's medicine worked wonders," the Guardian told him. "I'm raring to go. Have you had any rest?"

"I can't seem to," Devon said. "I keep thinking about things … Ogden, for one."

Montaigne nodded. "I've just come from drawing a pentagram on the floor of the garage," he said. "A pentagram is a five-pointed star …"

"Yes, I know what a pentagram is. It's used for protection."

"Precisely. We will place McNutt inside the pentagram

tonight. It will keep him from hurting himself or others when he changes tonight under the full moon. And hopefully in the next lunar cycle we will discover a more permanent cure."

Devon said nothing, just looked away toward the parlor.

Montaigne sighed. "I can see from your lack of response that you carry information from the future that we will not be successful with poor Ogden. But we must nevertheless carry on and continue to try. Without hope—"

"You are right, Montaigne. It would be impossible to do everything we have to do if we didn't have hope."

The day dragged by ever more slowly. Sitting in a chair opposite the immobile yet highly conscious Randolph, Devon at last dozed off for a bit. He awoke with a start, aware of the lengthening shadows in the room.

Randolph came to life as well, speaking not a word. Somehow, without communicating with Montaigne, he knew the plan. He escorted McNutt to the garage, Devon following. It felt like a play, with actors just going through their parts. Devon was a weary member of the audience, who'd seen it all before and knew how it ended.

Montaigne provided a chair, and McNutt took his place in the middle of the star.

"Tell me what happens," McNutt said to Devon, his voice calm and terribly sad.

How could he tell him? What could he possibly say?

Devon smiled, trying not to cry.

"Well, your daughter Gigi will grow up to be a lovely girl," he told McNutt, "and she'll find a happy home with a husband who loves her. And you will have a grandson, who will be one of my best friends, a really cool guy, smart and brave. And I promise you, if I ever get home again, I will tell both of them all about you: what a smart and brave and loyal Guardian you have been to us."

Ogden McNutt smiled. "Thank you, Teddy. Thank you. That's all I need to know." He closed his eyes, waiting for the moon to rise.

It did, and the transformation began.

"Now I remember!" McNutt shrieked. "The urge to kill! That's what came over me!"

He groaned as his body contorted left, then right.

"I don't want to kill! Don't let me kill!"

"You're safe within the pentagram," Randolph told him. "You won't be able to step outside it!"

But McNutt could no longer hear him. He had become the beast, snarling and gnashing its teeth inside the pentagram.

The thing howled at the top of its lungs. Devon recoiled from the terrible sound echoing through the empty garage.

The beast cried again, as if calling for help.

And someone apparently heard it.

"Look!" Devon shouted.

The pentagram was disappearing! As if smudged off by an invisible eraser, the white chalk drawn on the concrete was vanishing!

With his finger Randolph attempted to magically restore the lines of chalk, but as fast as he could draw them they were erased again. With enough of the pentagram broken, the beast was able to step free of its boundaries. It roared, and Devon saw its red eyes were filled with the lust for blood.

Instantly Devon and Randolph were covered once more in their silver armor. With a wave of Randolph's hand Montaigne was armored as well. The beast, letting out a long scream of frustration, turned and leapt through the garage window into the night.

"We've got to go after him!" Montaigne shouted.

"Not so fast," came a voice.

They turned. Standing there in the doorway, smiling at them in his black sorcerer's robes, was Jackson.

"Before you rush off," he said, his voice calm and almost friendly, "I think there might be something here a little more urgent."

Randolph took several steps toward him. "Listen to me, brother. Take pity on the poor souls in the village who have done you no harm. McNutt will kill someone tonight. Call him back."

A wide grin stretched across Jackson's face. "Do you think I have any feeling left for anyone after the way you all took my wife from me? Certainly not for the poor souls who will soon be my subjects!"

The Madman lifted his face and laughed, a sound that was even worse than the beast's howl echoing through the garage.

He dropped his eyes back to his brother. "Did you really think you could hide your family from me, Randolph?"

Devon saw Randolph's face go white.

"Oh, how many secrets the Guardians know, and today I have been inside the mind of a Guardian! There are no more secrets from me."

"Leave my family alone, Jackson!" Randolph shouted.

"A brilliant hiding place! Oh, yes it was! Right here! Right among us! Only in a parallel universe, vibrating at just a slightly different frequency than our own. Brilliant, Randolph! Just brilliant!" The Madman laughed. "The children could still run and play, go to sleep in their own beds. Only they would remain out of our sight, out of our reach."

Randolph readied himself, the terror written on his face.

"Once I knew where they were, it was easy to get them," the Madman said.

He reached his arm through the air. Suddenly it disappeared from the elbow down as he broke through to the parallel world and pulled back, as if from some invisible pocket, a frightened, a sobbing little Amanda.

"No!" Randolph shrieked.

"Oh, yes, yes," Jackson said, and instantly he was no longer dressed as a sorcerer but as Major Musick, the white-faced clown who had so terrified the little girl. He smiled with his big mouth and poked his bulbous red nose into her face. Amanda screamed.

Randolph lunged at him, but Jackson disappeared, Amanda with him.

"He's got my baby," Randolph stuttered. "He's got Amanda!"

"Be calm, sir," Montaigne advised. "He wanted to throw you off balance."

Devon watched as the great sorcerer visibly restored himself. A sense of purpose returned to his face, and he let out a long breath.

"Yes," he said. "You are right, Montaigne. We will win if we remain balanced." He turned his eyes to Devon. "The two of you must go after McNutt. Whatever destiny must be fulfilled is up to you. I will follow my brother."

"Do you know where he's gone?" Devon asked.

"There is only one place," he said, and disappeared.

Devon turned to Montaigne. "Follow me. I know where we'll find the beast. He'll be at East Seaboard Beach. And he's probably already killed a girl."

Indeed, when they got there, just as the newspapers would tell of it in the future, the girl was dead. Her body lay on the beach as the waves crashed steadily against the sand, the moon casting its terrible white glow against the rocky surface of the sea.

The beast stood over her, looking down. It howled, not out of rage or triumph, but out of grief.

I don't want to kill! Don't let me kill!

Devon stood face to face with it. The beast's cries were heartrending as it stood in the moonlight.

Montaigne came bounding onto the beach. The beast noticed him, made a low growl in its throat, and advanced upon him.

"Get back," the Guardian shouted, but the creature kept lumbering toward him.

"Ogden!" Devon shouted.

The beast paused in its approach.

"You don't want to kill!" Devon reminded it.

The beast turned once, and in its eyes Devon could see its humanity. He could see Ogden McNutt.

Then the creature turned again and resumed its menacing approach toward Montaigne.

"Ogden!" Devon shouted again.

But now the beast had nearly reached Montaigne, its giant arms outspread to maul him, its maw snapping with a thirst for blood.

Montaigne had no choice but to shoot, sending a silver bullet straight through the beast's heart. It staggered backward, letting out a long, wounded howl, and fell onto the sand.

And there, in the moonlight, another transformation occurred. The beast once again became the gentle Ogden McNutt. Devon hurried to him, cradling his head and shoulder in his arms as he died.

"Tell ... them ..." McNutt whispered.

"I will. I promise."

With that, Ogden McNutt closed his eyes and was gone.

It was a horrible experience, growing up.

Devon had arrived in this era a boy, but now, with the deaths of two people he cared about—two deaths he had been powerless to prevent—Devon no longer felt so young.

He had never really known the innocence of childhood, of course—not with the monsters in closet being real. But he had been lucky, up until now. No one had died. He had managed to save them all—Alexander, Cecily, D.J.—whenever any of them had been in danger.

Now he knew that his great powers would not always save the day.

He didn't like growing up. Not if it felt like this.

"I didn't mean to kill him," Montaigne said, the gun still smoking in his hand.

Devon let out a long breath and stood, looking down at Ogden's lifeless body. "He'd prefer it this way," he said, his voice cracking. "He didn't want to go on killing."

They brought the body back to Montaigne's cottage and made an anonymous call to the police about the dead girl on the beach. But the grief that threatened to overwhelm Devon had to be cut short: there was still the Madman to deal with, and Randolph was going to need his help.

"I know where they are," Devon said. "Take my hand."

Montaigne did so. They disappeared, and reappeared in the West Wing.

At the Hell Hole.

"Welcome!" Jackson cheered, still dressed as a clown and still holding a terrified Amanda in his arms. "I was wondering how long it would take for you to arrive!"

He faced Randolph, who stood in front of the Hell Hole, blocking his brother's path. Only a distance of about three yards separated the Madman from his ultimate goal.

"Just the boy to break our standoff!" Jackson sang in his clownish voice. "Tell my brother he's being fooooooooolhardy. It's an even exchange. His daughter for my Hell Hooooooooooole!"

"You can't be so monstrous," Randolph shouted. "She's just a child!"

"Monstrous?" The voice deepened, and the clown face showed its sharp yellow teeth. "You took my wife from me! The only woman I ever loved!"

"No one took her from you except you yourself, Jackson," Devon said.

The Madman snarled with one brightly painted red lip. "I had hoped you might be more reasonable, boy," he told Devon. "But I see you are as intransigent as my brother here!"

"Give me Amanda," Randolph said, trying to remain calm. "Give her to me, and then we will discuss whether I open the Hell Hole for you."

"Oh ho ho ho!" The Madman laughed. "I'm not letting this little lady go that easily!"

Devon could see Randolph was weakening. The harder Amanda cried and the more terrified she became, the less resolve her father had to hold the Hell Hole.

"Don't give in, Randolph!" Devon shouted.

"If he doesn't," the Madman cooed, smirking, "then I'm going to have to start *really* scaring my precious little niece here."

With that there came the sound of leather wings. Another bat-like demon, similar to the one Devon had defeated on the grounds of Ravenscliff, appeared above them. It screeched, stretching its enormous wings and flexing its giant talons. Then it perched on a bookcase, training its burning red eyes on the girl.

Amanda screamed, a bloodcurdling cry of terror from the two-year-old child.

"All right then!" her father shouted. "You can have the Hell Hole! Do with it what you will! Just give me my daughter!"

"No!" Devon shouted. "Think what he will do with all that power!"

Randolph was running forward, his arms outstretched. "I don't care! Just give me Amanda!"

The Madman's eyes grew wide with lust as the bolt on the Hell Hole began to slide away.

"No!" Devon shouted again.

The portal creaked open.

"It is mine!" Jackson exulted. "It is mine!"

He dropped the girl as he rushed forward to embrace his prize. Amanda was caught by her father.

This was it, Devon realized.

The moment Jackson Muir was defeated.

It all happened in the blink of an eye. Devon proved faster than the Madman. He made it to the portal before Jackson did.

And he dove straight inside.

I've been in here before, he told himself. *I can do it again.*

It was black and terribly hot, and the smell was overpowering.

I don't have to go in far. Just far enough to block the demons from getting out, and Jackson from getting in to set them free.

He positioned himself at the portal itself, his torso serving as a barricade to prevent anyone from coming or going.

"Move out of the way, foolish boy!" the Madman commanded. "You dare prevent me from claiming what is rightfully mine?"

Behind him Devon could now feel the demons assembling. Their filthy claws and scaly hands began grabbing at his back, pinching his calves, biting his shoulders.

"You'll have to kill me first!" Devon shouted.

"My minions will save me that trouble," Jackson replied, laughing as something behind Devon took a chunk out of his upper arm. Devon bit down on his tongue, drawing blood, to resist screaming out.

This is how it ends, Devon thought. *This is where I die. Randolph will overpower Jackson, but I will die, here in the Hell Hole.*

Something wet and slimy was at his ear.

Move aside, master. You can join us. Isn't that better than being slowly eaten alive?

Something else took another painful chunk out of his thigh. This time Devon couldn't help screaming.

"You see?" The Madman's voice came through from the other side of the portal. "Your death has begun! You will die in there, boy, you will—"

He was cut off in mid sentence. From outside the Hell Hole Devon could hear the sounds of a renewed battle. With Amanda safe once more, Randolph must have leapt back into action.

He knew I'd act, Devon realized. *Randolph waited for me to get back before he went into his plan. He knew I'd do what I did. He trusted me—that was why he stepped aside to save his daughter! He trusted me!*

And I did it!

Another set of teeth chomped down on Devon's butt. He took it as a cue to get out of there—fast!

But that was no easy task. The demons clung to him, holding him back.

Take us with you, master!

Don't leave us behind!

Devon shook them off with all his strength. "Back to your Hell Hole!" he shouted as he rushed forward, breaking free of the suction that held him inside. He fell face first onto the floor.

Montaigne was quick to slam the portal shut and slide the bolt back into place. "Seal it shut!" he yelled to Devon, who with a nod of his hand secured it once again from the hands of the Madman.

But when they turned around they saw Jackson appeared to have gained the upper hand on Randolph. Amanda had disappeared, back to her parallel time by the snap of her father's fingers, and the demon was gone, too, surely sent back to hell by Randolph. But now the two sorcerers were on the ground. The Madman straddled his brother, his hands squeezing Randolph's neck.

"You will die for usurping my rightful place," Jackson told him. "Die!"

Randolph's face was turning blue. Their powers, so evenly matched, were finally at the breaking point. Only one would survive this assault.

"I am Master of Ravenscliff!" Jackson shouted. His face was twisted with rage and he raised his eyes to look around at all of them. His clown costume was gone. He was once again the Apostate, and it did appear that he had won. Below him his brother had fallen still. Randolph's struggles had ceased.

"I am lord and master here!" Jackson proclaimed. "No one but me!"

"Not if I have anything to say about it!"

Devon turned. Someone else had suddenly appeared in the room.

Miranda!

She held a dagger in her hand.

Jackson was taken by complete surprise. He had been exulting in his victory, so he had no time to react, no time to stop Miranda from plunging the dagger straight into his heart.

"No," the Madman gasped. "To die at the hands of such as you—it can't be!"

"Such as me?" Miranda asked weakly. "You forget, Jackson. I am a Devon."

Blood spit from his mouth. Jackson's eyes rolled backward in his head. His moment of triumph had been obliterated. He fell backward.

Montaigne rushed to check his pulse.

"He is dead," he announced.

Could it be possible?

Devon looked down at the battered body of the Madman. Sorcerers they might be, but they were still human. A dagger to the heart, not caught in time, could still kill them in one quick shot.

"And Randolph?" Devon asked, kneeling beside the other fallen sorcerer.

Montaigne checked. "Alive," he breathed with relief. "Thank God."

Devon turned to thank Miranda, but she was gone. Montaigne helped Randolph to his feet. The great sorcerer looked down at the cold, unmoving body of his brother.

"He was my childhood hero," he said thickly, with emotion. "We had different mothers but we were brothers in every way. He had greatness in him. He should have been a great and noble Nightwing."

His eyes moved over to Devon's.

"Look at him and know the truth, my young comrade. Look at him and see the ways of the Apostate."

Devon did as he was told. Jackson Muir's black eyes stared silently up into the void, desire and greed and hatred still etched upon his face.

EPILOGUE
THE GRAVEYARD

The death of Jackson Muir was not announced right away. Too many deaths had occurred in such a short span of time that the authorities would grow suspicious. But when word was finally given, Randolph had a memorial built for his brother in the graveyard that read: Master of Ravenscliff.

"Perhaps in death it will give him some peace," he said sadly, placing his hand on Jackson's brownstone monument.

An angel, fully winged, stood on top, a symbol of the good that Randolph believed still lived, deep down, within his brother. Devon lifted his eyes to it, knowing that at some point over the next thirty windswept, stormy years, one of the angel's wings would break off. It would offer a silent statement on just how much good was left inside the Madman.

They headed slowly back to Ravenscliff. Despite the potions and salves of the gnomes, Devon still walked with a little difficulty, the wounds of the Hell Hole still not fully healed. He went directly to the tower room.

"Miranda?"

Devon knocked on the door.

She had refused to leave this place. Even after Randolph praised her for her courage, insisting she had restored the glory of her family, Miranda had not stirred. Her depression worsened every day, and she sat staring out of the window toward the cliffs. Even her final act of courage could not undo the Madman's invasion of her mind.

"Come on," Devon said. "We're going out dancing tonight."

Miranda smiled sadly at him. "I am never leaving this

room," she said.

"This is ridiculous. You can't stay here forever."

"I have but one reason to keep going," Miranda told him. "The child I carry. I must give her life. Then there is nothing more."

"You're young!" Devon protested. "You have your whole life ahead of you!"

"Not while the body of Emily Muir still floats lifelessly in the sea."

Devon sat back in his chair. "I have something for you," he told her.

"I don't want any gifts."

From his pocket he produced Emily Muir's prayerbook. "I think she'd want you to have this."

Miranda accepted it, opening the pages and reading the words. She closed the book and pressed it against her heart. "Thank you, Teddy Bear."

I've done all I can, Devon thought. *I can't change the course of history.*

He'd accepted now that it was his fate to live out his life in this time. It had been three months since the Madman was killed. Three months—and still no sign of the Staircase Into Time. *Then this it*, Devon thought. *This is my destiny: to live out my life here.*

What else could he believe as the months passed? The winter deepened, grew colder and icier. Devon continued his training with Montaigne, finally receiving the kind of Nightwing education he had dreamed about, apprenticing alongside Randolph Muir.

I really could grow up to be a great sorcerer now, Devon thought, *if only I had a guarantee that I was going to grow up.*

He confided his fears to Randolph. "Since Amanda and Edward won't remember me when I arrive," Devon said, "I might die here, and soon."

Randolph smiled. "Or you might move away, go somewhere else to train among the Nightwing."

Devon smiled sadly. "But I guess I'll never go back to my own time. I'll never play a video game or send a text message again."

"I'm not sure what those things are," Randolph said, "but you might yet go back to your own time. Just because McNutt didn't see you while he was there doesn't mean you *never* return. Maybe you return the moment he left!"

Devon allowed it was possible, and for the first time in his months he allowed himself to hope.

"Or else," Randolph said, considering the idea further, "maybe your destiny is to go to *another* time."

"But I need to go back *home*," Devon said. "I need to help Marcus. And—"

He stopped. He knew he couldn't tell Randolph what will happen in the future: that the Madman wasn't dead forever, that he would return, more than once.

And that his own fate at his brother's hands still lay in the future.

As the winter melted into spring, Devon concluded he would never return to his own time. He'd never be able to tell Cecily how he felt about her—how sorry he was now that they had broken up, and how much he wished they could start over.

I'll never see her again, Devon thought.

He'd been in the past for eleven months, almost a full year. *I'm almost seventeen now,* he realized.

In some ways, this era had become as much his own time as the one from which he came. He'd gotten used to the lack of computers and cell phones. He liked the music. And he reveled in his lessons in sorcery from Montaigne. Randolph had even talked of enrolling him in a special summer program for young Nightwing, held in England. That would be freaking awesome.

"But I miss my friends," Devon admitted to Montaigne.

"You'll make new ones here," his Guardian assured him. "We've been so busy staying alive you haven't had a normal life. We'll get you back to school. You'll meet lots of friends. Is it really so bad to think of staying with us?"

"Of course it isn't," Devon said. "I just don't know what else I have to learn in this time, aside from my lessons with you. What more was this trip into the past meant to teach me?"

A few weeks later he got the answer to that, when Miranda

gave birth to her daughter in the confines of her tower room.

"What will you name her?" asked the little gnome Gertrud, who'd been called in to act as midwife.

"I will name her for my mother," said Miranda. "Her name will be Clarissa."

Devon was staggered.

So Clarissa was—is—Jackson's daughter!

His surprise faded as he considered the idea fully, however. It made sense.

I had thought so once, and now I can understand why Mrs. Crandall had been so fearful of Clarissa.

She gets her powers from the Madman, and if she were to follow in her father's footsteps ...

Would Clarissa know who her father was? Or had she just been instinctively drawn to the Hell Hole, sensing her destiny—and her father—was there?

Devon wondered if he ever got to return to his own time, would he find Clarissa friend or foe?

"We will raise her with our own children," Randolph promised Miranda as he stood, holding the baby Clarissa, looking down at the frail, emaciated girl in the bed.

A day later, Miranda was dead.

It was just as she told them. Having given birth to Clarissa, Miranda found no reason to go on living. Assured of her daughter's care and protection, Miranda closed her eyes and slipped away, as if simply willing herself to die.

One more death. One more farewell to his youth. Devon shed tears as Miranda was buried—tears for his kinswoman, for a girl who had once been so filled with life. Wiping his eyes, he watched as the obelisk rose over her grave. It was a symbol of the magic of the enchanters of the islands. As was Miranda's wish, only the name Devon—the name of which she had been so proud—was etched upon the surface.

Later that night, Devon stood looking down at Clarissa in the crib.

So now I know who you are, he thought. *You'll grow up to be Crazy Lady, kept prisoner in this house once your powers assert themselves. But I'll break you free—and I hope you end up finding a life somewhere away from the evil legacy of your father.*

He reached in and stroked the baby's soft, fine hair. She cooed.

Devon headed out of her room, down the corridor and through the foyer, heading up the stairs to his own room. He was tired. More tired than he'd been since fighting off the Madman. All he wanted to do was fall asleep and have no dreams. He was all cried out—for Emily, for Ogden, for Miranda, for the friends he missed so much but whose faces he found it increasingly difficult to recall.

Except Cecily's. All Devon had to do was his close his eyes and he could see Cecily, the way he last saw her in his own time.

He continued heading up the stairs.

It took a moment for him to realize that something was different. The stairs were going on far longer, far higher, than they should have been.

Suddenly the light in the room had gotten very low. Looking up ahead of him, Devon couldn't see the top of the stairs.

It's here! At last! I'm on the Staircase Into Time!

He was exultant. Bursting into happy laughter, he started to run, taking two steps at a time. He could see the top of the staircase now.

I'm going home! I'm going home!

Devon reached the top. He looked around. Yes, he was home! The telephone on the hall table had *push buttons*! No more dials!

I'm home, I'm home, I'm home!

He looked around.

Aren't I?

Something seemed different.

The curtains … the light fixtures …

He heard a sound. Ahead of him, someone came through the door.

"You!" Devon shouted as his eyes opened wide. "It can't be!"

CONTINUED IN BOOK FOUR

Acknowledgments

Thanks to everyone at Diversion Books for bringing the stories of Devon March and the Nightwing back to life. Thanks also to Malaga Baldi and Tara Hart. And thanks to all the readers who have waited so long for this series to continue. I want to hear from you. Write to me at:

GeoffreyHuntingtonAuthor@gmail.com

—G.H.

@HuntingtonGeoff

www.Facebook.com/Geoffrey.Huntington

Printed in the United States
by Baker & Taylor Publisher Services